KV-514-835

Foolish Notions

FOOLISH NOTIONS

ARIS WHITTIER

FIVE STAR
An imprint of Thomson Gale, a part of The Thomson Corporation

Detroit • New York • San Francisco • New Haven, Conn. • Waterville, Maine • London

LIBRARY OF CONGRESS CATALOGING-IN-PUBLICATION DATA

Whittier, Aris.
   Foolish notions / Aris Whittier. — 1st ed.
       p. cm.
   "Published ... in conjunction with Tekno Books."
   ISBN-13: 978-1-59414-584-1 (alk. paper)
   ISBN-10: 1-59414-584-9 (alk. paper)
   I. Title.
PS3623.H58716F66 2007
813'.6—dc22
                                                    2006038245

First Edition. First Printing: April 2007.

Published in 2007 in conjunction with Tekno Books.

Printed in the United States of America on permanent paper
10 9 8 7 6 5 4 3 2 1

FOOLISH NOTIONS

CHAPTER ONE

"You can't be serious mom," James Taylor said as he absent-mindedly unbuttoned his double-breasted suit with his thumb and forefinger. His hand then moved to his neck and loosened the khaki silk tie that felt like it was slowly constricting around his throat, strangling him. Silently, he stared at the floor and reluctantly let the words sink in.

Marie sucked in a deep breath and shot her son a pleading look. "I'm afraid I am."

"Mom." He looked at her for a few seconds. "You know I'll do anything for you—"

"But not this," Marie said hesitantly.

"We'll find another way."

"But this is the best way. We can make it work."

James paced at the foot of the bed as he ran a hand over the day's worth of stubble on his chin and pondered over the recommendation again. He knew without a doubt that the suggestion was not only illogical but also impossible. "I'm sorry, but it's not an option."

"Why?" Marie's tone was soft.

"Because." He answered tiredly. He had left for New York at the break of dawn, spent four hours in a meeting that should have taken two, and then the company jet had been grounded for an hour because of mechanical difficulty. He hadn't slept on the flight home because he found he was more productive when alone in the jet. Now, he was thinking that he should've just slept. Maybe all this wouldn't seem so unbelievable if he had. The relief, which had consumed him when he touched down in Los Angeles, had been short-lived. If he'd known about the bombshell his mom was going to drop on him when he got home, he might have never stepped foot off the plane.

"What kind of answer is 'because'?"

His mom's words drew James back from his wandering thoughts. "It's the kind of answer that's given when something isn't possible."

"Anything is possible, Son," Marie said logically. "You of all people know that."

He shook his head. "Not this."

To avoid the disappointment in her eyes, he glanced around the room, which had been redecorated several weeks ago when she had moved in. The curtains were antique lace with a swirling rose pattern throughout. He had known she would love them the moment he'd laid eyes on them. They allowed the warm sunshine and the soft breeze drifting off the ocean to pass through the delicate weave with ease. The carpet was cream-colored and so plush it felt like you were walking on air. He had only the best installed.

The adjoining bathroom had been refitted for her needs. He had also had a television and small refrigerator, stocked with her favorite juices and water, put in. He'd tried to make it like a small apartment or, at the very least, a dorm. He wanted everything to be convenient for her.

Some people collected teddy bears or small figurines, but his mom's passion was roses. It didn't matter if they were living or not. She surrounded herself with their beauty. Not wanting his mom to lose the delight she derived from the roses when she moved in, James had the decorator hang massive pictures of roses and gardens on every wall. He had also made sure that she had fresh flowers in her room daily. It was the least he could do for her. He had done everything but physically force her to move in with him.

"It is possible, James," Marie insisted, lifting her hands in frustration.

He looked at his mom, who sat against the headboard, supported by several pillows as she spoke. "I've tried to do everything to accommodate you, but this can't be done."

She tried to reach for him as he walked back and forth. "You've been wonderful. Please, don't get me wrong, I—"

"We'll find another nurse to take care of you."

"We've already interviewed a dozen nurses."

"It's been more than a dozen," he mumbled under his breath.

"I'm running out of time, James. In just one more week—"

"I know what happens in just one more week," he snapped, as he stopped suddenly.

James turned to his mother. It didn't matter how many days or weeks passed; every time he thought about or heard someone say his mom had cancer he wanted to vomit.

Abruptly, he bowed his head in shame. How could he have snapped at her like that? The strain of constantly worrying about her health was creating an uncontrollable nervous tension within him. Combine that with the fact that over the last week he hadn't slept more than a few hours each night. And now his mom was asking for the impossible. No wonder he was stressed. Actually, stressed was an understatement. He was ready to erupt. "I think you're being a little hard on them. Not all of them could be as bad as you say."

"They're not bad, they're just not right." Marie tugged at the pillow behind her. "Don't you want me to have the best care possible?"

"Of course I do. What kind of question is that?" He took a seat next to her. "I love you. I want what's best for you."

"Then hire Samantha; she's what's best for me."

James allowed his head to sink into his hands. He was fighting a losing battle. He didn't want to fight. Not now, not with what they were going through, and not with what they were about to go through in a few days. He raised his head and looked at his mom. She looked tired and weak. Her hair was a limp, lifeless white. New, small lines seemed to etch their way across her face at remarkable speed. Her lovely brown eyes had lost their sparkle, which had been present for as long as he could remember. The toll the cancer was taking on her body was painfully evident.

When he reached for her hand and took it in his, he realized that it was cold and much too thin. Why couldn't he just scoop her into his arms and make everything better? He was used to making things better; that's what he did. If there was a problem, he solved it. If he couldn't solve it, he went around it. If it couldn't be avoided, he manipulated it until it went his way. But not this. No amount of solving or manipulating was going to fix this.

He felt her softly squeeze his fingers and he smiled tenderly before he spoke. "My secretary faxed me over another list of nurses this morning. I went over it and there are a few that we haven't interviewed yet. I'll give them a call and set up some interviews for tomorrow."

Marie nodded. "What about work? I know you're busy. Did you get everything taken care of in New York?"

Busy didn't even being to describe what he was up against. Weeks of work had piled up. He was so behind that it didn't matter now. "Yes, most if it is taken care of. I won't have to go back to New York for a while." He was supposed to fly to Seattle tomorrow but he would send someone else. "I'll take the day off."

"Are you sure?" she asked wearily.

"Of course." He kissed the backside of her hand and then

held it against his cheek briefly before he stood. "I'm going to make the calls." He reached for the door and turned back and looked at her. "You get some rest. I'll check in on you in a bit."

"James?"

"Yes?"

"If they don't work out, can we call Samantha?"

He remained silent for a moment as he stared at the floor. Finally he looked up. "We'll talk about it, if or when that time comes."

"I'm not trying to make this hard on you."

"I know you're not."

"I love you."

"I love you too, Mom." He closed the door quietly.

James didn't go straight to his office—instead he went down the long hall to his bedroom. He changed from his suit into cotton socks, sweatpants, and a T-shirt. It felt good to get out of his work clothes.

He moved to the window across from his bed and stared at the rolling waves of the Pacific Ocean. He felt the tension between his shoulders slack and his clenched jaw relax. The calming sensation that was generated by the vast body of water moved to his stomach muscles and swept throughout the rest of him. He hadn't realized how tense he had been or how uptight he'd gotten until now.

The window opened with a gentle slide and he was greeted with a light, salty breeze. He leaned against the window frame, and thought about what his mom had suggested. She wanted his ex-girlfriend to move in with them and take care of her when she was going through her treatment. Boy, he hadn't seen that one coming.

"Samantha." He hadn't spoken her name in over a year. Her beautiful face appeared before him, her hair swirling in the waves, her eyes glistening in the whitecaps. The echoing of her name penetrated his ears as each wave crashed against the beach, and slowly drifted out again. It was as if the foamy surf spoke her name, calling her, pleading for her to come back.

The suede-colored sand, which stretched on for miles, reminded him of her skin. The crisp blue of the sky was reminiscent of her eyes. And the air, which smelled like a tropical paradise, was the scent of her body. It had taken him a long time not to see her in everything that was beautiful, in everything that meant something to him. He drew in a long breath, breathing her in.

He had met Samantha at a bar three years ago. She was out celebrating, with some classmates, their recent graduation from nursing school. He was celebrating his new position at Parker & Wells with some colleagues, when he saw her come through the door. She was breathtaking. He had never been so struck by a woman before. He couldn't decide what he liked best about her as he watched her move across the room. Could it be her brilliant smile, the way she tossed her head when she spoke, her laugh that rang throughout the room, or the lazy way she drank her beer? He didn't know if it was one or a combination of all these things, but she was mesmerizing. A solid elbow to his ribs from his friend Rick drew him out of his trance.

"Are you going to drool all over yourself or are you going to talk to her?"

James took a swig of his beer and shrugged his shoulders as if it didn't matter.

"I saw the way you were looking at her. I think you're in love." Rick puckered his lips and blew a few kisses in the air as he gave Ed a high five.

"Come on, I wasn't looking at her. Besides she looks young enough to be my daughter."

Ed laughed. "What's wrong with that?"

James glanced back at the young woman who had captured

his attention so completely. She was sitting in a booth directly across the room from him. She was intently listening to a member of her party speak. He watched her nod, smile, and then affectionately reach for the other woman's hand. She then stretched across the table to give a sentimental hug before they all started laughing again. James made a mental note that she was a touchy-feely type, before Rick's words drew him back to the group.

"What's the matter, is our new CEO shy? What happened to the tough son-of-a-bitch that bullied his way to the top?"

He looked back across the smoke-filled bar. Why couldn't he keep his eyes off her? Beautiful women were a dime a dozen, so he knew it wasn't just her beauty. Although she was exceptional, he admitted. It was something else he couldn't put his finger on. But there was definitely something different about her.

He watched intently, as the nameless beauty sat with her arms crossed in front of her. Her long blond hair was tucked behind her ears as not to obscure her golden complexion. Her face was nude of makeup, or at least that was how it appeared. He watched as she lifted the long-neck beer bottle to her sun-kissed peach lips.

Ed leaned over. "If you're not going to go over there and talk to her, I'm gonna." He smiled wickedly. "As it stands right now she's fair game."

James's eyes remained fixed on the young woman. "Fair game for what? You're married."

"Point being?"

For this, James broke his gaze, looked to Ed, and raised a brow. "You're bad." He shook his head. "I don't think Barbara would appreciate hearing you say that."

Ed's grin was a mile wide. "What she doesn't know won't hurt her."

As the guys laughed, James looked back to the woman, who

was now sitting alone. Her friends had moved to the small, wooden dance floor in the middle of the room. Turning to the bartender he said, "Two beers." He tossed some money on the bar, took the beers, and grabbed a basket of pretzels. He paused momentarily to look at his friends. "Don't wait up for me."

"Go get her, boss," they said in unison.

James slid into the empty seat across from her with confidence. She was even more beautiful up close. "Drink?" he asked, as he held the beer in font of her.

Slowly, blue eyes turned on him. "Got one."

James's eyes settled on hers. He liked the fact that she wasn't intimidated easily. The last thing he wanted in a woman was meekness. He found that just the opposite made for a much more interesting, though slightly more turbulent, relationship. He watched her raise her beer in a nonchalant manner as she drove her point home.

Somehow he managed to hide his smile as she set her drink back down. She could act unimpressed all she wanted, but James caught the intense sparkle in her eyes and knew that she was anything but indifferent. He slid the drink in front of her anyway. "Save it for later."

"Later?" she asked curiously.

"Yeah, later." Before he finished his sentence, she looked at her friends on the dance floor, completely disregarding his comment and the offered beer.

With her attention on something else, he was able to focus on her profile, without appearing to be ogling. The dim corner booth and the lights on the dance floor made for a perfect silhouette of her face. There was a delicate slope to her nose and he could see her long lashes brush her cheek each time she blinked. The dark outline softened as it contoured at her chin and curved slightly higher at her cheek. He cleared his throat. He wasn't going to let her blow him off that easily. Besides, he was having way too much fun to stop.

She looked at him.

"Pretzel?" He gestured toward the basket he had brought with him.

Never taking her eyes off him, she reached to her left for the basket of pretzels. She waved them before him. Dropping them, she said, "Got one."

"Ride home?" This time he didn't give her enough time to look away.

"Got one." She took a swig of her beer.

"Boyfriend?" He was waiting for the "got one," and when he didn't hear it his confidence grew. He drew his gaze from her eyes to her mouth, where a touch of a smile was apparent. She moistened her plump lips with the tip of her tongue. They were lips that some women, women he knew, paid thousands for.

After a long, slow drink, James leaned in and spoke. "How about I give you something that you don't . . . got?"

She moved forward, leaning in, pretending she was interested. "I think I pretty much have everything. Thanks anyway."

It was his turn to take a pretzel. He played with it, shifting it from one hand to the next until it was a pile of broken pieces. "So, you're saying you have everything you want?"

She appeared to be biting her tongue not to smile. "It seems that way."

"You're forgetting one thing."

She puckered her lips. "Is that so?"

He raised a single brow, hooked a finger around the beer bottle's long neck, and took a drink. His bottle chimed against the table when he set it down.

"And just what might that be?"

He sat back with bold smugness and said, "Me."

She raised a perfectly arched brow and contemplated for a moment. "Does 'me' have a name?"

"James Taylor."

"Well, Mr. James Taylor, and just what is it that you got, and you think I need?"

"You'll find out in due time."

Her lips broadened into a soft smile. "Your confidence is"—she looked heavenward as she contemplated—"paramount."

"I like to think so."

"Do you?"

"Yes, it's my greatest weapon."

"Weapon for what?"

"My line of business."

"Perhaps you can tell me about your line of business sometime." She paused for a moment. "I'm Samantha."

James broke a smile too and extended his hand across the table. "Samantha. I like that."

"Is this how you approach all women?" she asked cautiously.

James shook his head and took a drink. "No, you're the first."

She wrinkled her nose. "That's good to know."

"Does it work?"

She stuck her tongue in the side of her cheek as she thought. "It might."

His thumb tapped against the table with the beat of the music. "When will you let me know?"

"By the end of the night."

That was good enough for him. "How come you're not out on the dance floor?" He looked over to the group that she had come with.

She straightened her leg so it poked out from beneath the table. "I broke it two months ago. I just got the cast off yesterday. I don't want to push my luck, so I'm sitting this one out."

Looking a little closer he could see that below the knee was a few shades lighter than the rest of her leg. "What happened?"

She shrugged. "I had a little surfing accident."

"First timer?"

"Nope. I've been doing it all my life." She rolled her eyes as she thought about it. "It was pretty embarrassing to be carried out of the water by two lifeguards I grew up with."

"I can imagine."

Her facial expression was of mock contempt. "Thanks, that makes me feel better."

"I'm only teasing." He reached for her hand. "Promise me a dance when you're healed up."

"I think that can be arranged."

They had hit it off. They dated for one incredible year before he asked her to move in with him. He had had no reservations when making the transition, but he had never dreamed that living together could have been so unbelievably fulfilling. Everything between them was heightened. Their passion grew deeper as they discovered new things about each other. He had never been so in love or happier. He had had it all: a meaningful relationship with a beautiful, intelligent woman, and a great job. Who could have asked for more? It had been all his for the taking, until the unthinkable happened. She had caught him in another woman's arms. Before he had a chance to explain, Samantha was gone. He raced home but she had already left; she hadn't even bothered to take any of her things.

James balled up his fists and sucked in a deep breath of salty air. "What happened to us, Samantha?" His eyes closed briefly; it didn't matter. Not now.

He reached for the list of nurses he had set on his nightstand and left the room.

Chapter Two

James held open the front door as the last nurse left. He'd managed to organize seven interviews in two days. "Thank you for coming. We'll be in touch."

He looked at his mom across the room as he walked into the living room. "Well, what did you think?" He shuffled through the stack of résumés sitting on the coffee table as he took a seat on the sofa. "I like number six, what's her name? Karen, that's it. It says right here that she has eight years of experience with this kind of care."

"Yes, number six," Marie said absentmindedly.

"I like number two also. Lots of experience, great personality." James looked over the papers before he tapped another résumé. "Rita is a good candidate too." He glanced up to see his mother looking out the sliding glass window at the ocean. "Mom, are you listing to me?"

"Yes."

He shook the papers in his hand. "Then what do you think? I'd like to hear your input."

Marie didn't look at him. "I suppose they're nice."

"What do you mean you suppose they're nice? You didn't like any of them?" He set the résumés down and ruffled his hair in an agitated manner.

"Number two was too old." Her eyes moved to James and then immediately back to the window.

"Too old? Mom, she was your age."

Marie lifted her shoulders to her ears. "A little older."

"What about number six?" Frustration was setting in. "She was half your age."

"Yes, pretty young thing, but she didn't look fun." She watched a seagull dance in the wind. "I don't want some humdrum person to take care of me. I'd get bored and you know how I hate to get bored."

James gritted his teeth. The dull ache at the base of his neck was slowly traveling upward. He rolled his head from side to side. He needed an aspirin. Hell, he needed an entire bottle. "We're not looking for a playmate." He felt his beeper on his hip go off for the third time in the last hour, reminding him of all the work that was still waiting for him at the office. He looked at the number; it was his secretary again. Annoyed, he turned it off and tossed it on the table.

"It's important that I get along with whoever takes care of me," Marie continued.

James looked up at his mom, who was sitting on the edge of the overstuffed chenille chair that nearly consumed her small frame. "I personally don't care if you get along or not. If she is qualified and administers good care nothing else should matter."

"How can you say that? If I like the person, my recovery will be much quicker." Her tone grew stronger as she pleaded her case. "You remember what the doctor said—positive thinking, mind over matter, all that kind of stuff."

"B.S."

She frowned at him. "James."

"Well, it is."

"I don't want her just to be a nurse. She needs to be more. I need someone who will enjoy sitting on the deck and watching the ocean and the birds as much as I do. Who will help me tend to the roses out front when I'm too sick to walk? You took the time to have them moved here," she pointed out. "I want someone who will enjoy them with me." She reached for the glass on the coffee table in front of her. "James, there's nothing wrong with wanting a nurse and a companion. This person is going to spend almost every waking moment with me."

He rubbed his eyes. "You realize that your treatment starts in four days and we have no one. No one." He leaned back against the sofa, discouraged to the point of giving up. "I don't think you know how serious this is."

"Of course I do."

"Mom, I can't take care of you. I wouldn't know what to do." Hell, he was having problems just *finding* someone to take care of her.

"I don't expect you to."

"Then what do you suggest we do?" He threw his hands in the air. "I'm out of ideas. I've called every nurse in this town. There is no one left to call."

"There's Samantha."

He stood up and grumbled, "Let's not start this again. It's been a long day." He moved into the large eat-in kitchen, which opened up from the living room to create one large room. "What do you want for dinner?"

She followed him, taking a seat at the small breakfast table. "She liked to walk on the beach. Remember?"

How could he forget, they had some of their best times on the beach. Walking, talking, thinking, making love. It was where they had preferred to be over anywhere else. The sandy seaside was their special place and the infinite crashing of the waves was their special song. It was a place that allowed them to reflect and preserve what they had shared and what was still yet to come.

"She loved my roses. The 'Crimson Glory' tea rose she gave me for my birthday is still one of my favorites."

Swinging open the refrigerator door, he stared at its contents. "You want to barbeque?"

"She was fun. Her enthusiasm seemed to be contagious. I remember some of our shopping trips. She would have me giggling like a child and buying frivolous items I didn't need." Her eyes drifted to her hands in her lap. "She was intoxicating."

James went still.

"Intoxicating." Marie repeated the word slowly. "Lovely word, isn't it?" She watched her son closely before she continued. "That's the kind of person I need around me during my treatment."

James's hand gripped the door handle as he flashed back to a moonless night on the back deck of his mom's house. He tried to will the memories away but it was a waste of time. The word his mom had just spoken was an unwanted tap that reached deep into his mind, extracting memories that he didn't wish to remember.

He had pulled Samantha outside to steal a few kisses in the cool night air while his mom went upstairs to freshen up for dinner. He had taken her by the arm, guided her across the deck, and pressed her backside against the railing. In the dark, his lips had found hers in a needy, captive kiss. He had never needed anything more in his life right then, than to kiss her. She had that affect on him. One moment he was fine, and then suddenly, out of nowhere, he needed to touch her, be with her.

"We can't do this," Samantha had said.

"Sure we can," James had murmured as he had nudged her head back and his lips had followed the curve of her slender neck, leaving a moist trail of tingly kisses.

"We better stop."

"Why?" he had half-heartedly whispered as his tongue teased the sensitive area.

"Your mom is inside. I don't want her to catch us."

James had laughed, but his lips had never broken contact with her skin. "I'm not sixteen. I think she knows that we kiss. After all, we live together." His tongue had traced lazy circles over her neck. "She probably suspects that we do other things, too."

Samantha had given him a tender shove. "James, don't say that."

"I want you." He had pulled her closer to him. "Why can't I seem to get enough of you?" He had moved his lips to her ear and nibbled on the tender lobe. "You're intoxicating, you know that? You're like a drug that I can't get enough of." His words had been hot against her ear. "I love you."

"James?" Marie repeated his name for the second time.

He came out of the unyielding image suddenly and had to orient himself with what he had been doing. "Leftover casserole, how does that sound?" He rummaged around the refrigerator for several moments, trying to regain his composure. "I don't see much of anything else in here. We need to go grocery shopping." It was another errand that he added to his list of things he didn't have time to do.

"Call her."

"I'm not calling her." He lifted a clear container and examined it. "There's soup from last night. How about soup and salad?"

"Why won't you call her?"

"She left me. She hasn't spoken to me in over a year. That sounds like a good enough reason to me." Anguish washed over him. The dull ache that had started at the base of his neck engulfed his entire head, pounding violently against every surface for release. "Mom—"

"Mom, that's right. I'm your mom." She pointed a slender finger at him and sent him a look that only a mother could give her child. "At one time I was your mommy who fed you, changed you, and took care of all your needs."

"Don't leave out the forty-six hours of labor you endured," he said dryly.

"I haven't forgotten. How could I ever forget? They were the longest days of my life. By the way, it's up to fifty-six hours now."

"Do you even remember how long you were in labor?"

Her eyes narrowed. "Trust me, I'm still feeling the pains."

"I bet you are."

"My point is, you can talk to me just like you always have."

He placed a tall, empty glass in front of her. "This isn't some bump you can kiss and make all better."

"I'm not saying that it's going to be better. I just want you to talk about it."

"You wouldn't understand."

She raised her hands, giving up. "Let's make a deal."

He was too tired to argue. He felt irritation slithering through him, ready to settle permanently. God, he hoped she would make it fast. "What kind of deal?"

"If Samantha—"

"Mother, I don't want to talk about this." He pulled out a saucepan and turned on the stove.

Marie swallowed hard. "Just hear me out."

He tried to hide his temper, by busying himself with making dinner. "We went over this two nights ago."

"Yes, we did. However, we never settled anything."

He looked up swiftly. "She'll never be your nurse," he said undiplomatically. "There, it's settled."

"That's not fair."

He wasn't in the mood to be fair. "Maybe not, but it's settled."

"James Anthony Taylor, I raised you—"

James sighed heavily. "Let's not start this."

Marie's hand found its way to her chest, where she tapped it lightly over her heart, and then looked heavenward. "Lord, I don't know where I went wrong—"

"Please, let's not start with the Lord stuff." He cast an uneasy look at his dramatic mom and then said, "Okay, I'll hear you out. What's the deal?"

Marie smiled kindly as she leaned back in her chair. "Thank you."

"Oh, no, thank *you*," he said sarcastically.

"If Samantha can't take care of me, I'll pick one of the other nurses. It's as simple as that."

As James took out place settings he contemplated the deal. This could be the answer to his prayers. What were the chances of Samantha accepting this job? She hadn't spoken to him in a year; she would never agree to move in with him and take care of his mom.

"Well?"

"If Samantha declines, you will pick one of the other nurses without a single word of complaint?" He wanted to make sure they completely understood each other, because once it was settled he didn't want to hear another word about it ever again.

She placed a hand over her chest in mock contempt. "I never complain."

He could only roll his eyes at the proclamation. "No more of this nonsense about how you want a nurse who will enjoy your roses and also keep you entertained. We will hire the most qualified nurse. Is that what you're telling me?"

"By the way, it's not nonsense." Her mood turned serious. "All that nonsense happens to be documented in some very prestigious medical journals."

He looked up at her.

"Yes, that's the deal," she said swiftly.

"Despite her age or her floral preference?"

"That's what I'm saying," she agreed. "Should I have my

lawyer call your lawyer?"

"Just for the record, you're not funny."

Her smile never faded. "Then what else do I have to agree to? Do you want me to sign something in blood?"

God, how he loved easy deals. Why couldn't all his deals be this easy? "That won't be necessary. You have a deal."

She leaned forward and said, "Seal it with a kiss."

And he did.

An hour later James had cleaned the dishes and, even though she refused, he had helped his mom to her room to get settled for the night before heading back downstairs to his office.

Now, he sat in the deep leather chair in his office, his elbows rested on the arms, his chin supported by his hands, his gaze on the phone. He had tried to concentrate on his paperwork, but all he'd managed to do was waste forty-five minutes staring at the phone. He was dreading the call he knew he was going to have to make.

The thought crossed his mind, several times, to lie to his mom and tell her he had called Samantha, and she'd turned down the job. He would be avoiding a very awkward moment, not to mention opening old wounds. He thought about another half dozen lies before he quickly plucked up the receiver and dialed the first six digits of Samantha's number. He held the phone to his ear before punching the last number. It took forever for the phone to ring.

"Hello."

James suddenly couldn't speak. His words caught in his throat like a dry cotton ball. He swallowed hard against the bittersweet feeling of knowing she was at the other end of the line. He shifted in his seat.

"Hello, is anyone there?"

"Hi, Samantha."

"James?"

Well, she hadn't forgotten his voice. He gained a little pleasure from that fact. "Yes, umm . . . I hope I didn't call too late."

"No, I just got home."

He hadn't realized how much he wanted to hear her voice or how good it would feel when he did. Her distinct soft tone penetrated the phone, and swirled through his head. He had loved that voice. He had loved to hear her sing as she had worked around the house, when she had spoken on the phone, or whispered to him at night. That was the voice he couldn't get out of his head. It spoke to him when there was no one else there. He closed his eyes and remembered how he had loved to hear her murmur against his ear when they had made love. Her low moans of fulfillment had driven him wild with passion and love. Her voice had always reached deep within him; it still did.

"James, are you there?" Samantha cleared her throat. "James?"

"Excuse me?" He shook his head abruptly as the oversized picture on the far wall came into focus. What the hell was wrong with him? Get it together, he demanded. "Yes, I'm here."

"Are you okay?"

"Yes." He started to doodle on a yellow legal pad. He had to do something to divert the nervous tension.

"Why are you calling?"

"My mom's sick." Losing interest in the pen, he picked up a paper clip and began to fiddle with it.

Concern jumped into Samantha's voice immediately. "Marie. What do you exactly mean by sick?"

"She has cancer." James's stomach churned as a bitter taste formed in his mouth. He hated saying the word.

"Oh, God, I'm sorry. How is she doing?"

"She's hanging in there." He wasn't. He wished that he had

taken the news as well as his mom had. Oddly, he'd felt like it had devastated him more than her. "She starts chemotherapy in three days."

"You'd be amazed at what they can do these days. Treatment has come a long way in the last few years." Her tone was encouraging. "The drugs they are using are more effective—"

"Yeah, I've heard."

"James?" She paused for several seconds. "James, are you okay? You don't sound good."

"Yes, I'm fine it's just that—" What was wrong with him? Why was he fumbling for words? He was a top corporate executive, he reminded himself. He ran a huge company, interacted with some of the most powerful people in the world. He stifled a laugh; his communication skills were honed to perfection, and yet it took all of him just to talk to his ex-girlfriend.

"What is it?" Samantha's voice softened. "You can talk to me." She paused. "Do you have medical questions? Is that why you called?"

"My mom wants you to take care of her." Oh, hell, he hadn't meant to blurt it out like that. His intentions were to ease the topic into the conversation after they had some time to get used to the fact that they were talking with each other.

"Pardon?"

Well, at least she didn't hang up on him. "She has requested that you be her nurse during her treatment. I know it sounds crazy, but she has been very persistent about this."

"I don't think that's a good idea."

Of course she wouldn't.

"I can give you the names of some good nurses if you'd like," she offered.

James pressed his thumb and pointer finger into his eyes—his migraine from yesterday was returning. The intense pressure across his forehead promised to rival the pain he'd experienced the previous day. "We've probably already interviewed them," he said as he pinched tighter.

"What?"

"Nothing." He sat up tall in his chair. The motion cleared his head enough so he could think. "She wants you. I've tried to explain to her that it wouldn't work, but she refuses to listen. Normally, I wouldn't have called, but I'm becoming concerned because her treatment starts so soon and she won't decide on a nurse until she talks to you."

"Maybe if I give her a call I can explain that it just isn't possible."

"That won't work." He picked up his pen again and tapped it in an erratic fashion as he gazed out the window. A phone call wouldn't be enough for his mom. She would want to see Samantha in person. "Come see her."

"Come?"

"She's staying with me."

"I see."

"If you're not busy, why don't you come over to the house tomorrow? That way you can tell her in person that you can't work for her. Make something up if you have to. It's the only way she's going to back down."

"Well—"

James heard the hesitation in her soft voice and guessed correctly that she didn't want to risk seeing him. He ground his teeth together and took a slow deep breath. "I won't be home."

"It's not—"

"I have to work all day. Just stop in. It would be a wonderful treat for her—she would love to see you."

"Yes, I would love to see her, too." There was a moment of silence before her gentle voice rang through. "Tell her I'll be by."

"Sam—Samantha—"

"Yes?"

"Thank you. You don't know how much I appreciate this."
The phone dangled in mid-air before he gently set it back.

CHAPTER THREE

James buttered the two slices of cinnamon toast lightly and set a cup of coffee on a bed tray. He eyed Ginger, his housekeeper, as she came out of the utility closet. The flashy gold-toned earrings that dangled from her ears matched the rhinestones embedded around the collar of her shirt. He smiled at his flamboyant housekeeper. "You are a miracle worker with flour and baking powder," he said as he took a bite of toast. "This is my third piece."

"I'm glad you like it." Ginger ran her hand across a strip of molding, checking for dust on the stark white cloth she had sprayed with cleaner. "I should have made two loaves."

He nodded in agreement and polished off the rest of the toast. "Might I ask why you are cleaning houses when you can bake like this? You should have a bakery in old town somewhere." He held his hands up. "I can see it. A quaint little shop nestled between two antique stores. The aroma of baking yeast would permeate the store and seep outside, drawing in people who were looking for right-from-the-oven goodies."

"It does sound tempting. But if I were to do that, people like you would be living in filth."

"People like me? Are you trying to imply that I'm dirty?" He stumbled back and made sure he kept his amusement out of his voice. "You wound me, Ginger."

She rolled her eyes at his drama then laughed. "Not at all. However, you are a very busy bachelor who doesn't think about separating his white clothes from his color clothes or the ungodly amount of dust that accumulates on the ceiling fans."

He tilted his head suspiciously. "You clean my ceiling fans?"

With an overexaggerated nod, which caused the large hoops in her ears to swing, she said, "See what I mean? You're not dirty, just busy." She wrapped the leftover cinnamon bread in plastic wrap and stored it in the cabinet nearest to her. "Have you found a nurse yet?"

James's mood instantly shifted from enjoyable teasing to somber. "No, we're working on it."

Ginger gave him a sideways glance. "Marie being stubborn, or are you?"

As James watched Ginger meticulously sweep the dining area, it dawned on him how much they had really gotten to know one another over the last year. Ginger was more than just a housekeeper, she was a friend. When she had found out Marie was sick she started to come in an extra day a week. Fortunately, she usually brought a little something to eat, too. "I think it's a little of both of us. We can't seem to agree on a nurse."

"The two of you are too much alike." She bent to sweep a pile of dirt into a dustpan. "You'll agree."

James made a grunting sound.

Ginger looked up and eyed him. "You will." She stood and moved to the trashcan. "And when you do, everything will work out. You'll see."

"We have one more nurse coming today. My mom will do the interview. Her name is Samantha. She should be here around noon." He took the tray on the counter. "I'm going to take this up."

"Good morning." James handed Marie the paper he had already read and neatly refolded. When she tucked it under her arm, he set the tray across her lap.

"Thank you," Marie said as she viewed the tray. "What would I do without you?"

The question was, what would he do without her? That was something he would not allow himself to think about. If he did, it would be like he was admitting she wasn't going to make it. "You'll never have to find that out."

She smiled tenderly at him.

"Sleep well?"

"Yes. It's the first time in days that I've been able to sleep through the entire night." She stretched her arms over her head and looked out the window. The morning sun cast warm golden light into the room, highlighting particles of dust and lint, which appeared to float weightlessly through the air in all directions. "It must be the beautiful weather."

"You look good." He wasn't just saying it to encourage her, either. Her cheeks held a hint of soft, pale pink. He noticed how her blue eyes had flickered brightly—with mischief—when he had leaned over and set the tray across her lap. She must have gotten up early, because her hair was neatly combed and she wore a matching jogging suit instead of her nightdress.

"I feel good," she added. "I think that was all I needed, a good night's rest."

"No pain?" He moved to the window and cracked it open to allow the richly scented breeze in.

"Just a little. Nothing to worry about." She nibbled on a piece of toast.

"I can get you something." He turned toward the bathroom.

"I don't need anything. I'm fine, really." When he stopped, she smiled at him. "Nothing I can't handle. Besides, I'm not going to pop a pill every time I feel a little twinge."

James took a seat in a Victorian floral tapestry chair, which was only a few feet from the bed. "Ginger made a loaf of her famous cinnamon bread." He motioned to her plate. "It's delicious toasted. I think I should hire her as our cook instead of our housekeeper."

Marie took a bite of the crisp bread. After she swallowed, she spoke. "This is delightful." After a moment she added, "Did you call Samantha last night?"

"Yes, I did."

"And?"

"She's coming over some time today."

Dropping the toast, she clasped her hands together and smiled. "Thank you."

He lifted a brow. "That doesn't mean she'll be able to take the job."

"I understand, but it will be good to see her."

He looked at his watch. "I need to go. I have to get in early so Shelly can type up a proposal. The earlier I get there the happier she will be." He pushed out of the chair and kissed her cheek. "Call me if you need anything. Don't forget Ginger's here, too."

"I'll be fine." She lifted the tray off her lap and set it aside. "I need to get my lazy butt out of bed, that's what I need to do."

He looked over his shoulder. "Just don't overdo it."

"Have you ever known me to overdo it?"

James stopped midstride and slowly turned so his large frame faced into the room. His eyes locked with his mom's. By her expression, he knew that she was very aware of the huge can of worms she had just so unwisely opened. "You really don't want me to answer that, do you?" he asked, as his disdainful gaze challenged her.

She cocked her head hopefully. "Is that a rhetorical question or an authentic one?"

"Take a guess."

She looked heavenward, her hands quickly folding into prayer. Her expression was split between wholesomeness and sheer determination as she began to speak. "Please, Lord, have mercy on me and I'll never ask that question ever again nor will I ever—ever—"

"Don't bring the Lord into this." He watched her wince when he interrupted her prayer.

"He's the only one who can save me now."

"Perhaps. However, I have a feeling you're about to make a promise you can't keep," he said dryly.

Marie drew her eyes from the ceiling to glance at him. "Oh, I'll keep it if the good Lord spares me this conversation."

"You will not be saved today, Mom," James said as he moved back into the room. "Let's see, where shall I start?" His finger popped in the air suddenly. "Let's start when I was six and I had the chicken pox and wasn't able to go see Santa at the mall."

"Must we really do this?" Giving up on the prayer, Marie found her way back to the edge of the bed and let out a long breath as she sat. "I'm beginning to feel tired."

"I bet you are." He watched her take the coffee from the tray and sip it slowly. "You brought Santa home."

She shrugged her shoulders. "Naturally, you start with the Santa story—"

"I start with the Santa story because—"

"I know, I know. Because, according to you, it's the most traumatizing of all the things that I've done." She thought for a moment. "I didn't want you to be disappointed. Besides, it's what any good mom would have done."

His eyes widened, and when he spoke his voice was an octave higher than normal. "But you reconstructed the entire wonderland in the living room and Santa's workshop in the dining room."

Marie nodded and smiled at the same time. "It was magnificent wasn't it?"

"Mom—"

"You were surprised when you came downstairs, weren't you?"

"Startled was more like it."

She waved a hand at him. "Oh, that was just the fever."

"Mom, there were reindeer in the kitchen."

Marie shook her head in objection. "Don't exaggerate. There was only one reindeer and it was supposed to be Rudolph." The delight on her face grew as she thought about it. "In retrospect he should have remained outside on the deck. And that red nose wasn't a very good idea either." She took another sip of her coffee. "I should have listened to your dad on that one." She looked up at James and smiled. "Live and learn."

James's eyes narrowed in disbelief. "And you see nothing wrong with that. You don't feel that's overdoing it just a tad?"

"Nope."

He watched her for a moment, wondering if his mom was truly a sane woman. "Do you know any other mothers who did anything like that?"

"Nope, but that doesn't prove anything."

"It proved everything," he snapped. "It proves that no one is crazy enough—"

"Crazy? That's a little extreme." She pointed a finger at him. "I like to call it creative, not crazy."

"What about the time—"

Marie lifted her hands helplessly. "Will I be tortured for the rest of my life just because I tried to be a good mother?"

James shot her a look. "I don't believe you're the one who was tortured."

"You know, you don't always have to be right."

"But I am right about this." James paused for an instant. Someday, he swore to himself, he would make her see how crazy all of it was. "On my tenth birthday, when I requested a cowboy theme, reconstructing the Bonanza set was going over-board."

"Maybe, but you had a great time."

"There was a blacksmith in our back yard." He could do nothing but walk out of the room when he heard her gleefully go into detail of how the horse corral had been created.

"It's not like I committed a crime," she called out to him as he went down the stairs. "And if I'm so crazy then why did all your friends want to stay the night at our house?"

James smacked his hand against his desk as he looked over to his vice-president, Raymond Stewart. "Goddamn it, I took special security measures to ensure our competitors didn't find out about this." He shoved away from his desk suddenly. "Shit." He began pacing in front of a large row of windows that stretched from floor to ceiling. Reaching his hand around the back of his neck, he rubbed the stiff area. Being the CEO of a major consumer electronics company was a curse sometimes. Currently, his company was working on secretive new technol-ogy that, once launched, would not only change the face of the industry but also double his company's revenue base. A situa-tion like this could be catastrophic depending on how much information was leaked. "How the hell did this happen?"

Raymond shook his head as he sat calmly on the edge of the chair opposite the desk. "I'm not sure. I've got a hunch that it's from within."

James turned and stared at him.

"Security is so tight, it makes the most sense," Raymond added.

"It can't be from within. None of our employees would leak the information."

"If they were paid enough, they would."

James pinched the bridge of his nose, not even wanting to

consider the thought.

"Perhaps it's one of the senior managers."

"A senior manager?" James went down a mental list of managers and couldn't fathom any of them selling company secrets. He not only treated his employees well, he paid them well, too. "I don't see that happening."

Raymond propped his elbows on the sides of the chair and stared at his boss.

"I think it's more plausible that ISAC hired an investigator." James's hand shot out in air. "Hell, we know a lot of corporate espionage is done by professional investigators who specialize in it."

Raymond sucked in a long breath. "True."

There had always been competition between ISAC and his company. But James had believed it to be healthy and fair. Perhaps he was mistaken. "Now that I think about it, I wouldn't put it past McDonald." McDonald was the CEO of ISAC. He had an unbridled rivalry with James. But James thought the rivalry was completely normal, and even valuable, because it fueled motivation and diversity between the two.

"The man has absolutely no ethics," Raymond stated firmly. "You know I've always thought that."

James knew Raymond didn't like the man. McDonald was too brash and cocky for Raymond. "When we're back against the wall, we all get down and dirty, too."

"Not like him. We maintain a moral code. He doesn't. What we are releasing is huge. So huge that I think he'd stoop this low. I think it's worth looking into."

"I agree. But first we need to see how much information has been leaked." James turned and stared out the window.

"What do you want to do?"

"Call Al."

Raymond's expression turned to surprise. "Are you sure?"

James was quiet for a moment and then nodded. "Yes. I want this over and done with, fast." He shook his head. "If they have an excellent investigator on their side, which I suspect they have, I want the best on my side. Al's the best. Besides, we've worked together before."

"Okay, I'll call."

James turned. "Keep this between you and me."

Raymond stood and walked to the door. "I'll let you know when and where we'll meet."

Chapter Four

Samantha smoothed out her blouse, tucked her hair behind her ear, took two deep breaths, and knocked on the door. She quickly stuffed her raised hand into her pocket when she noticed that it was slightly trembling. She hated being apprehensive—it made her feel weak and vulnerable. The rolling in her gut matched the rolling of the ocean's waves that she could hear crashing behind the house. She sucked in a few more breaths, taking command of the emotions running through her. Within a few seconds she felt a little of her anxiety diminish. Her yoga instructor would be proud of her. And to think she used to struggle with the technique. She was confident that over the next hour or so her relaxation skills would be tested to the limit.

Pulling back her sleeve, she glanced at her watch. She knew she hadn't been standing at the door for more than a few seconds but it felt like an eternity. Time was cruel. It stood still for things dreaded and flew by for things enjoyed. It wasn't fair.

The door swung open suddenly, and Samantha's head snapped up. "Hi, I'm Samantha." She smiled weakly at the unfamiliar face. "Marie is expecting me."

"Yes, she's been waiting for you. I'm Ginger," the woman said as she waved a friendly hand. "Come on in."

Samantha nodded and took a cautious step forward as the woman stepped aside and allowed her in.

"Marie is in the guest room. Up the stairs and it's the first door to your left."

Samantha observed Ginger, whose bright pink lips offered a surprise flash of color in her otherwise fair-complected face. The cheery woman held a feather duster in one hand and a can of furniture polish in the other. She smiled and pointed over her shoulder toward the stairs.

"Yes, I know the way." She didn't have to be told where the guest room was. She already knew every room in the house.

Tucking the duster under her arm, Ginger shifted her weight. Her gum snapped at the back of her mouth as she slowly nodded. "Holy crap."

Samantha looked over her shoulder and then back to Ginger. "What?"

"When he said a nurse named Samantha was coming by, I didn't think he meant *the* Samantha." She chewed her gum with a wide mouth. "He calls you 'Sam,' " she nodded. "I think that's what threw me. The little devil didn't tell me."

The woman's statement took Samantha by surprise. Puzzled, she said, "Excuse me?"

"Your looks gave you away." She nodded in agreement with herself. "You're just as he explained." She shrugged. "Of course, that was some time ago, but you still look the same."

Samantha felt like she had just walked into an already existing conversation. Was she missing something? "Who explained?" Her stomach was beginning to flip-flop again. She swallowed hard against the queasy feeling. Is this how Alice in Wonderland felt? Lost, confused, and a little out of place.

Ginger moved forward and cocked her head. "I have to see these eyes." She focused in on Samantha as she rolled her gum from side to side and began to nod. "Yes, I do see it. He said 'angelic' and he was right. What is that, a hint of gray around the edges?"

"Angelic? Gray?" Samantha shook her head. She knew she shouldn't have come. Something wasn't right. She couldn't even carry on a conversation with this woman. She was beginning to feel like an unintelligent idiot who wasn't able to follow the simplest of conversations.

"Boy, he has you down to a T. I didn't believe that gray bit, but he was right," Ginger said with an aloof shrug of her shoulders.

Samantha was certain the woman was either confusing her with someone else or she was having some type of reaction to the ungodly amount of makeup on the woman's face. Whichever it was, Samantha didn't take offense to her babbling. If anything, it eased her into the awkward situation by keeping her mind off the fact that she was standing in what used to be her home. She couldn't really dwell on the reality of where she was and what it meant to her, while Ginger was constantly talking. The woman had a way of worming her way into your head and allowing nothing else in.

"The hair is nice too. I can see what the fuss is all about. It's not easy to have a good head of hair, because it's all in the genes." Ginger poked her finger in the air and waved it from side to side. "But them there eyes are something else." She gave a long soft whistle as she let her breath out. "You know, it's been a long time since he talked about you but—" She tapped her temple with her finger. "I remembered every detail he said." She shook her head. "I've never seen a man talk about a woman the way he talked about you."

With the intense way Ginger was staring at her, Samantha felt she had no other choice but to watch Ginger's eyes too. They were caked with mascara and narrowed when they examined her. For a brief moment she thought the woman was going to reach up and touch her hair. "I must apologize," Samantha said quickly. "I'm not normally this scatterbrained. I have a lot on my mind at the moment." She smiled faintly, feeling flustered once again. "To be quite honest with you, I don't understand what you're talking about."

"Oh, don't mind me, I'm just thinking out loud." Ginger snatched the duster from beneath her arm and waved it wildly in front of her. "If you need anything just give me a holler. I'll be around here somewhere."

Samantha stood in the foyer after the woman had disappeared into the living room, trying to make sense of the last few minutes. Ginger was like a whirlwind that left those in her wake a little confused and disoriented. She had never met anyone quite like her. Samantha smiled. Given the chance, she could really like this woman. Understand her, not likely—but be fond of her, definitely. Ginger was unique to say the least.

Her awareness shifted from Ginger to her surroundings. She was standing in a house that had once been her home, the place she thought she would raise her children and grow old in. It was surreal. She had never dreamed she would see this place again. But now that she was inside, it enveloped her like an old familiar friend.

She took a few steps forward. The house looked the same. It smelled the same. It smelled of pungent salt, rich leather, and James. She fingered a large, glossy green leaf that belonged to the massive plant next to her. She had moved the tree from the dining room into the foyer because the afternoon sun was burning it. She had been correct in thinking that the indirect light was better. It must have grown at least a couple of feet in its new location. She smiled at the beautiful ceramic pot it was in. She had almost forgotten about it. It had been one of her best flea market finds. One Sunday a month she and Marie would scout the local flea market for treasures. James had frowned when she had brought the pot home because he had thought it was too ugly to put in the house. Yet, it was still here.

Samantha abruptly clutched the strap of her purse with both hands. Horror shot through her when the reality hit. Was she completely out of her mind? This wasn't some fun little walk down memory lane. She was here to see Marie and that was it. The last thing she needed to be doing was reminiscing.

Squaring her shoulders, she stood tall. The small act made her feel stronger. *It's only going to take a few minutes,* she told herself. "In and out," she said aloud, as she expelled a long breath.

She hurried up the stairs and stopped several feet before the opened door. Moving slowly, she peeked into the room. Marie was sitting in bed looking out a huge window at the endless blue ocean. She didn't look well. Her once-enchanting eyes were now bleak. Her posture was stooped, her demeanor somber. All these traits were so unlike the woman she had known only a year ago.

Samantha couldn't ignore the intense urge to run away from the pain, even as her heart ached for this woman. The powerful sensation swept through her, demanding she get out of the house, get into her car, and drive as fast as she could to the safety of her apartment.

But she couldn't do that to Marie. She wouldn't do that to Marie. It wasn't going to be easy but she had to at least speak with her. She stepped into the room and said softly, "Marie."

Marie's face lit up as she turned. "Hi, sweetheart. I've been waiting for you." She gestured for her to come in.

Samantha went to her bedside and immediately gave her a hug. "It's so nice to see you."

"It's wonderful to see you, darling; it's been a long time. Too long."

Samantha nodded her head in agreement as she pulled away. "Yes, it has."

"I wasn't sure you would come."

"Of course I would." She tried to smile, but couldn't force it. Lying didn't come naturally to her.

Marie arched a brow.

She would fess up. Starting their meeting off with a lie was a daunting thought. "The truth is, I turned around three different times on the way over."

Taking Samantha's hand in hers, Marie patted it reassuringly. "Yes, but you're here and that is all that matters now."

Samantha looked at their hands. She felt dreadfully guilty that she hadn't made the effort to see Marie before now. It didn't matter how painful it might have been; she should have come and visited or, at the very least, called. "You're too kind to me, Marie. After everything—"

"Stop." Marie touched the bed beside her. "Sit. Let me get a closer look at you."

Samantha sat next to her on the big bed.

"You look just as beautiful as you did the first day I met you," Marie said.

"Thank you, that's very kind." Samantha remembered the day James had taken her to meet his mom. James had tended the barbeque as Marie had showed her around her prized rose gardens. As she and James were driving home at the end of the day she could remember thinking that she would love to have Marie as a mother-in-law. She had felt an instant closeness to Marie. Even though she and James had only been dating for three months, she knew that he was the one. They were compatible in every way. They thought alike, they had a lot of the same interests, they liked the same music, and they even appreciated the same type of art. They were well matched, to say the least.

She blinked to clear the thoughts. She couldn't have been more wrong about a person than she had been about James. She didn't want to think about it. It made her sick to think about the mistake she had made. It had not only cost her several years of her life but the torment she lived with was unbearable at times. She turned her attention to Marie. "How are you feeling?"

"Oh, I have my good days and my bad days. Today happens to be one of the good days, since you're here." She rested her hand on Samantha's. "Did James fill you in on everything?"

"Yes, he did."

"What do you think?"

Samantha thought for a moment. "I think you'll pull through this just fine. It's amazing what doctors can do these days."

Marie shook her head. "Do you want to take care of me?"

"I would love to take care of you, Marie, but I can't."

"Why?"

She raised her shoulders. "Because I have my job at the hospital. I can't just get up and leave."

"Don't you have any sick-leave time coming?"

Samantha shook her head. "I'm sorry, I don't."

"How about vacation time?"

"Afraid not."

Marie dropped her shoulders and looked down at her hands, her expression forlorn. "I need you," she said in her best pathetic voice. "I can't get through this without you. I just don't know what I'm going to do."

"Don't say that, Marie. You don't need me." Samantha leaned in. "I know this is going to be hard but you can make it. You're strong and you've taken good care of yourself. Besides, you're not alone. You have James, who will support you through this."

Marie hung her head. "James isn't taking this well and it worries me tremendously."

Samantha found Marie's hand, took it into hers, and squeezed it. She waited until Marie was looking at her before she spoke. "He's a strong man. I think you are underestimating him. We both know what James is capable of."

"But you haven't seen him."

No, she hadn't seen him. When she had spoken with him, he had obviously been distraught, but not to the point that she was overly worried about him. "The both of you will get through this."

"I hope so."

Samantha took a deep breath, eager to comfort the woman. "I'll stop by from time to time and check in on you. I'll give you my number. You can call me anytime if you have any questions or just need someone to talk to." She hoped her consoling was working. She took both of Marie's hands in hers. "You can do this, I know you can."

Marie's demeanor didn't change. "You know what they are going to do to me."

Samantha nodded.

"I don't want a stranger taking care of me. I don't want some stranger to hold my head up when I'm being sick or bathing and dressing me when I'm too weak to do it myself. James doesn't understand how I feel, but I know you do." She looked directly into Samantha's eyes. "You understand, don't you?"

Tears caused Samantha's eyes to gloss over. She cared deeply for Marie. They had been good friends once. Marie had been like a mother to her. It was killing her inside to see Marie like this. "I understand," she said softly.

"Do you?"

"Yes, Marie, I do." It was one of the truest statements she had made while she was there. When she had been in nursing school she had to spend time in a cancer ward. The pain that cancer patients went through was insufferable. Sometimes the cure made them sicker than the disease. She knew what Marie had ahead of her. "But that doesn't mean this kind of arrangement would work."

"If you're referring to James, he is never here. You know how much he works. And since—well—you left, that's all he does.

I'm asking you to do this for me, not for James."

"If it were that easy I'd do it in a minute. But it's not," she said.

Marie coughed into a Kleenex before speaking. "I don't know what happened between you and my son; that is between the two of you. But I need your help to get me through this." A tear rolled down her cheek. "I'll beg if I have to. You can't even begin to understand how important this is to me. Honestly, I'm afraid of the treatment, but I'm also afraid that we're not going to find someone to take care of me. It's all approaching so fast. We only have two days to get everything in order before my first treatment starts. I've depended on James too much as it is. I need someone to help me. I feel so helpless, I'm not sure what to do." Marie paused for a moment. "Samantha, if it's the money, you know I can pay—"

"For heaven's sake, Marie, it's not the money. How could you ever think it's about money?"

"Then what is it?" Her hand pressed against her chest. "Is it me? You just don't want to work for me? If that's the case just tell me."

"Of course that's not the case." Samantha stared at Marie in the huge bed as she considered the situation. She raked her teeth over her bottom lip and took a deep breath. She couldn't allow Marie to think it was because of her when it wasn't. God, what kind of nurse was she? What kind of nurse refused to help someone because they didn't want to see their ex-boyfriend? She should be ashamed of herself. And to think she always prided herself on the fact that she went the extra mile as a nurse, and as a friend. "Two days until your first treatment?"

"Yes."

"That doesn't give me much time to get everything done."

Marie cried as she pulled Samantha to her. "You won't regret this. I promise."

Yeah, right, Samantha thought, as she held the woman in a tight embrace.

"I'll never be able to thank you enough." Marie sobbed in her ear.

Samantha pulled away. "I'm going to need your doctor's name and number so I can talk with him. And I also need to call my work."

CHAPTER FIVE

James didn't even bother to take his briefcase into the office or hang his jacket in the closet when he walked into the house. Sheer exhaustion drove him to let the items fall to the floor in a heap in the foyer. He would worry about them later, preferably in the morning after a long night's sleep.

As he rolled his neck, it snapped and cracked a few times, relieving the pressure, which had increased to extreme pain, the moment Raymond had told him about the leak. A loud growl came from his midsection; he was not only dog-tired, he was starving. He hadn't eaten since Shelly, his secretary, had brought him a blueberry muffin at noon. Coffee was all he had managed to get down before that. No wonder it felt as if he was going to collapse alongside the things at his feet. He rubbed his stomach. Food would have to wait—he wanted to see his mom first.

Taking a step toward the stairs, he stopped instantly. Moving his head from side to side he sniffed the air. That scent. He closed his eyes and savored the fragrance that engulfed his senses.

Under the influence of her perfume, dozens of memories popped in his head. Images, of Samantha's lips, her fingers, her hips, and her toes. Lovemaking and picnics. Visions of how their bodies intertwined together as they slept in every Saturday, and visions of late romantic dinners on the patio beneath the stars, teased and tricked him. He believed she was there. He sensed her. He felt her.

The ache in his stomach changed into an intense hunger that no food could ever sedate. The powerful memories took him by surprise. Images uncontrollably inundated his thoughts. Some were of times they had shared together. He could see her in the kitchen cooking, in the garden planting, and in his bed smiling. But some were also of events that hadn't happened, although he had wanted them so desperately to. Visions of children popped into his head, small fingers and toes to kiss and tickle.

Suddenly his eyes sprang open; he gripped the railing at his side. God, he was glad he hadn't come home any sooner. If this was what happened just smelling her perfume, he didn't dare to think of how he'd have reacted if he'd actually seen her.

As he climbed the stairs he redirected his thoughts to his mom. He hoped her spirits hadn't been broken after speaking with Samantha. She had seemed so cheerful this morning, and he didn't want her to lose that.

"Hi." He was pleasantly surprised to see his mom sitting in a chair by the window. She was typically in bed by this time of day. She was never one to stay up late. And now that she was sick she seemed to retire even earlier. He kissed her softly on the brow. "It's good to see you up."

"It feels good to be up," she said enthusiastically. "For some reason I'm not tired."

He said a silent thank-you to Samantha for letting his mom down easy. Marie obviously didn't show any ill effects from the reunion. He should have known Samantha would come through. She always did. "Good. You need to be in good health and spirits when you start your treatment." He leaned down again. "What's that smell?"

"I believe it's the perfume you bought me for Mother's Day." Marie raised her wrist. "I haven't felt like getting myself all fixed up lately. It just doesn't seem worth it if I'm going to be sitting around the house all day. But like I said, I'm feeling really good today."

"It smells nice." God, if this is what Samantha could accomplish just by talking with his mother, he should have called her weeks ago. The transformation was amazing.

"How was work?" Marie asked seriously.

"Long," he said with a sigh. "I finally closed the Malone deal, though," he added with a positive tone.

Marie smiled proudly. "Wonderful. You've been working on that one for awhile."

He held his fingers up. "Three months."

"Maybe a celebration is in order," she said with a wink.

A smile spread across his face. "Wow, you are feeling better." His eyes narrowed mischievously. "What did you have in mind?"

"Let's go bar hopping."

The burst of laughter couldn't be contained as he tilted his head back and expressed his amusement. He indulged her. "Where to?"

Marie drummed her fingers. "We could start at that bar down on Sunup Drive. I heard that's where you young kids go to do . . . what do they call them? Shooters?" She turned and looked at him seriously. "Now, what exactly are shooters?"

"Never mind, Mom."

She shook her head, disregarding the thought. "What's the name of that place? Do you know which one I'm talking about?"

Of course he knew which bar she was referring to. That was the nightclub where he had met Samantha. They had gone there often while they were together. It was their exclusive place that reminded them of when they met. "Nightlight."

"Nightlight, that's it. Well, we could start there and end up God only knows where," she said with a hoot.

"I don't know if I'm up for a night of bar hopping." He moved to close the window. "I have to be up early tomorrow."

"Spoilsport."

"I know, I know. But one of us has to—"

"Marie—"

James halted in mid-turn when he heard the voice. His smile disappeared as his gaze moved to the other side of the room, searching the vicinity the voice had come from. It took only moments for him to find the object that was causing his heart to pummel against his chest like a drum keeping a turbulent tempo. The glimpse prompted his eyes to find hers in hopes they weren't viciously deceiving him. When his eyes met with Samantha's for the first time in a year, her words trailed off into an uncertain whisper. She slowly faded into a blur and then came back into focus. He shook his head to clear it.

James's gaze went to the neatly folded stack of clothes in her arms before it shifted upward to the golden streaks that highlighted her hair. The gorgeous, blond mane was swept back into a loose ponytail. The warm hues enhanced her face, which didn't have a trace of makeup on it. Her slender figure was clad in capri pants and a silk tank top. He studied her eyes.

His gaze remained fixed on her, just as it had the first time he had seen her—an unbreakable stare. She looked the same. Her natural beauty still radiated from her, producing a wholesome, sweet glow. If he hadn't known some of the things they had done together he would have thought her childlike innocence was authentic. Yes, she looked the same. She blinked, and it caused him to really inspect the clear blue surrounded by sandy lashes. Something was missing. Physically, she was as stunning as always, but there was definitely something different about her. He took an unconscious step forward. Her eyes didn't shimmer like they used to. They were sad eyes.

"James? Did you hear me?" Marie asked.

"Huh?" He reluctantly moved his attention from Samantha to his mom. "Sorry. What?"

"We have found our nurse," she said happily. "Samantha is

going to take care of me. Isn't that wonderful?"

His eyes darted back to Samantha. "I—I thought—" He stuffed his hands into his pockets. "Are you going to—" He cleared his throat.

"James," Marie said firmly. "James?"

"May I talk with you?" James muttered to Samantha.

Samantha opened her mouth, closed it again. Then said, "Sure."

"Alone," he said as he turned and left the room.

"Sure." The word snapped out much too fast.

Marie said nothing as she watched Samantha leave the room.

Samantha's heart boomed as she followed him down the hall. She paused at the top of the stairs to catch her breath as he continued on. Her hand covered her heart as she fought to control her breathing. Oh, my God, oh, my God. The phrase not only echoed inside her head but in her heart, too. Had she made the right decision? This was going to be much harder than she had planned. She hadn't been prepared for what she was going to feel when she saw him.

The feelings that she had for him so long ago couldn't still be lingering inside her, could they? She knew the answer to that. She had loved him too deeply, too completely, for them to just fade away. Even after what he'd done.

For the last year she had tried to forget everything about James, especially how handsome and masculine he was. At night was the hardest, alone in her bed. Memories of how it felt to be held and loved by him consumed her. She would lie awake for hours aching for someone to hold her and touch her. She thought the absence of a man in her bed for a year had somehow made her exaggerate how virile James was. It was just the opposite. He was that and more, no exaggeration was needed. Seeing him tonight was proof of that.

She found him in the kitchen. He was rummaging through the refrigerator for something to eat. Neither one of them spoke as she took a seat at the bar. She could tell he was contemplating what to say. He always busied himself when he was deciding on something he wasn't sure about. If his back were not to her, she would be able to see the deep crease that formed between his brows when he was in thought. She had seen it many times. When they were playing a game of chess or when he was poring over reports. She would touch that deep crease, rub it until it softened, and then tell him he was too serious. The gesture always caused him to smile.

"Want one?" James asked, as he tossed the fixings for a sandwich on the counter.

"No, thank you." She tried to interpret his expression. "Are you angry with me?"

He shook his head, unable to look at her. "Anger is not what I'm feeling."

"Then what is it?" As she watched him she realized that he truly didn't appear to be angry. Instead, he looked confused. It wasn't often that James Taylor was at a loss, but clearly he was now.

"I didn't think you'd be here. I didn't think that you'd—" He was quiet for a moment. "I just didn't think you'd be here," he finally said.

"I'm sorry to disappoint you."

"I'm not disappointed." For the first time since they'd come downstairs he looked at her. "I'm not disappointed, I'm surprised."

She stifled a nervous laugh. "To be honest with you, so am I."

James returned to arranging cheese and greens on a slice of bread that he had coated with mayo. "Why? I don't understand."

"I think she really needs me."

"I'm sure she does, but . . ." His voice faded away and he moved back to the refrigerator.

"But what?" she asked curiously.

He shook his head and lifted his shoulders as he dropped more items on the counter. "How is this going to work?"

"I'm going to take care of your mom."

There was a long silence, and then he looked up at her again. "And it's as simple as that?"

"It has to be as simple as that."

"And if it's not?"

"We don't have to make this complicated, James." Good God, it wasn't going to be that simple but she couldn't tell him that. She didn't even know how to explain to him why she had agreed to the job, because she herself didn't know the answer. Maybe it was her sick way of trying to prov to herself that she was over him. Or perhaps she was trying to conquer a deep emotional yearning. Hell, maybe she just wanted to torture herself. Who knew? She sure didn't.

"Isn't it already complicated?"

"It doesn't have to be. We'll make this work," she said confidently. "We have to make it work, for Marie."

Nodding, he said, "You don't have to do this."

"I want to do this."

James pressed the completed sandwich together. "You're sure?" He took a bite of the sandwich, chewed, and then swallowed. "I'm afraid I won't have enough time to find a new nurse if you change your mind."

"I won't change my mind." She watched him take another bite before adding, "I love her, too."

The intensity of compassion and warmth in her voice made him turn toward her. "I know you do."

"I'm not going to back out, if that's what you're worried about." She was a woman of her word. Once she decided to do something she did it.

"What about your job? This is a full-time position."

"I've already taken care of it. I was due for some time off." The truth was, after she left James, she had worked nonstop. Her supervisor had expressed concern that she might be working herself too hard. In a year she hadn't taken any vacation time or sick leave. She was always the first to volunteer to pull a double shift or to cover for someone else. When she called her supervisor this afternoon and told her she needed some time off, she was more than happy to give it to her.

His eyes found hers. Staring deeply into the warm blue pools, he spoke. "I don't know what to say."

She didn't either. "A thank-you will do."

His voice dropped. "Samantha, you know I thank you. I just don't think 'thank you' is adequate. You have gone beyond the call of duty as a nurse and friend." And ex-girlfriend. "This job isn't going to be easy and the circumstances are just as difficult, yet you are willing to do this. I thank you more than you'll ever know."

Samantha gently smiled. He was making her sound like a saint. She wasn't entirely certain her motives for taking the job were that commendable. Right now, there wasn't much she was sure of. "I spoke with her doctor today. You know her treatment is going to be aggressive. I don't know what you've been told but this isn't going to be easy on her. She is more than likely going to be very sick and weak."

James's jaw tightened. He moved to the cabinet, got a glass, and filled it at the sink. "They have explained the treatment, but I'm not sure if I understand it all."

"Would you like me to explain it to you?" she offered.

"Yes, and please do it in layman's terms so I can comprehend what you're saying."

"Sure. The chemotherapy drugs that Marie will be given will

travel throughout her body to slow the growth of cancer cells and, hopefully, kill them. The doctor has chosen to inject the drugs into the bloodstream through an intravenous needle that is inserted into a vein." She fought the urge to reach for his hand. "Chemotherapy is usually given in cycles during which you have treatment for a period of time, and then you have a few weeks to recover before your next treatment. This is how Marie is going to have her treatments."

Samantha stopped when she saw the flash of anger and hint of sadness flicker across his face. She would explain the rest another time. "I know this is hard on you." She tried to offer him a reassuring smile as she slid out of the chair and walked around to him. "We're going to get her through it."

Setting the glass down, he braced his arms on the counter; his head was dropped slightly, and his voice was resigned as he spoke. "Why did this have to happen to her? She's always been healthy. I can't remember her ever being sick."

The urge to console him and soothe his pain shot through her with fierce intensity. James was the strongest person she knew. Nothing intimidated him. He wasn't weak in any sense of the word—physically, mentally, or emotionally—but his mother's illness was taking its toll. It hurt her to see him like this.

Taking a small step toward him, she reached out her hand and rested it against his cheek. Her fingers moved over the planes of his face as his eyes dropped closed. The gentle touch brought back memories, which she attempted to stuff back into the depths they came from. "You need to be strong for her," she whispered reassuringly.

"I'm trying."

Her hand lingered, her fingers caressed, and when he opened his eyes and looked at her, the connection she felt was deep. "I know you are."

"It's hard to watch her go through this. I hate knowing that there's a disease in her body that's—"

"Shh," Samantha said softly.

He shook his head. "God, I can't even stand to think about it."

"We're going to get her through this. I'm going to do whatever it takes to get her through this as easily as possible."

"This is out of your and my control. Damn, I hate this." His jaw clenched. "I feel like I'm looking down an endless tunnel with no goddamn light in sight."

She raised her other hand, holding his face. He was used to being in control and having control of almost everything that affected him. She knew having that vital attribute taken away left him extremely vulnerable. And that was one thing he'd always prided himself on not being. "We just have to be strong and have faith. We have to put our trust in God."

He tried not to laugh. "Put my trust in God? I have little faith in Him right now." His eyes followed hers. "He's the one who is trying to take my mom. I think I'll put my faith in something or someone who is on my side, because God definitely isn't."

"You don't believe that."

"The hell I don't," he snapped.

"James—"

He covered her hand with his and fiddled with the silver thumb ring that rested against his jaw. "*He* took you from me, too." A heart-wrenching expression crossed his face. "Why would *He* take the two most important things in my life from me?"

His words came out in the form of a soft breath against her face, causing her own breaths to come in small, short gasps.

"I've already lost you. I can't lose her, too." He pinched his eyes shut. "I'd rather die myself."

"You're not going to lose her."

"Can you promise me that?"

"You know I can't."

He held her face, gently stroking her hair. "I never thought I'd lose you and look what happened."

"I didn't die."

"It felt like you did."

She withdrew her hands and stepped back.

James reached for her. "Samantha—"

Samantha held up a hand not only to avoid contact with him but also to silence him. "Don't."

"Don't what?"

She moved across the room. "Don't say anything."

"Why?"

"Because, I don't want to hear anything you have to say."

"Christ, Samantha, I've waited a year to explain what happened. You never gave me that chance." He paused as he tried to control a year's worth of frustration and anger. "You left before I could justify myself."

"I don't want to hear any justification. I didn't want to hear it then and I sure don't want to hear it now."

"That's not fair."

"Not fair?" The words flew from her mouth in disbelief. "Not fair. How's this for not fair? I gave you everything I had, my love, my heart, my soul. And what did you do with it? You betrayed it all." The change in her eyes was sudden and fierce. "I don't think you want to talk to me about what's fair and what's not." Their eyes held for an uncomfortable minute. "Your infidelity damaged more than just our relationship."

"What are you taking about?"

"You broke emotional bonds, which can never be fixed. You tore me in two."

"Jesus, Samantha." He was shaking his head. "I didn't betray

59

you or anything we shared. If you knew what really happened, you would understand that."

"I know what happened, James. I saw her in your arms." She blinked back the tears that instantly formed. There was no way she was going to let him see her cry. She was finished with crying. She had stopped crying a long time ago. "You were kissing her, and holding her. I'm not stupid or blind, so don't talk to me about understanding. I understand what happened perfectly."

"You understand nothing."

"I don't want to discuss this anymore. Me moving in here and taking care of Marie is strictly professional. My relationship with you is strictly professional. What happened in the past doesn't matter. I am here as a nurse and as a friend to Marie. That's all."

"Sam—"

She cut him off. "Do you have a preference about what room I'll be staying in?"

He blew out a long breath. "Take your pick."

CHAPTER SIX

James cradled the hot cup of coffee in one hand and closed the sliding glass door behind him with the other. He wandered across the deck toward a table that was shaded by a huge green umbrella and surrounded by matching chairs and cushions. Beyond the arrangement of chairs, plants, and flowers there was a built-in barbecue and a wet bar made of brick that hadn't been used in over a year. To his right, there was a covered hot tub that also hadn't been used in some time. Surveying his unused amenities, he realized that he hadn't done much over the last year but work. And once his mom had been diagnosed with cancer, every spare moment thereafter had been dedicated to her.

"Good morning," Marie said as she squinted against the bright morning sun. "Isn't it just a beautiful day?"

James looked toward the edge of the deck, where the stairs led down to the beach. He moved to his mom's side, resting his hand on the back of her chair. "What are you doing out here?"

"Enjoying the sun, the breeze, the water." She pointed to a chair next to her. "Sit down, it's wonderful."

"Here, hold this." James handed her his cup of coffee. "It'll warm you up." He disappeared into the house, and then returned with a blanket. He shook it out to its full length. Reaching for his coffee, he balanced it on the railing before he draped the thick material over her and tucked it around her shoulders.

"What are you doing?" she asked curiously.

"It's cool."

"It's refreshing," she countered as he awkwardly tried to cover her.

"Call it what you will." He worked the blanket a little more.

"Don't be silly, Son. I'm fine." She pushed at his hands to illustrate her point. "See, as snug as a bug in a rug."

James touched her hand, holding it tightly in his. "Your hand is cold. Maybe we should go in; the breeze might be too much for you." He looked up into the gentle morning wind rolling off the ocean. It didn't feel overly cool to him but he had to consider her condition.

"Stop fussing and sit with me for a minute." She gave him a soft smile. "Thank you."

James pulled a chair next to hers and sat. It wouldn't hurt for her to be out for a little while, he determined. "For what?"

"For calling Samantha, for asking her to be my nurse."

"I didn't ask her to be your nurse," he said matter-of-factly.

"Maybe not directly."

"Not at all."

"But you got her over here so I could ask her." Marie was quiet for a moment. "I wasn't sure the deal was still on."

He looked at her. "What? Couldn't overhear much from the top of the stairs?"

"Not really," she said sourly.

"I'll make sure to speak louder when I'm having a private conversation."

"I wasn't sure she was even in the house until she came in to say good night."

"Did you think I'd throw her out?" he said as he took a sip of his coffee.

"No. I raised you better than that. However, after you demanded that you speak alone with her, I thought she might run out the door and never look back. You looked a little unsettled."

"Unsettled, is that how I looked?"

"I should have called and told you she was going to be here." She adjusted the blanket. "I wanted to surprise you."

"You surprised me all right." His tone was gruff and little irritable, too.

"I realize now that that wasn't fair. I'm sorry." She glanced at him. "You're not happy about her being my nurse, are you?"

He stared down at his coffee.

"You can tell me how you feel about this. After all, it's your house."

"I want what's best for you." It was the truth, he thought, as he reached for her hand. "And if you feel Samantha is the best person to help you get through your treatment then I have no qualms about it. Besides, we both know she is an excellent nurse."

"Yes, she is. And you're okay with her living with us?"

"We're all adults."

"I don't want you to be uncomfortable in your own home."

"I won't be."

Marie nodded and then raised her hand. "Look over there."

James's eyes followed the direction of his mother's pointed finger. In doing so, he spotted Samantha several yards from them on the beach. Her hair tumbled around her face and formed soft tangles in the wind as she bent over to pick something up. Her left hand rested on her thigh and held a handful of the red cotton dress she wore. The remaining material danced around her calves. The hem was slightly wet from the water. Red toenails peeked through the sand as her fingers rooted around beside them. She was breathtaking.

As she stood, the morning light outlined her body and caused warm hues of sunlight to spread through her hair, growing lighter toward the tips. The rising surge had her quickly gathering more of her dress into her hand to keep it from getting wet. The small movement caused a long, golden leg to appear as the dress inched further upward. His gaze followed the shapely curve of her calf to the firm contour of her brown-sugar thigh. From there the lightweight material clung gently to the curve of her bottom.

James silently groaned as he remembered all the times he had casually touched, gently kissed, or passionately loved the areas he was looking at.

"Isn't she just a vision?" Marie turned and looked at her son. "James?"

He blinked. "What?"

"She looks angelic with the ocean behind her and the wind looking like it could scoop her up and carry her away."

His body hardened at his mom's words. He had been thinking the exact same thing.

"Do you think she has any idea that she looks that radiant?"

James simply shook his head.

"I didn't think so." Her gaze moved between James and Samantha. "If she knew the way the sunlight filtered through her dress revealing her figure I'm sure she'd be self-conscious of it."

James silently agreed.

Marie smiled. "I think that simple fact makes her all the more beautiful."

He didn't want to take his eyes off Samantha, but he tore his gaze away and tossed a stern looked at his mom when her overly innocent tone registered with him. "What do you think you're doing, Mother?"

"Don't call me Mother. You only call me Mother when you're mad." She gave him a condescending look. "I've done nothing wrong."

"I also call you Mother," he said the word slowly, "when you've overstepped your bounds."

Her eyes flickered. "I have no idea what you're talking about. I was merely pointing out that she's very beautiful."

"Mother—"

"Oh, stop. I'll mind my own business," she promised cordially.

Samantha caught sight of James from the corner of her eye when he stepped out of the house. She was glad she had worn her sunglasses so he couldn't see her gaze. As she watched him she couldn't help but notice the power that oozed from his magnificent body, which was clad in a crisp white shirt and dark slacks. The stark material stood out against the mute colors of the house and the beach. It wasn't just the material that made the distinction. He would have stood out no matter what he was dressed in. She watched him as he sat next to his mom, holding her hand, flashing his disruptive smile, sipping his coffee. She absorbed the sudden sentiment, reminding herself that she was here as a professional, before she started toward them.

"I found three more," she said as she climbed the redwood stairs. She walked past James and handed Marie the shells. "These are prettier than the last bunch."

"Darling, they're just beautiful." After inspection, Marie put the shells in a pile with the rest. "Now, we just have to figure out what we're going to do with them."

Samantha dusted the sand off her hands and looked over at James—after all, she couldn't just ignore him. "Good morning. We're just about to eat. Would you like to join us?" She looked toward Marie. "I'll see what I can scrounge up and we'll eat out here. It's too nice of a morning to eat inside."

Samantha moved toward the door, not waiting for James to give her an answer. She didn't really care if he ate with them; she was just trying to be polite.

James excused himself and followed Samantha to the door. "Why is my mom outside?"

"Because she wants to be." She raked her feet over the twine mat as she slid the door open.

"She can't do everything she wants," he pointed out.

Samantha stepped into the house and turned. He was inches from her. Had his eyelashes always been that long . . . the colors of his eyes that deep . . . she'd never noticed him swallow before . . . Quickly, she moved into the kitchen. "She woke up this morning and said she wanted to walk on the beach and collect seashells. We compromised. I would collect the shells if she sat on the deck and enjoyed the fresh air and sunshine." Pausing, she put her hands on her hips. "I don't see anything wrong with that."

"Well, I do. It's cold."

She slipped her sunglasses off and tossed them on the counter. "Cold? Are you joking?"

His voice was deep and weighty as he stepped toward her. "Do I look like I'm joking?"

No, he didn't. However, that didn't take away from the fact that what he was saying was ludicrous. "I have two words for you: Southern California."

"The doctor said she must stay in perfect health. Even a slight cold could—"

"Who is the nurse here?" Samantha paused as she fought for a little poise and self-control. After their confrontation last night she had vowed to herself she wouldn't fight with him again. She was not only above that, she was beyond it, too. "I know what a cold can do."

"She starts her chemo—"

Her eyes narrowed; he was making it very hard to maintain the restraint she dug deep for. "I know when she starts her chemo."

"If she gets sick—"

"I know what can happen if she gets sick," she bit out angrily.

66

"Then why is she outside?" he demanded.

"For fresh air, sunshine, and a change of scene. It appears you've kept her cooped up in the house for the last week and a half."

"I call it safe and healthy." His hand slapped the counter and his voice was a low growl. "Damn it, Samantha, this is one area I will not back down on."

The look on his face wrapped around her heart like a vice, squeezing all anger from her. She didn't want him to back down. The protectiveness that he was showing was a part of him. She understood how important this was to him. They were dealing with his mom's life, for God's sake. If the shoe was on her foot, she wouldn't back down either, especially if she thought her mom wasn't getting the proper care. But that wasn't the case now. He was going to have to turn over some of the control he held on to so tightly, so she could do her job. "I understand." She softened. "But you can't fight me every step of the way."

"I don't want to fight." His voice was weary and honest.

"Let me do my job, James. If you have any questions about decisions that I've made then ask me about them. But don't doubt my capabilities as a nurse."

"I want what's best for her."

"And so do I."

He shook his head regretfully. "I know you do."

"I'm the one with the training. That is why you hired me, to monitor and maintain her health. You need to let me do that."

He pinched his eyes shut momentarily.

"If this is going to work you're going to have to let go and give me the responsibility for her health. You're also going to have to put a little faith in me." When he opened his eyes, she continued. "As a professional, I say she's well enough to go outside and enjoy the sun."

"Okay." He raised his hands in defeat. "You're right. If you say she's fine, then she's fine."

"Thank you. I appreciate that."

For a very long moment he just stared at her.

"What? What is it?"

He shook his head. "Nothing." He turned. "I need to go. I have an appointment."

"What about breakfast?"

"I'll grab something on the way."

"You always used to eat breakfast with me . . ." The words faded as she realized what she was saying.

"Yes, I did, didn't I?"

"That's not . . . I'm sorry . . ." Samantha watched him as he turned swiftly away from her. He went outside to say goodbye to his mom. Through the window she watched him as he gave Marie a quick kiss on the cheek before he reentered. He didn't speak a word as he walked past her. The click of the front door closing was the only thing left in his wake.

CHAPTER SEVEN

When James arrived home that evening, he found Samantha in the kitchen, sitting at the bar as she artfully glued seashells onto a terracotta flowerpot. Soothing instrumental music flowed through the house and the light scent of burning candles filled the air. The sliding glass door was open, allowing the roar of the ocean to mix with the relaxing ambiance. "Good evening."

Samantha looked up from her project. "I didn't hear you come in."

"Has my mom turned in already?" James asked as he strolled into the kitchen, looking at two flickering candles.

"Yes." She turned her wrist and looked at her watch. "About an hour ago."

His head popped up. "That's a little early. Is she okay?"

"Yep." She smiled gently. "She was just a little tired, that's all." She fiddled with a small shell while she scrutinized the clay pot from several angles. "We had a busy day of getting things in order." She looked up. "But we are all organized. How was your day?"

"Good." James worked off his tie as he studied her creation. "What is that?"

Samantha's gaze slid away from James to what she held in her hands. "What do you mean, what is it?" She tried desperately to collect the long, stringy strains of glue that were draped all over the pot, her hands, and the glue gun. Once the majority of them were contained, she spoke. "Isn't it self-explanatory?"

He shook his head, enjoying her antics. "Not really."

"This is a one-of-a-kind, hand-crafted flowerpot, with genuine seashells collected by," she gave him a brilliant smile, "yours truly." She held the pot in the air with pride.

He stared at the pot quietly for several moments, before saying, "One of a kind, that's the truth."

She squinted as she glared at him. "Are you mocking my creation? It's a work of art."

"A work of art, that's a stretch."

"Okay, craftiness isn't one of my finer talents. However, I think Marie will love it."

"Yes, she will, and no it's not." He seized a long strand of glue that had found its way into her hair. He allowed his fingers to glide down the length, enjoying the slight contact with her. After he rolled the string into a ball, he flicked it into the trashcan and watched her for a moment. Damn the wind for tousling her hair like that. Damn the sun for giving her skin that magnificent glow. Damn the air for making her smell sweet and heavenly. He took a step away from her. Waking up to her presence in the house this morning had been hard, but being with her right now was torture.

"I've been working on this for almost an hour."

"Really, that long?"

She lifted the pot, careful not to damage any of the shells, and regarded it. "Do you know how hard it is to glue onto a round surface?"

"I haven't a clue," he said dryly.

She adjusted a few shells. "It's not that bad."

"If you say so." He picked up the mail on the counter.

"You have to have an imagination," she explained. "Picture it with a beautiful flowering plant of some sort in it. Glossy green leaves cascading over the edge."

"For some reason the vision just isn't coming to me." He

dropped the mail and moved around her to the pantry. "I bet for twenty bucks you could go and buy one of those so-called one-of-a-kind pots at the local florist's with a plant already in it." Her expression, one of complete exasperation, made him smile, so he carried on. "Hell, I think they sell them down on the boardwalk for ten."

"You're mean, do you know that?"

"No, I'm honest."

"You're cruel." She pulled the pot close, shielding it. "Besides, homemade is always better."

He tore open a bag of potato chips and stuffed a handful into his mouth. "Not always," he said, watching her search through the pile of shells on the counter to fill the remaining empty hole. After trying several, she decided on a small silver dollar that nestled nicely with the others. She coated the backside with a huge glob of glue, and then pressed it to the pot.

"Ouch." The glue gun dropped and landed on the ceramic tile with a loud tap; the legs of the stool sputtered across the floor as she jumped up.

James dropped the bag of chips on the counter and grabbed for her hand, which she was shaking wildly. "Let me see it."

She batted his hand away. "No, don't touch it, it hurts."

"Samantha, we have to get the glue off your hand or it will just keep burning." He pulled her by the arm toward the sink and put her hand under the cold water. After a few minutes he looked at her. "Is it feeling any better?"

She nodded. "Yes, a little."

"Do you want to take it off or should I?" James asked as he looked at the dab of clear glue on her skin. Somehow he managed to integrate a smile into the question.

"I'm not touching it." Her eyes narrowed. "And would you please quit looking so smug."

"I don't know what you're talking about."

"Obviously, the thought of torturing me appeals to you or you wouldn't be looking so amused right now."

"Do I look amused?"

"Yes, you do," she snapped.

He raised a brow and said absolutely nothing as he stared at her lips.

"Ugh, you're impossible."

Carefully, James reached for her hand. "If you're not touching it, then I'll do the honors."

Samantha pulled her hand close to her and then took a step back. "No, you won't."

"Samantha, you can't leave it there." He moved toward her. "Stop being a baby—you're a nurse, for crying out loud."

"What does that have to do with anything? I may be a nurse but that doesn't mean I like pain."

"Pain?" he scoffed. "You've got to be kidding me. It's a small dot of glue." His eyes drifted gently over her face. "I don't remember you ever being this much of a sissy."

As she looked down at her hand, her bottom lip protruded into a pout. "That isn't small. It's at least the size of a penny."

He frowned. "Maybe a small pea." He cornered her against the counter and refrigerator. "I have a plan."

She looked back up and stared at him. "So do I."

He disregarded her words with a shake of his head.

"You haven't even heard what I'm going to say."

"I don't need to hear it to know it's not going to be a good plan." When her eyes turned threatening he blew out a long breath and said, "By all means. Let's hear your plan."

"I think I should let it wear off."

"Really?" He watched her with fascinated interest. "I take it you didn't think that plan all the way through."

She didn't say a word.

"Okay, now we can move on to plan B, which should have

been plan A in the first place." Carefully, he took her hand in his. "Don't pull away. I just want to look at it." He turned her hand over. It was still very red. The clear bead was thick and completely dry. "If I were a nurse and I had a patient with this type of injury I would—"

"Not call her a sissy and a baby," she offered, her brows angled defiantly. "It's called good bedside manner."

"I would handle the situation very carefully. You see it's not easy dealing with a patient who has such a low pain tolerance." He looked heavenward as he thought. "I believe that fast and quick would be the right procedure in this case." In one quick motion he ripped the glue off.

"Ouch." She shot across the room and glared at him. "You wouldn't make a very good nurse," she said as she examined her hand, clearly sulking. "I can't believe you did that."

He was about to suggest she say "thank you," but when he looked at her his words caught in his throat. Every muscle in his body turned taut as need swept through him in a burning wave of heat. Good Lord, she was breathtaking.

She was leaning against the wall that separated the kitchen and the dining room, pouting as she inspected her hand. The setting sun cast dark shadows over the entire room. Samantha's face was hidden in a shadow; however, a single bar of golden light fell across her bare feet. Frayed white thread from her faded jeans adorned her slender ankles. He hadn't noticed the worn denims before, because she had been sitting behind the counter. They fit like a glove and that was what he liked about them. They sat low on her hips and exposed just a touch of her belly. If she hadn't been in a shadow he would have been able to see the slight depression of her navel. The dark outline revealed every round curve on her painfully perfect body. God, she was beautiful. Her red toes began to flick in a restless rhythm. He watched them shine in the light before he looked up. "Do I make you nervous?"

Deliberately, she crossed her ankles to remove her feet from the illumination as he stared at her. Now her entire body was engulfed in darkness. He knew she had done it to feel protected. The shadows shielded her from things she didn't want to encounter. Or at least gave her the illusion she was shielded. When she stuffed her hands in her pockets, James's gut tumbled because it caused her jeans to ride even lower on her hips. "Answer the question, Samantha. Do I make you nervous?"

"No."

"Then what is it?"

"I'm not used to being stared at like that." The low whisper came from the darkness and was barely audible over the music.

"Like what?" he said gently. Even though it was dim, he could see the clear blue of her eyes gradually smoldered to a dark gray. He had seen the change many times before and knew instantly that her emotions were stirring and beginning to take over. She wouldn't like this and he knew without a doubt she would fight them and push them as far away as possible.

When she didn't answer, James spoke. "I used to stare at you all the time." Hell, almost every man stared at her the way he was staring at her, she just never noticed. When they had been together it was almost impossible not to see the way men would eyeball her. At times he could even read their blatant, nauseating thoughts, which would infuriate him to the point of confrontation. Of course, he never confronted anyone in front of Samantha. Several momentous occasions popped into his head, of times when he had gone back into a restaurant or store to put a man in his place for the impolite glances, but Samantha never knew about them.

There was a side of him that he didn't allow her to see often. It was a side of him that allowed him to succeed in his business. It allowed him to cut raw deals, sometimes unfair deals, without batting an eye. It was an impersonal side, filled with arrogance and shrewdness. However, he'd gone to great lengths to make sure that Samantha was never a part of that world. Her soft voice drew him from his thoughts. His eyes lifted.

"That was then. Things are different now."

"They are different, but I'm not some stranger." His voice was deep. Samantha stared at him, unmoving. He didn't want to be put in some category with other men. He wouldn't be.

"I didn't say you were." She raked her teeth over her bottom lip anxiously.

James had to dig deep to fight the urge to move closer. It made him sick, but he was no better than a stranger. He couldn't just walk over and touch her. The truth was he had no right to be looking at her the way he was right now. He had no right to be thinking the thoughts he was thinking right now, either. The realization was sudden and powerful. A year ago he would have placed a kiss against her neck without a second thought. Now, he had no right to behave that way. He had no right to feel so possessive of her. "You know what's strange?" His eyes held hers in a heavy stare. "To have someone in front of you that at one time had been entirely yours and now you have no right to her. It's an odd feeling, Samantha, that doesn't sit right in here." He placed his hand over his heart. "It makes no difference how much you loved her, or how long you held her, or how deeply you cared for her. You no longer have a claim to her."

She swallowed hard. "Things have changed."

James's voice was curt and his eyes were cold. "They shouldn't have." She had been an angel sent to him to keep him grounded, focused, and human. She'd been the balance that he needed to survive in the crazy world where he did business. He smiled at the thought of how it used to be. How would he ever find the strength to watch her leave again? He shuddered.

"Move, so I can see you." He spoke the words softly. When she made no attempt to move, he repositioned himself so he could see her better. Her eyes were wide, her expression meek. The look she was giving him didn't sit well with him either. "I won't pounce on you."

"You look like you will."

"But you know I won't," he said with absolute control.

She sucked in a shaky breath and nodded.

"I'm glad you agree." Moving slightly, he asked, "Tell me what you're thinking."

"You've never looked at me like this before." She paused. "Not even when we were together."

"I can't touch you—that's why I'm looking at you this way." He angled his head. "It's a position I've never been in, and to be honest with you, I don't like it." Her expression changed as a flicker of reserve twisted her lips and filled her eyes. She was looking at him like she didn't trust him. "If I can't touch you—"

"Please, stop."

He moved to her and pulled her hand out of her pocket. "Then don't look at me like that." He brushed her hair away from her face and ran the back of his hand across her cheek. "You look at me like I'm going to hurt you." He lifted her chin. "You know I'll never hurt you."

"I'm so confused."

A smile slowly transformed his mouth. "Is that what that look is?" He had to admit, she did look a bit baffled. Raising her hand, he said, "Did I get it all?"

"Yes, and a little skin too."

"Good thing I'm not a nurse." He brushed his lips over the tender spot, lightly.

"It's fine."

He watched her briefly. "Are you?"

"If you take a few steps back so I can think and breathe, I

will be." She pulled her hand free from his, taking a deep breath. "I'm tired."

"Me, too." His smile was almost destructive. "You want to go to bed?" He was so amused by the look in her eyes, he laughed out loud. "In separate beds, Angel." He leaned in and hovered just above her ear. "At least, separate beds for now. Good night."

In separate beds for now. What was the man thinking, Samantha mused, as she got into the car and pulled out of the driveway. How the hell was she supposed to sleep after a comment like that? How was she supposed to lie under the same roof after he'd looked at her like that? James was an arrogant son-of-a-bitch, she decided, as she sped down Pacific Coast Highway.

She tapped her fingernail against the steering wheel—spite mounting until she was trembling. "I should have told him he was a son-of-a-bitch, too." She looked over her shoulder and changed to the fast lane. "Why I kept my mouth shut is beyond me." She should have set him straight then and there. She should have—

When the odometer pushed past seventy she lifted her foot and sighed at how ridiculous she was being. She couldn't have spoken up if she had tried. Her entire body, even her voice, had seemed to grind to a halt the moment his gaze had fallen on her. Confusion had swarmed through her head, tackling any thoughts she might have had. Hell, she was happy that she had managed to stay erect because what she'd really wanted to do was slide down the wall and force herself to forget he was even in the room.

His smile had been seductive. His arrogance had been persuasive. The biceps that flexed against his crisp shirt had been devastatingly visible. Her fingers tightened around the steering wheel as her insides exploded into a raging fire. A sharp ache scattered through her entire body, starting from the pit of her stomach and spreading outward in a sudden wave of intense heat.

What had she been thinking when she thought she could take care of Marie and just ignore James? Thinking they could live peacefully together was a mistake—a huge error on her part. How was she going to get out of this situation? She couldn't stay there. She couldn't live under the same roof with him. It would never work. It wasn't working.

What she really needed was to talk to her best friend, Marisa. They had been practically inseparable since age seven. Marisa would put everything back into perspective for her. She was often the more practical of the two and she was definitely the take-charge one. Marisa would help her find her way out of this mess.

Glancing down at the dashboard she saw that it was almost nine o'clock. Hopefully Marisa would still be up. Pulling off the highway, Samantha steered the car into an upscale residential neighborhood. She was thankful when she pulled up to the curb in front of the house to see that there were lights on.

Instant relief filled Samantha when Marisa appeared at the door. It was so good to have a best friend, particularly at a time like this.

"You don't look good. What's wrong?" Marisa said quickly as she pulled Samantha into the house and put a protective arm around her. "What happened? Is everything okay with Marie?"

"Yes, Marie is fine."

Marisa's hand went to her chest. "You scared me for a minute."

"I'm sorry." Samantha shook her head. "Everyone's fine." She blew out a breath. "I know it's late, but I really need someone to talk to."

Marisa closed the door and walked Samantha to the living

room. "You want me to fix some coffee or tea?" she asked, moving toward the kitchen.

Samantha shook her head.

"You want a glass of wine?"

"No, nothing to drink."

Marisa's eyebrows shot up. "This is serious." She moved to the sofa and pulled Samantha down next to her. "What's going on?"

Samantha couldn't stop the tears that filled her eyes. "It's harder that I thought it would be."

"Why? Tell me what's hard. Is it seeing Marie sick?"

She shook her head, wiping her eyes with the back of her hand.

"I didn't think so. It's James, isn't it?"

"Being near him like this is so difficult."

Marisa pulled Samantha into a tight embrace. "Oh, God, Samantha, I'm sorry."

"It's so hard to be there."

"I know it is."

"I don't think I can do this," Samantha said as she closed her eyes and rested her chin on Marisa's shoulder.

"Of course you can do this."

"No, it's too hard."

"It's only the first day. Give it more time."

"Time isn't going to make any difference. I bit off way more than I can chew. I've made a huge mistake."

Pushing her at arm's length, Marisa grabbed Samantha's shoulders and said softly, but firmly, "You have to do this. For Marie."

"I can find another nurse. With the kind of money James is paying—"

"Marie needs you," Marisa gently reminded her. She leaned over, plucked two tissues out of a box, and handed them to Samantha. "Not some other nurse. You can't lose focus on that. That's why you're there."

"Focus," Samantha repeated with a hysterical laugh. "I can't stay focused with James so close."

"You're going to have to, because Marie needs you."

Samantha nodded and sniffled at the same time. "You're right. She does. That's why I agreed to this in the first place." She lifted her shoulders. "But this is killing me. I haven't even been in the house for two days and—"

"And what?"

"It's still there." She buried her face in her hands. "I don't want it to be, but all the emotions and feelings are still there." She lifted her head. "God, sometimes he looks at me like he's going to eat me alive and then other times he looks at me like *I'm* the one who betrayed *him*."

"He still cares for you," Marisa said logically.

"I don't want him to care for me."

"You and I both know that feelings can't be turned on and off. It's going to be okay. It's only temporary."

"You're right." Samantha wiped her eyes with the back of her hands.

"You want me to get that wine now?"

"No." Samantha stood. "It's getting late and I need to go."

Marisa walked Samantha to the door, stopped, and pulled her close. "Call me in a day or so and let me know how things are going."

"I will."

"It's going to be okay," Marisa insisted. "Take care of Marie. That's all you have to do."

"I know." Samantha said as she kissed Marisa on the cheek and smiled thankfully. "I love you."

CHAPTER EIGHT

At Marie's insistence, Samantha finally agreed to take the walk on the beach that she had desperately wanted to take but kept putting off because she'd find something else that needed her attention. The peaceful stroll would be greatly appreciated, because tomorrow was going to be a busy day and it might be the last time she had a free moment to herself.

Moving about her room, she unpacked the rest of her belongings, which she had fetched earlier that afternoon when Marie had been napping. Pausing, she thought about the woman down the hall. She had left Marie comfortably settled in bed with a crossword puzzle less than twenty minutes ago. Tomorrow night she might not be as content. In less than twenty-four hours she would be in the middle of her first treatment.

Samantha slid the dresser drawer shut and moved across the room to the window. Pressing her palms against the glass she stared spellbound at the endless ocean. She wondered why this vast body of water enthralled her. She felt amazingly small when she was near it. For some unexplainable reason, it reinforced her belief that people truly do not have control over destiny. She had no control over the outcome of Marie's cancer or her own feelings for James. She felt destiny was like the ocean—it was sometimes merciless and almost always unpredictable.

A motion from below caused her gaze to drop. She watched James from the second-story window as he sat quietly on the beautiful deck. He must have changed from his work clothes when she was getting Marie settled in for the evening. She vaguely remembered hearing the car pull into the drive, but she assumed that he went right into his office. She hadn't seen him since the night before when he had mocked her flowerpot and ripped off a layer of skin.

She could tell he was deep in thought because he didn't take notice of the seagulls that were perched on the railing crying for food, nor did he respond to the couple walking hand in hand down the beach who turned and waved. She speculated that his apparent bleak mood was why he hadn't rushed to his mom when he had gotten home. That surprised her.

Reluctantly, she turned away from the window. She knew she was going downstairs and it wasn't because she was going to walk on the beach. She was going to see James. She plucked up the tennis shoes, which were sitting on the bed with socks stuffed in them, and tossed them back in the closet. She did the same to the yellow windbreaker. The beach was going to have to wait a few hours longer.

She found James sitting on a chaise lounge. Two beer bottles sat on the weathered wood below him: one full, one empty. His arms were folded tightly across his chest as his gaze penetrated the setting sun. The brilliant oranges and reds drenched his solemn features with color.

Quietly, she closed the door behind her. She moved alongside the lounge. As she sat, she folded her legs Indian style next to his beer. She looked out at the setting sun and squinted her eyes against the gentle wind. The sun was a majestic, bright orange-red globe that dipped behind the waves, slowly sinking into the water. Long fingers of color stretched in each direction as far as the eye could see. The sight was postcard perfect.

"Tomorrow is the day," James said, as he reached for his beer. "Is everything ready?"

She drew her eyes from the setting sun. "Yes, it is."

"What time does she go in?"

"One-thirty."

"At the hospital or the doctor's office?"

"It is standard procedure for the first treatment to be administered in the hospital."

"Do I need to be there?"

"Not really."

He took three big swigs and after a few minutes said, "It doesn't matter. She doesn't want me there anyway."

"Did she say that?" She pulled her hair over her shoulder so the wind wouldn't blow it in her face as she turned and looked at him.

"Not in those exact words. But I got the message."

"She doesn't want you to see what she has to go through." Samantha wanted to touch his arm and then decided against it. "She is a mother protecting her child."

"I don't need protection." He said the words with such force his body stiffened.

"Try telling a mother that."

As he put his beer back down, his hand lightly brushed her bare knee. "How hard is it going to be on her?"

"I'm not going to lie to you, James. It's like I told you yesterday. The therapy is aggressive."

He turned to her. "Everyone keeps saying aggressive, what exactly does that mean?"

"It basically means that they are using some intense drugs to destroy the cancer. Most likely she will have some side effects from them."

"A reaction to them?"

She nodded. "That's right."

"Like what?"

"It all depends on how her body responds to the drugs." She paused for a moment. "Let's not worry over the inevitable. We'll take it as it comes."

He gave an irritated laugh as he looked at her. "Worry? My mom has cancer and you're telling me not to worry." He stood up in one swift movement. "Well, please, excuse me if I do, but it's kind of hard not to." Without another word he went into the house.

Samantha looked at her feet. It took every ounce of will not to get up and run after him. She wanted to take him in her arms, hold him against her breast, and gently stroke his hair as she spoke soft endearments that soothed his pain away. A voice echoed in her ears—she was here to take care of Marie, not James. He could take care of himself. This would be hard on him, it might even test him, but he would survive. He would handle this misfortune just like he handled any hardship that was thrown his way. He would fight his way through it. He was resilient.

She raised her knees and dropped her head on them in frustration. But this was his mom and he was hurting. She cursed her softer side as she looked up at the last rays of the setting sun. She sat in the dusk contemplating whether she should go comfort him or go get her shoes and take that walk.

What kind of person was she if she let him go on feeling this way without even trying to help him through it? The least she could do was let him vent the agony he must be going through. No one should have to suffer alone through the pain of having a sick loved one. She got up and went into the house. James was in the living room, slouched on a black leather sofa with a fresh beer in his hand.

"James, I'm sorry for how that might have sounded. I'm not saying 'don't care.' Of course you care." She stood before him and consoled, "I understand what you are going through."

"Do you?" He looked at her questioningly.

"Yes, I see it almost every day. I see children who are so sick they can't hold their heads up. I see parents who would give anything to take that sickness away. I see husbands worried about their wives and vice versa. And I see children who are hurt and concerned about their parents."

She sat down. "Your mom is starting out with more of an advantage than most. For starters, she's going into this with a good outlook. If you want my opinion, that's half the battle." She tallied on each finger as she spoke. "Plus, she's strong and healthy, and mentally, she is ready for this. She has a son who will move mountains for her. And she's got one hell of a good nurse to take care of her."

He lifted his beer but didn't drink. "Then why do I feel so helpless?"

"You're not going to evade that feeling no matter what you do. No one is. All we can do is be there to support her. Be there when she needs us." She touched him on his leg, because she simply couldn't refrain any longer. "She's going to be fine."

He looked at her slowly, thoughtfully. It wasn't her business what he was feeling, how he was reacting to his mom's sickness, yet she was reaching out to him anyway. Her compassion and concern left him speechless. She was an amazing woman. And she had been his.

"What is it? You can tell me."

He cleared his throat and shook his head. "I'm sorry for getting so angry. And I'm sorry about the other morning, too. I haven't been myself lately," he said.

"Understandably. These next couple of months are going to be long and hard."

He nodded in agreement.

"I want us to be friends," she explained further. "We need to work with each other, not against each other."

"We used to work well together." As he looked into her eyes, she didn't move; she only stared back at him. Was it just her unique kindness that prompted her to move into his home and take care of his mom or was there another reason? He needed to know. And there was only one way to find out.

His gaze dropped to her mouth and he focused on her lips, which were parted slightly. They were an amazing soft pink; slightly damp from her running her tongue along them, and staring at them caused his mind to wander. They had always kissed like it was the first time. The faraway hunger that he'd felt when he'd come home and found her there, stirred and spread as he remembered how her mouth tasted, how it felt pressed against his. Her lips were dewy and yielding and her bottom lip fit perfectly between his teeth. They had an exceptional flavor reminiscent of a mysterious exotic fruit. When he leaned toward her and she didn't move, he took it as a sign, and cupped the side of her face to guide her to him. His mouth melted against hers.

Using his tongue, James subtly, gently, teased her lips until they parted. The lingering little nibbles were so he could taste her well-known warmth. He hadn't tasted her in so long he wanted to savor every drop.

He was consumed by the sensation of her hair in his fingers, the softness of her cheek against his palm, the sweet taste of her in his mouth. Her lips were warm satin, inviting to the point of madness.

He wanted her more than he had ever wanted her before. The need to touch every part of her body shot through him with unexpected force. The intensity was astonishing, even to him. He was desperate to reacquaint himself with every square inch of that body, which he had known so well.

Samantha's nails slid along his scalp as her fingers ran through his hair, down to his neck. A moan of pleasure escaped from her lips as her hands pulled him closer to deepen the kiss.

She leaned into him, pressing deeper into the sofa.

"Oh God, Samantha," he said. He wanted her and his voice was saturated with that want. He couldn't get closer even if he tried. This was how he remembered it, captivating and sensual.

Instantly Samantha broke the kiss and abruptly moved to the other side of the sofa. Her hand flew to her mouth, touching her swollen lips as her trance-like gaze remained fixed on the cushion in front of her.

"Samantha? What's the matter?" James sputtered as he tried to figure out how she had moved from his arms so quickly. He looked down the sofa at her. She looked as if she had just been slapped, not kissed.

She took a deep breath and commanded, "Don't ever do that again."

James's eyebrows shot up. He was totally unprepared for the demand she hurled at him with poignant intensity. "Excuse me?"

Her words came out slowly as she carefully punctuated every last one. "Don't you ever touch me again."

He scoffed at her statement, turning her threat into nothing more than a hollow retort. "That wasn't just me. You were enjoying it just as much as I was." He looked into her eyes. "Or was that moan I heard a moan of protest?"

She jumped up from the sofa and raked her hair behind her ears in an agitated manner. It took her a few seconds to recover her composure. "I don't enjoy being manhandled."

James's laugh echoed throughout the room when he stood up. He moved toward her and in a low, taunting voice said, "I've touched and loved every inch of your body." He moved a step closer. "And I don't ever recall you accusing me of manhandling you."

She closed her eyes as he brushed his thumb over her lower lip.

"Don't tell me you're going to deny it."

She turned her head to the side, breaking all physical contact with him. "Y-yes. I am. This might come as a shock to you but I no longer want your caresses." She squared her shoulders. "I don't want you to ever touch me again."

He raised a single brow. "Ever is a long time, Samantha."

"I don't have to stand here and listen to this."

James followed her around the room as she paced about uneasily. "Listen to what? The truth? You wanted me just as badly as I wanted you."

"Nonsense."

He cocked his head to the side. "I've never known you to lie, Samantha."

She stopped suddenly, held a level gaze, and replied, "I never have."

The doorbell chimed and both sets of eyes shot in the direction of the front door. James started forward but stopped when Samantha raised her hand and said, "It's for me." She turned and left.

"Hi, Paul," Samantha said as she held the door open. She wore a smile that looked pasted on.

Paul leaned in and placed a kiss on her cheek, then looked at his watch. "Sorry, I'm late. It took me a while to find it." He laughed as he looked around the enormous foyer. "I'm not used to these fancy neighborhoods with private driveways."

Samantha touched the guy's shoulder, giving a gentle squeeze. "Don't worry about it. Your timing is perfect. All I need to do is get my bag and I'll be ready." She called over her shoulder as she left the room, "I'll be just a minute."

James stood in the foyer sizing up the man as Samantha went upstairs. Paul appeared to be around their age, perhaps a little older. His hair was a deep brown and slightly thinning at the top. He was wearing gray sweatpants, a white T-shirt, and the athletic sneakers were spotless white. He stood about an inch shorter than James and had a good, strong build.

"Hi, you must be James." Paul stepped forward and extended his hand in a friendly greeting.

"I must be." James instinctively reached out and shook the man's hand. His stomach turned not only at Paul's wide smile but also at the way he surveyed his home. Would throwing him out be too rude? What did he care—after all, it was his house. He tossed the idea around for a moment before deciding against it.

"Love the house," Paul said after looking at the wrought iron on the sweeping staircase.

James could care less what he loved. "And who might you be?"

"I'm Paul."

James puckered his lips in agitation. He didn't like him. And what was with that stupid smile? "Yes, I heard your name." He was way too chipper. What was Samantha doing with this guy? He wasn't her style.

Samantha came down the stairs quickly, holding a gym bag. She raised it in the air. "Got it. I'm ready."

Paul moved in front of her and took her by the shoulders when she came to stand by him. "Sammy, I haven't seen tension like this in you for a long time." He worked the muscles that stretched across her shoulders.

"I need this so desperately tonight."

"Relax," Paul said softly as his hands moved down her arms and then back up to her shoulders and neck.

"That's easier said than done." Samantha rolled her neck from side to side as Paul's fingers manipulated her muscles. "Oooh."

Paul smiled at her heartfelt groan. "It's going to be torture, but we'll have a good time tonight."

Did he just wink at her, James wondered. If Paul touched her again James would throw him out, and he would enjoy every minute of it. He felt a hint of satisfaction as he pictured hurling the nuisance over the perfectly trimmed hedge by the front door, past his mom's roses, and into the driveway.

"Told you I needed it," Samantha said.

"Sammy, you look flush." Paul pressed the back of his hand against her forehead. "Are you feeling well?"

James shifted his position. *Of course she's flushed, she just got done kissing me, you idiot.*

"I'm fine. Really." She raised her shoulders and then let them fall again. "Things have just been a little busy lately."

"That's all?"

She smiled. "That's all."

Paul's thumb brushed her chin. "If you say so."

James raised a brow when his gaze met Samantha's. "Forget I'm here?"

She shook her head. "No."

"Good."

Samantha took a step away from Paul as she made introductions. "Paul, this is my boss, James Taylor. James, this is Paul—"

"Yes, we've met." James's tone turned hard, and he never took his eyes off Samantha.

"Well, then . . ." she said awkwardly.

"Sammy, we better get going," Paul said.

"Yes, we better." She turned her attention back to James. "Good night, James."

Paul raised his hand in a friendly wave. "It was nice meeting you, James. Your home is very impressive."

James followed Samantha to the door and reached for her arm. As she was about to exit, he spoke, "Will you excuse us, Paul?" He pulled her back into the house. "Samantha," he put great emphasis on her full name, "and I will be just a minute."

"What do you think you're doing?" Samantha managed to get out as James hauled her through the foyer, past his office, and into the living room.

He didn't release her arm as he whipped her around and stopped. "I could ask you that same question."

"I beg your pardon."

"Just where the hell do you think you're going?"

Samantha yanked her arm from his grip. "Wherever the hell I want to."

"Samantha, I'm in no mood for your sarcasm," he all but growled.

"You are completely out of your mind if you think you can intimidate me." Her eyes narrowed. "You can inflict your rude, appalling, and extremely nauseating manner on me, but how dare you do it to Paul? He's an innocent bystander."

"Innocent my ass."

"Excuse me?" she shot out furiously.

James's hands were planted on his hips, his eyes glistening like daggers as he stared at her. "What's this Sammy crap?" He made a sour face at the nickname. "Who the hell does he think he is, calling you Sammy?"

"I don't have to answer to you. Where I go on my time is my business. Whom I choose to spend that time with is also my business." She looked at her watch. "Look at that, it appears to be my time."

Oh, Jesus, he couldn't even say the word. He wanted to ask her if Paul was her boyfriend but his mouth wouldn't form the words. He hadn't even considered her having a boyfriend. He swallowed hard, opened his mouth, closed it, and then opened it again. "I don't like the way he touches you."

Her gaze leveled, her eyes narrowed. "And that's my problem how?"

"He touches you like he knows you." His jaw clenched as his

eyes moved over her. "Like he knows your body." Swallowing, he finished. "I don't like the thought of anyone knowing your body but me."

"I'm leaving." She turned. "Like I said before, good night, James."

"Stop," James demanded. "Tell me who he is."

She stopped and then turned. "He's a friend," she said after a moment.

"He doesn't look at you like he's just your friend."

She shifted the gym bag to her other hand. "I'm sorry you don't like the way he touches me or looks at me. There's nothing I can do about that." Lifting her shoulders, she added, "Not that I would."

He sucked in a long breath, trying to control his annoyance. "I don't recall you ever being this sassy before." If it wasn't for the hint of jealousy he was feeling, he knew that he would be enjoying her brazen ways. "I guess I'm going to have to start calling you my sassy angel."

"I'm not your angel anymore."

"Are you Paul's?" Irritation crept through him. He didn't like feeling this way. When Samantha had been with him there had never been any reason for jealousy. She had been his, without a doubt. No one else mattered.

"I don't understand what your problem is." She lifted her shoulders, then dropped them. "You don't want me; you never did."

"I was devoted to you."

"That's bullshit," she snapped angrily.

He pushed the words through his teeth. "Answer the question, Samantha. Who the hell is he?"

She, too, gritted her teeth when she spoke. "I don't believe that's any of your business. And I don't believe I have to answer any of your questions."

"Perhaps Paul would like to know that only moments ago you were passionately kissing—"

"I told you, he's a friend. And you're mistaken if you think there was passion in that kiss."

His gaze fell to the floor as he tried to control his emotions. "How good of a friend?"

She hesitated and adjusted her bag in her hand again. She looked over her shoulder toward the door before she spoke. "Good enough to be my yoga instructor."

He looked up swiftly. "Yoga instructor?"

"Yes. He also happens to be my chiropractor."

"Chiropractor?" James puckered his lips as he said the word. "That's all? He's nothing more than a friend, instructor, and chiropractor?"

"Why, are you going to beat him up if he is?"

"I've thought about it."

"Will you grow up?" she snapped, shaking her bag in irritation. "There is nothing between us."

"At least not on your part."

"On his part either."

"I saw the way he was looking at you." The muscle in his jaw flexed again. "I'm a man. I know what's going through his mind."

"I promise that's not what was going through his mind. We are friends. That's all we've ever been; that's all we'll ever be." She looked down at her watch. "Are you satisfied now?"

A smile slowly pulled at the corner of his lips. "Not nearly as satisfied if the kiss—"

"I don't have time for this. Good night, James." As she walked out of the room she said, "And that's the last good night you're going to hear tonight. I'm going to be late for class."

"There is one more thing." He didn't respond to her twisted frown as he stepped behind her. "Don't ever introduce me as your boss again."

"You're paying me, so that makes you my—"

James just shook his head. "I'm not, nor will I ever be your boss." That was the last thing he wanted to be in her life. He reached his hand out and touched her face lightly. His fingers glided over the arch of her cheekbone and down the length of her jaw. The blond bun that had gold wisps of hair shooting in different directions begged to be freed. The gold hoops in her ears were as delicate as her facial features. When Samantha raised her arm indicating the time, he nodded and leaned into her ear. He lingered for a moment before he spoke softly. "Have a good class, Angel."

CHAPTER NINE

James and Raymond decided against the company car and they each took separate taxis to Sharp Plaza Bar & Grill, downtown in the heart of the business and financial districts. James had chosen the restaurant not for its location but because the casual bar provided private rooms where business could be conducted. Raymond arrived five minutes after him. They sat and made idle conversation as they waited for Al.

"How's your mom?" Raymond asked.

"She starts her treatment today."

Raymond only nodded, with a grim expression. "Samantha's taking care of her right?"

"Yes."

"How's that working out?"

"So far, so good."

Raymond stared down at the table. "I feel helpless in a situation like this, but if there's anything I can do you'll let me know?"

"Of course I will."

"Cynthia sends her best."

"Thank you. I appreciate it." James then asked about Raymond and Cynthia's kids. They had two daughters. One had just graduated from college and the other had just started. They talked for a while before they moved on to the stock report. It was another ten minutes before Al was quietly shown into the room.

"Thanks for meeting us here," James said as he stood and extended his hand.

Al nodded and then reached for Raymond's hand after shaking James's. "Thank you for being discreet. You know how vital I believe it is."

"Yes," James said, gesturing to a chair. "I haven't forgotten."

After they sat, a waitress immediately appeared. Once their orders were given and they were alone, Al spoke. "Is it the same thing as last time?"

"Honestly, I'm not sure," James said as he shook his head. "In less than three months we are going to release a new electronic program that will essentially transform programming as we know it."

Al nodded. "Serious stuff."

"Very," James acknowledged. He continued, "I've gone to great lengths to keep this confidential. I learned my lesson last time. Or at least I thought I had."

Flipping open a small, rectangular notepad, Al wrote and spoke at the same time. "If you have anything that gives you an edge over competitors, rest assured that your competitors will make all attempts to find out about it. You might have learned a lesson last time, but in this business, methods of gathering information are always evolving. That means we must keep up."

James grimaced. "That's why I've hired you, to keep up with them." He looked over to Raymond, then back to Al, who was still writing. "However, we're not so sure if it's the competition this time or if it's internal."

Al looked up. "It won't take me too long to figure that out."

With a serious expression, Raymond stared at Al. "We implemented all your suggestions from last time and still there was a leak. It's beyond me how this happened."

Al nodded. "It happens. What's been going on with the company? With the exception of this new technology that you're going to be releasing, tell me about any other major happenings."

Between them, James and Raymond filled Al in on all the particulars. Their food came and as they ate they conversed; they made certain to touch on everything, no matter how minor. They knew they couldn't leave anything out. If they did, it could jeopardize Al's investigation.

"Internal or not, I think your guilty party may be thinking the commotion from the Europe merger will divert your attention," Al pointed out.

James nodded in agreement. "We figured that much."

"I'd like to have a list of the names of the associates who are involved in this merger. Both here and in Europe."

Raymond plucked a pen from his breast pocket. "I'll take care of that."

"You just let me know what you want to do. I want this done and over with as soon as possible," James said firmly.

"I understand, Mr. Taylor. I think I'm going to look at the managers first while you're getting me the information on the merger." Al stopped and thought for a moment. "You have cameras in the parking garage, don't you?"

"Yes, for security reasons," James said.

"I'll need the footage from the last two months sent to my office. I'll get the license plate numbers from all the managers' vehicles and then we'll see who's coming and going and at what times."

Raymond kept writing. "I'll have it sent to your office."

Al nodded and closed the small notepad.

"Is that all?" James asked. He wiped his mouth with a cloth napkin, then dropped it on his empty plate.

Al slid a two-page contract across the table to James. "Confidentiality clause."

James stared at the papers for a long moment, fingering them until one corner was tattered. Irritation and frustration crept through him. Contemplation wasn't necessary—he knew what his responsibility was—but he didn't like the position it put him in. He felt Raymond shift uncomfortably next to him.

"Mr. Taylor," Al began, "I can't begin the investigation until—"

James looked up briefly, his expression silencing Al.

"You know I make all my clients—"

James quickly signed the papers. "Thanks for coming on such short notice," he said firmly.

Al stood up and nodded curtly. "I'll be in touch."

James gripped the long-stemmed roses in his hand as he ascended the stairs. He had agonized over whether he should call the hospital to see how his mom was doing, but then he decided against it. This morning she had given specific instructions that he was not to worry about her or go to the hospital. He respected her wishes although it was extremely hard to do so. Besides, that was what Samantha was there for. She could handle anything that came up. Turning on his heel he stopped and knocked softly on the bedroom door. He didn't want to wake her if she was sleeping. It was seven-thirty, nearly five hours since her first treatment.

"Hi. You're home early," Samantha said as she opened the door just wide enough to poke her head out.

"It's seven-thirty." James pointed out.

"Is it that late already?" She glanced at the gold-linked watch around her wrist. "I didn't realize what time it was. When did you get home?"

"Just now. I had a meeting that ran late. How is my mom doing?" He stepped forward. "May I see her?"

Samantha hesitated. "This isn't a good time right now."

"Is everything all right?" James felt a lump form in his throat, and he began rapidly firing questions. "Is something wrong? Why didn't you call me? If something's wrong you should have phoned." His hand moved from his beeper at his hip to the small cell phone in the breast pocket of his suit. "Shelly didn't say—"

"Shelly didn't give you a message because I didn't call you." Raising her hand in a calming manner, she rested it against his chest. "Everything's all right. The treatment went fine. She's just a little queasy right now."

At that moment, James heard his mom retch in her bathroom. The repulsive sound instinctively propelled him forward. He clutched the soft, feminine hand that pressed against his chest, trying in vain to stop him. The bouquet of roses in his free hand fell to the floor, unnoticed, as he reached for the door. "Queasy? You call that queasy? What in the hell do you call sick?" He bit back a few foul words. "Goddamn it, Samantha, you should have called me."

"James—"

"Shouldn't someone be in there with her?" His eyes searched hers as another gagging sound reached them. "Why are you just standing here?"

Samantha took hold of the fingers that wrapped through hers and leaned her weight into the door with her shoulder. "This is a normal side effect from the chemotherapy. I've been with her the entire time." She shifted her weight. "Stop pushing on the door."

"I want in."

"No."

"How long has she been like this? How long is it going to last?" he asked as he tried to look around her into the room. He knew he wouldn't be able to see anything. A wall at the far end of the room conveniently blocked the bathroom. He had reservations about going in anyway. The sounds of his mom retching were ghastly.

"Not long." Samantha's tone remained calming.

His head dropped and worry saturated his voice, making it sound strange and distant. "Oh, God, I didn't know it was going to be like this. I didn't know she'd be going through this."

"No one knows how they are going to react to a drug until it's given to them."

He nodded.

"Why don't you go downstairs," she suggested.

"Downstairs?" The words flew from his mouth in an all-but-crazed voice. "Are you asking me to leave? It sounds like my mom is dying in there and you want me to leave? There's no way in hell I'm leaving."

"What are you going to do for her that I can't?" she said reasonably. "Think about it, James. If you go in there right now, how are you going to be able to help her?"

He knew she was right but he still didn't want to leave. He covered his face with his hand while he tried to think logically. Logic was worlds away from him right now. His gaze lifted and found Samantha's eyes. "I can't leave. Please don't ask me to leave."

"I've made her as comfortable as possible. There's really nothing you can do for her right now."

He nodded methodically. "What kind of son would I be if I just left?"

"You'd be the kind of son who's taking care of himself so he'll be able to take care of his mom when she does need him." She paused. "Besides, you're only going downstairs. Staying here in the hall isn't going to help her."

There was the logic he was searching for. There was the reasoning that he so desperately needed right now. Possibilities and crazy feelings swirled through his head erratically, making him feel helpless. Samantha steadied all the turmoil in him.

"Go, have some dinner," she suggested.

"I can't eat."

She nodded in understanding. "Then try your best to relax. I'll let you know if we need you."

"You'll call me."

Samantha nodded. "You know I will." She looked over her shoulder. "I need to be with her." She softly closed the door.

As James leaned against the door he listened to the muffled sounds on the other side. A feeling of nausea overcame him. He moved his hand to his stomach and unconsciously began to rub it. Samantha didn't need two sick people to take care of. Shit, this had to be the worst day of his life.

He moved the few feet down the hall into his room. Several buttons flew from his suit and shirt as he tore them off and tossed them to the floor. The dresser drawer abruptly slid off its tracks when he yanked it open to get a pair of sweat pants. He struggled with the drawer for only a moment before he became too irritated to realign it. He left it hanging awkwardly and moved to the closet to retrieve his jogging shoes.

Ten minutes later he was running full speed down the beach. His feet dug into the sand with fierce rage, and his arms pumped with all their might at his sides. He ran hard and fast, so his thoughts wouldn't have time to form. His head was filled with the pounding of blood, and the crashing of waves, and nothing else. Just how he wanted it.

The miles ticked by and he still didn't stop. He couldn't. He was running from something he could never escape—yet he still tried. It wasn't until his muscles ached with fatigue and his lungs burned like an inferno that he slowed the cruel pace. It was a few more miles until he completely stopped.

He leaned forward, his hands resting on his knees, and he gasped for air as he tried to catch his breath. Finally, he raised his head and took notice of his surroundings. The moon struggled to be seen through the thin layer of clouds that had blown in. He looked at the houses neatly aligned and all-aglow. He realized he didn't recognize any of them.

It was then he dropped down to his knees in the sand and allowed himself to think of his mom and what she was going through. As his labored breathing returned to normal, he contemplated her condition. He grasped how sick she really was. He'd understood the seriousness of it, but he had never permitted himself to let the reality of it sink in. The reality of what the end result could be. A voice shot through his head like a colossal, unexpected wave: *She could die.* He shook his head abruptly to ward off the voice. Beads of sweat scattered like raindrops, causing the sand to form little clumps all around him. He had vowed he would never speak those words, yet they had popped into his head anyway. He picked up a handful of sand in anger and tossed it as far as he could. The curse words he yelled were pure anguish—the crashing of the waves drowned them out and the wind flung them back in his face.

The tirade wasn't like him but it felt good. So good in fact, that he roared into the wind again and didn't stop until his voice was hoarse and he was exhausted. The painful swell of sorrow that raged deep within him fed the sadness, which relentlessly flowed from him. Closing his eyes he wallowed even more as it consumed him.

Slowly, he began to realize that amongst the torment and fear something began to rise. Empty holes were filling, and as he surrendered to the feeling, awareness took over—he was healing. Suddenly, unexpectedly, he felt himself begin to calm.

He struggled to his feet and squared his shoulders. He pulled himself together by taking a few calming breaths. He would get through this. They would get through this. Between the three of them they would be there for each other and they would support each other. There was a time when all he needed was his mom and Samantha. They were all he needed now.

Slowly, he started back home. He felt better. Maybe all he needed was a good breakdown. If his coworkers could see him, they wouldn't believe their eyes. He had been dubbed "the man of steel" in the industry, not only because he was very successful at what he did but also because he rarely allowed his emotions to run loose. When things didn't go his way he wasn't one to yell until he got what he wanted. He knew it wasn't effective. He waited patiently, quietly, for things to change his way, because he knew they almost always did.

That's precisely how he needed to handle his mom's cancer and her treatment. Getting excited about it wasn't going to make a bit of difference. He would do what he did best—hold his ground and wait. Besides, there was nothing else he could do.

"James?"

James looked up and unexpectedly saw Samantha sitting on the top step of the stairs to the deck. He hadn't realized he was so close to the house. "How is she?" He reached for a beach towel draped over the railing and wiped the perspiration off his body.

"She's better." Samantha watched him closely. "Are you okay?"

"Is she—"

"She's resting in bed. The bout of nausea has passed." Her voice was low and soft as her eyes found his. "I asked about you." She looked at his body and clothes soaked with sweat. "You okay?"

He took the towel and ran it over his damp hair. "Don't worry about me."

She touched his hand to stop him. "It's hard not to." She moved down two steps, so she was eye level with him. Leaning forward, she cupped his face into her palms, as he remained silent. Finally, she ran her fingers the length of his jaw to the tip of his chin. "Talk to me."

It was a moment before he spoke. "I've never heard anything like that before. And I went to some pretty rowdy parties in college." He closed his eyes momentarily. "It almost killed me to listen to that."

Samantha nodded.

James opened his eyes and stared at her as relief inundated him. "I'm glad you're here." He pulled her against him hard. "She was right. My mom was right, you're the only one—"

Samantha stroked his back and ran her hand through his hair. "It's okay."

"Knowing you're here—that it was you in there with her. If it had just been me I wouldn't have known what to do. If it had been some stranger it wouldn't have felt right."

"Shh . . ."

He buried his face in her hair and exhaled a long sigh. "Thank you for coming."

"You've already thanked me," she said as she released him.

"Did I?"

"Yes, you did."

"She's okay?"

"Yes," Samantha patiently confirmed.

"You're okay?" he asked seriously.

"Yes. Remember I do this for a living. I can handle it." She put her hand over his. "Relax."

"I'm trying."

Smiling, she said, "Good. You can see her now if you want to."

"Does she want to see me?"

She nodded. "Go see her. I'll fill you in on the treatment later. I have to run into town anyway. It will give you two some time alone." She touched his bicep as he walked by. "She's fine, really. It sounded worse than it really was," she reassured him. "And she does want to see you."

His voice was hoarse and low when he spoke. "What do I say to her?"

Samantha stood very still. "She's your mom; you'll know what to say."

He just nodded and headed into the house.

James presented his mom with a bouquet of a dozen yellow roses as he opened the door. Samantha must have brought them downstairs, because he had found them on the kitchen counter when he had come in. "How's my favorite mom?"

She brought the flowers to her nose. "Are you going to bring me flowers every day?"

He winked as he kissed her cheek. "If you want. A different color every day." He studied her. He didn't know what he expected her to look like. She looked the same as she did when she left this morning, just a little more tired. However, the cotton ball taped to her left arm didn't escape his notice.

Marie set the roses across her lap. "Why are you looking at me like that? My hair isn't going to fall out in just one treatment."

"What was it like?" He had to know.

She fingered a sprig of baby's breath. "Boring. All I could do was sit there. I tried to read but I couldn't focus. I just kept thinking about what they were putting into me."

"What they're putting in you is what will save you." He felt numb as he said the words.

"That thought was what made me stay." She looked down for a moment. "I wanted to run."

James moved closer when she took a deep breath. She looked powerless and vulnerable. Those were two things she had never looked in her life. How could a disease take away everything that defined who and what you are and leave nothing in its wake but an unrecognizable shell?

"I can't tell you how much I wanted to tear out that I.V. and run." Her body shook as she spoke the words. Goose bumps formed on her arms. "I was terrified."

It killed him to see his mom having to go through this. Before his dad passed away, James had promised his father that he would take care of his mother. And he had, all these years. They had spoken every day and had seen each other at least twice a week. Their connection was one that ran deep. It went beyond just a mother-and-child relationship. It was so much more; they were friends. But right now he felt like he was letting his dad down. His dad would have handled this situation much better. He would have stood strong, letting nothing waver him or his family. James felt like he was going to crumble as he looked at his mom. "How do you feel?"

"A little weak, but good considering they pumped me full of chemicals." She grimaced. "I think I threw half of them up."

He bit back the sickening feeling. "I heard."

"I think most of the neighborhood heard, too. I hope I didn't scare you."

He shook his head.

Marie lifted her shoulders. "Well, if this is as bad as it gets I'm not going to complain." Her expression softened when she spoke the next words. "How was your day?"

"It was just like every other day. I wake up too early, go to ten different meetings, make a lot of decisions, and come home too late." He smiled. "Same old, same old."

She took his hand in hers and stroked it affectionately. "You work too hard, honey."

"I'm the boss—that's what they pay me for." He gave her a devilish grin. "Besides, all this work has made your son rich."

"I don't care if you're rich. I want you happy."

He shook his head from side to side. "Happy, rich. Rich, happy—"

"They're not the same," she reprimanded firmly. "I raised you better than that. You know the difference."

"There is no difference. If you have one, you have the other."

"I hate to hear you talk like that."

"It's the truth." He'd given up on happiness after Samantha had walked out.

"You don't believe that."

He nodded and winked. "I know I'll be both when you get better."

She eyed his damp hair and clothes. "Did you go for a run?"

"You could say that."

She patted his hand in understanding. "I can't begin to tell you how glad I was to have Samantha there with me. I couldn't have done it without her. She was so supportive and comforting." She smiled. "You should have seen her take care of everything. She was amazing."

"I'm sure she was."

"She has this remarkable ability to calm me with just the touch of her hand." She shook her head. "I don't know how she does it."

James knew exactly what she meant. "Have you eaten?"

"A little after I got home. Samantha fixed me some broth. It was the only thing I could tolerate. I don't have much of an appetite anyway. What about you?"

"I grabbed a bite on the way home. You must be exhausted; it's very late." He moved to the door. "I'll let you get some rest."

"No, please stay," she said quickly. "Let's watch an old movie." She flipped back the covers and fluffed the pillow next to her. "Like we used to."

James sensed that she didn't want to be alone, and the truth be known, he didn't want to leave her just yet. He kicked off his shoes. "I'm probably sweaty and stinky."

"Mothers are supposed to overlook that stuff."

"We haven't done this since I was ten." He slid into the bed next to her. The cool sheets smelled like her. They were reminiscent of days gone by. Bits and pieces of his childhood flashed before him. He shifted around, trying several positions. "You know this was much easier when I was half the size."

She aimed the remote at the television. "What sounds good?"

"I don't care. You pick."

CHAPTER TEN

Once Marie had fallen asleep, James slipped out of bed to take a much-needed hot shower. The scalding water had relaxed him enough so he could work on a presentation that was due the following day. As he entered his office he unconsciously turned on his laptop, checked the faxes, and scanned through the numbers in his pager.

Moving to his desk, he sat and viewed the room, which was slightly more disorganized than he would have liked. He had once made it a rule not to bring work home from the office, but that had changed when Samantha had left him. There was no longer a reason not to bring it home. Besides, he had to fill his evenings up with something. You could only drink and go out on meaningless dates for so long. He had tired of that quickly.

Samantha was the only one he'd ever wanted. There was no point in trying to fill what could never be filled. He was a realistic man. Replacement could never be obtained, so why bother? During the first few months she'd been gone he had found that if he submerged himself in his work he became numb. When he was numb it didn't hurt and that was a relief to him.

Right now, he didn't want to feel. So his intention for the next few hours was to immerse himself in work—that way perhaps he would forget the gruesome sounds of his mom being sick and forget the fact that Samantha living with him again made him want her more than he had ever wanted her before.

For over an hour James squinted as he stared at the glowing screen of his laptop. Typing words at a proficient speed, he'd managed to get caught up on several reports and tie up loose ends that had been all but forgotten over the last few weeks. After transferring several reports to a CD, he placed the disk in its hard plastic case and then tossed it into his briefcase.

He shook his head as he dove into another stack of folders piled on his desk. Thankfully, the pile dwindled quickly. The last file caused him trouble—it was missing several pages. He flipped through a mound of papers to his left. Not finding what he needed, he cursed and tried looking in another stack. He tossed that bunch aside, retrieved his briefcase from the floor, and rummaged around the narrow compartments. He blew out a long breath. What he really needed was Shelly to come and organize this dump.

"Pulling an all-nighter?"

James looked up and rubbed his hand over his face when he heard her voice. "I didn't hear you come in."

"You look deeply involved."

"I'm trying to catch up," he said as he shuffled through more papers.

"It looks like you're trying to find something." Samantha motioned to the papers on his desk. "Lose something?"

"No, just misplaced it."

Her lips twitched, suppressing a smile at his serious statement. "Nothing is ever lost, only misplaced."

"Exactly."

She moved into the room. His spacious home office was awash in valuable piles of papers and projects. "You always did work too hard."

The papers in his hand went still as his eyes met hers. He held the beautiful blue for a moment before speaking. "Not always."

Samantha didn't look away nor did she argue with his words. Instead she watched him closely, with her lips pursed thoughtfully.

James lifted his hand. "See, found it." He swiveled in the chair and looked down at the computer screen. As his fingers skimmed over the keys, he spoke. "There was a time when something else came first. There was a time when work was the farthest thing from my mind when I got home."

"Things—"

"Yes, I know. Things change. Even when we don't want them to." Contempt crept into his eyes as he glanced at her, then he looked back down at the screen and began to type.

"Wearing glasses would help you with that squinting problem."

"I don't have a squinting problem."

"You can barely see the words on the screen."

"I can see perfectly fine. I don't need glasses," he replied evenly.

"That's what you said a year ago, too," she reminded him.

Deliberately he allowed his eyes to relax. "I didn't need them then, and I don't need them now."

"That's ridiculous." She leaned across the desk and peered down at him. She waited for him to look at her before she spoke. "You do know that wearing glasses doesn't make you a nerd."

"That doesn't concern me because I'm not getting glasses."

Samantha laughed. "Yes, heaven forbid James Taylor wear glasses. That might knock you off the top-ten list of CEOs." She was quiet for a moment. "You know that's what this is all about. You're worried about what people would say."

Peering up he said, "You know I don't give a damn what people say."

"Yes, that's true." She cast him a serious glance. "Squinting damages nerves, which can lead to headaches—"

111

"Did this little lecture work a year ago?" he challenged.

She shook her head. "But I thought you might have come to your senses by now."

James reached for a paper coming out of the printer. Using a paperclip, he attached it to the front of a folder. "Did you come to give me a bad time about my working habits and my lack of vision or is there a reason why you're here?"

Raising her arm, she glanced at her watch and asked, "When was the last time you took a break?" Her eyes narrowed. "That's what I thought."

"Long hours are the mainstay of my profession."

"Do you know that long hours are linked to heart attacks?" She thought for a moment. "I read a recent study that said people who work for more than sixty hours a week and miss out on sleep are far more likely to have a heart attack."

"Really?"

"Yes. And the combination of the two could raise blood pressure and heart rate and trigger an attack."

"I didn't know that."

She smiled sweetly. "You do now."

"Trust me, it isn't the long hours that are going to raise my heart rate and cause me to have a heart attack." There was irritation in his tone.

"An average night's sleep—"

"Samantha." Her name came out in a growl.

She raised her hands in the air. "You're right. If you want to squint for the rest of your life and risk having a massive heart attack, then so be it." She turned. "I went grocery shopping. Come help me unload the car."

James stood back and looked at the trunk of her car, which was filled with brown paper bags. "Leave anything at the store?"

"You had no food in the house. All I could find for lunch

today was a can of broth." She lifted two heavy bags and handed them to James. "To keep your mom's strength up she's going to need far more than that. Good nutrition is an important part of this battle."

James lifted the bags from her arms. "Yes, I know, mind over matter, positive thoughts, healthy food, spiritually strong." He looked over his shoulder at her as he walked into the house. "Does the actual medicine the doctors are giving her play any type of role in making her better?"

Samantha shook her head as she followed him. "You're not that naïve, James. You know it's a combination of everything."

They made several trips from the car to the kitchen and once the last bag was brought in, they started to put everything away. James took out numerous strange-looking vegetables that he didn't recognize. "I forgot how much of a health nut you are."

"I'll take that as a compliment." She grabbed the plastic bags from his hand and tucked them into the bottom drawer of the refrigerator.

"I'm not eating any of this stuff," he said as he pulled out a container of unidentifiable grain.

"You used to."

"Not this stuff." He held the container high to examine the contents.

She pulled a large bowl from the cupboard and set an assortment of fruit in it. "Actually, I fixed you a pilaf made with that *stuff* and you enjoyed it." She set the bowl in the center of the counter and reached for another bag. "It was when you closed that big deal with the Japanese. Remember? We ate out on the deck." She laughed. "It was so cold—"

He laughed too as he cut in, remembering the long-ago dinner. "That we turned the heater on and opened the door so we could feel its warmth."

"So, you do remember. I don't recall you complaining about

the food." She shot him a teasing glance as she pulled out a carton of eggs and several loaves of bread. "In fact, I think you liked it so much you asked me to make it again."

He hadn't complained about anything that night—not even the pilaf made with strange grain, because the entire evening had been amazingly perfect. He had walked through the door and had been immediately met by Samantha in a little black dress, which had been sinfully short. She had wrapped her arms around his neck, placed a kiss against his lips, and congratulated him for several minutes before she had taken him by the hand and led him outside.

She had fixed a tasty dinner, complete with appetizers, wine, dessert, and coffee. The deck had been transformed into a romantic haven with dozens of lit candles and flowers. Halfway through the meal the temperature had dropped and the breeze had turned cold. They had moved the table in the path of the door to obtain the maximum amount of heat. The candles, which had been lit to set the mood, were used for warmth.

Samantha took the grain from him. "I think that must have been the coldest night in the history of Southern California." She came out of the pantry wrinkling her nose. "Why didn't we just come inside where it was warm? Dinner would have been just as good inside. I could have set something up in front of the fire."

James shook off the vision of Samantha shivering in warm candlelight before he spoke. "Because we were crazy." His voice lowered. "Besides, it didn't stay cold for long. Or at least you didn't look cold wrapped in my goose-down comforter on the chaise lounge." His eyes found her. "Now, *that* was crazy. Why were we on a three-foot-wide lounge, when we could have been making love on a six-foot bed?"

Samantha fumbled with the three cans she held, before one of them fell to the floor. The loud noise caused her to jump.

James watched her as she bent to retrieve the cans. He moved behind her and gently placed his hands on her shoulders as she stood. She became immobile. "Do you ever get crazy anymore?" He turned her and guided her to the window. Reaching over her and pulling back the curtain, he spoke softly against her ear. "It was that lounge, right there." His finger tapped on the window. "I can tell by the broken strap. Amazing that we fit on it."

Samantha closed her eyes.

"Open your eyes and look at it," James whispered.

Her eyes slowly opened.

He knew the instant she looked at the lounge, because her body responded with a shiver as the episode flooded her memory. "Sometimes I look out this window and I see that broken strap and all I see is you. Do you remember which one of us broke it?"

Samantha shook her head.

"Me either. But when we made love we never noticed anything other than each other." He turned her around, took the cans from her hands, and set them on the counter. "Do you miss it?" Her cheeks were red, but not from embarrassment; rather, from desire. He knew what she was experiencing. He had brought her there too many times not to recognize that she was almost there now.

"Miss what?" she asked in a serious voice.

His arm enclosed her small waist, pulling her closer to him. "Do you miss the type of desire that makes two people make love in freezing weather on a lounge chair?" He tucked her hair out of her eyes. "Do you miss the uncontrollable hunger that accompanies that type of desire?" He felt her quiver against his body.

"What makes you so sure I don't have that now?"

She could pretend his touch wasn't doing crazy things to her but he knew what she was feeling. His smile was solid conviction as he traced a thumb slowly across her lips. "Because you haven't been with me lately." He shook his head arrogantly. "Samantha, no one can make you feel the way I made you feel."

Her forehead creased as she glared at him. "How arrogant—"

He stopped her words with his finger. "No one."

Lifting her chin slightly, she said, "You're not the only man who knows how to have sex."

Need tore through him, hunger gnawed at every nerve, but he controlled it. "Having sex and making love are two completely different things." His fingers continued to play with the full curves of her lips. "Sex is simple and uncomplicated." He ran the length of her jawline. "Satisfaction is an intricate pleasure that's not always as easily obtained."

"You are absolutely absurd," she bit out.

He smiled with both his mouth and his eyes. "Perhaps, but I'm also right."

Why did his lips have to look so kissable? Samantha thought as she watched his mouth form the words that were causing her body to respond in ways it shouldn't. His expression was gallant, and the flicker in his eyes did nothing to deter it. His voice was borderline hypnotic. She found herself hanging on his every word. It was true. Sex and satisfaction were two completely different things. But when she had been with him they had been one and the same. She shuddered at the thought.

"What level of satisfaction have you reached lately?" James asked, his eyes very intense as they moved over her features.

Warm, creamy desire saturated her skin, sinking into her body, touching every part of her. She struggled to answer the question, because forming sentences was becoming more difficult by the second. "I refuse to answer that question."

"Why?" his brow arched into a soft curve. "Do the others pale in comparison?"

What others, she wanted to yell in his face. She also wanted to scream that the level of satisfaction she had reached in the last year was a big fat zero. It wasn't from a lack of trying either. She had been out with several men, but when it came down to it, the thought of making love with any of them had repulsed her.

"Your silence gives you away." He brushed the tip of her nose with his finger. "That's okay. I like knowing that no man has given you what I gave you." Slowly, he dipped his head and kissed her as innocently as a child might kiss a parent. "Speechless, that doesn't happen often, now, does it?" he whispered against her lips.

Samantha's head was reeling with thoughts. She wanted him; there was no denying it. Her body made it painfully clear, because it ached to the very core for him. The discovery was appalling. After a year of loathing him, how could she possibly want him?

"I like to see you aroused and fighting it." His lips met hers again but this time he barely brushed them over her.

"Stop kissing me," she demanded as she pulled back. "And I'm not aroused."

He laughed. "I also like seeing you deny it," he said as he turned and began putting the groceries away. "You won't be able to stay that way for long."

"You're right. I won't be able to stay that way for long because I'm not aroused."

Turning, he watched her for a moment. "I meant denying it, Angel." He retrieved the cans off the counter and handed them to her. "There will be a time when you won't deny what you're feeling right now."

"Don't hold your breath."

"I won't have to. I'm patient."

"This conversation is over," she snapped irritably.

"Sure." He shook his head. "If we keep talking about it we might just end up on that broken lounge—"

"James!"

He raised his hands in the air. "You won't hear another peep out of me."

Samantha was a jumbled mess of nerves as she reached for the cans. The area just beneath her skin tingled violently. She could barely concentrate on the task of stacking cans in the pantry. When she came out of the small room, she didn't make eye contact with him for several minutes. She needed enough time to force her body to stop shaking and her heart to slow its erratic pace.

She put the rest of the groceries away like she was on a strategic mission. She was so focused on the task that she hardly noticed James working around the kitchen beside her. She spoke only when she knew her voice was steady. "Do you want me to fill you in on how your mom's treatment went today?"

"Of course. We talked a little about it, but she didn't really say much. How did she handle it?"

Her calming breaths were working. "I think she handled it well. I could tell in the beginning she was very apprehensive. Eventually she relaxed a little."

He folded the last paper bag and tucked it into a narrow cupboard. "Do you want some coffee?"

"Sure, I'll have a cup." If he could pretend nothing happened so could she. He wasn't the only one who could be flippant.

CHAPTER ELEVEN

Over coffee, they talked about his mom's treatment for almost an hour. Samantha took him through the entire process step by step. She didn't want him to feel like he was being left in the dark, because James was the type of man who needed to know what was happening at all times—it kept him in control.

On the way to the hospital, Marie had shared with her that she had asked James not to come. Samantha knew that type of request would test James's dependable and loyal nature to the limit. She wasn't sure it was the best choice, but she understood Marie's decision and she respected it.

"The most important thing we can do right now is protect against infection." Samantha ran over a list of symptoms of infection so he would know what to look for. "Make sure to wash your hands frequently, especially after you come home from work. I think we should limit her visitors for the next few days, too."

James nodded. "I don't think she's up to seeing anyone anyway."

"Not likely." She stretched her legs, resting them on the coffee table.

"So, this is as bad as it will get?" he asked hopefully.

She swallowed a mouth full of coffee and shook her head.

"It could get worse?" He spoke the words bleakly. Picturing his mom even sicker than she already was, was daunting. He couldn't fathom that she could possibly get any worse.

"Maybe, maybe not. Since this is the beginning of her treatment it could go either way. I've seen it at both ends of the spectrum. Some people are mildly affected; they don't lose much hair, their appetites don't decrease, and they don't get nauseated. Then there are people who have every reaction imaginable. There's no telling what else could happen. It really depends on how her body handles the drug." Restlessly, she got up and moved to the window; pulling aside the curtain, she looked out at the black ocean. "I've already called the doctor and requested a stronger anti-nausea drug."

He watched her curiously. Her attention had been divided between him and the window most of their conversation. "I never knew there was even such a thing."

"There are many new drugs available to help with the side effects of chemo. The trick is to find the right ones for each individual. If we find the right combination for Marie, she'll have an easier time with her future treatments."

"If there is anything I can do, you'll let me know?"

"Of course I will," she said as she looked over her shoulder at him. "What? What are you looking at?"

He motioned to the window. "You've been staring out the window for the last ten minutes."

"It's beautiful out there. The moon is almost full and it's just amazing against the sand," she said as she let the curtain fall back.

"You want to go for a walk?"

She glanced at her watch before looking at him. "It's getting late and I really don't think—"

"Come on, we won't be long." He took her coffee from her and placed it on the table with his. "I think we could both use it."

She hesitated, but after a moment she nodded.

"Good."

Once outside, she moved across the deck to a chair. "Wait."

"What are you doing?" James asked as he watched her sit.

She bent down and untied the laces of her shoes. "The only way to walk on the beach is barefooted."

They strolled down to the water and allowed the cool surf to lap around their ankles. Silently, they walked up the beach, enjoying the cool breeze, the crashing of the waves, and the twinkling lights from the endless row of prestigious houses. The exclusive area had miles of private sandy beach.

Samantha looked over at James when she spoke. "Ginger came in this morning, and when she saw me she all but danced out of the room, saying 'I knew it, I knew it.' " She scrunched her nose. "I don't understand her."

James chuckled. "Don't even try."

"I feel like I'm missing half of what she's saying when I have a conversation with her."

"Join the crowd."

"So, I'm not alone."

He shook his head. "Don't even attempt to figure that woman out or you'll go crazy trying. She's a mystery that can never be solved." He raised his hands. "All I know is, she's one hell of a housekeeper, and she makes a mean loaf of cinnamon bread." Several moments of silence lapsed before James turned to her seriously and asked, "What have you been doing for the last year?"

She shrugged and tilted her head into the wind. "Not much. Mostly working."

"You're still at Mercy Hospital?"

The salty air filled her lungs and Samantha nodded. "Of course. I don't think I'll ever leave. I love the staff."

"How's your brother doing?"

"He's doing well. He and Connie are expecting another baby."

"So, that'll make three?"

"Yes."

"I can imagine that Casey and Lynn are excited about the new one." Casey had only been an infant the last time James saw him. He was probably walking and talking by now. And the beautiful, big-eyed Lynn had been starting kindergarten. He could only imagine how much they'd changed over the last year.

"They are. Casey wants it to be a boy and Lynn wants it to be a girl."

"Sounds about right. Things have been so busy I haven't gotten to ask how Marisa is doing. Is she still photographing the rich and famous?"

"Yes. She's opened another studio, too."

"Business must be good."

"It is. She's worked hard for it, so she deserves it." She looked over at him. "I see you've been busy, too."

His eyes met hers. "How so?"

"You've been in the newspaper three times in the last two months. And that's just in the paper I get." She pulled her hair to the side as it caught in the wind. "And let's not forget the little blurb in *Fortune 500.*" Her gaze drifted off into space. "What was the headline? 'The Greatest CEO Ever.' "

James shook his head and tried to deny the title. "I don't think it said that."

"Okay, it was more like 'James Taylor Is Taking the Industry by Storm, Conquering Deal after Deal.' "

He smiled at the animated authoritative tone she used.

"What, is this modesty I'm detecting?" She gave him a gentle shove. "Don't forget who you're talking to."

James gave her a sideways glance and said, "How does it feel to be walking on the beach with one of the world's top ten CEOs?" He stuck his chest out and strutted around her.

She laughed. "Now, that sounds more like it." When he

stopped and resumed his position beside her, she spoke, "I'm proud of you. I know it's not easy doing what you do."

He noted the change in her tone. She was serious. "I think that can be said about both our jobs."

A big wave crashed against Samantha legs. "This feels wonderful. Do you still jog every day?"

"I try. Although since Mom moved in I haven't had much time."

Samantha kicked at a wave and then laughed as it splashed around her, sending small droplets of water in the air. "When did she move in?"

"A little over two weeks ago. She still has her condo in Beach Point. I thought it would be best if she wasn't alone." He reached for her arm, pulling her away from a surprise wave that had surged unexpectedly far up the beach and wrapped around her calves and knees.

"I agree." She looked down at her soaked pants, amused.

"She was very reluctant at first," James continued. "Believe it or not, she claimed she couldn't leave because all her roses would die if she did. She was going on and on about feeding schedules, proper watering cycles, and she even claimed that she needed to be there to talk to them."

"Yes, that sounds like your mom." She stopped and picked up a shell. "How did you get around that one?"

"I reminded her that she not only has an automatic watering system but also a gardener. That made it pretty hard to argue with." He regarded the shell she held in her hand. "You're not going to attempt to make something with that are you?"

"I might." She looked over at him. "Why, would you like to put in a request?"

He shook his head. "Just be careful."

Another wave licked her legs and she sighed in enjoyment. "Walking on the beach in the moonlight is good for the soul. I haven't done this since—" Her words trailed off.

The tone in her voice was an instant giveaway. Instinctively, the hairs on the back of James's neck prickled. An uneasy feeling consumed him. Something just happened but he wasn't sure what it was. The mood definitely shifted. "Since when?" he asked firmly.

She shook her head carelessly, looking down at the water. "It's just been a while, that's all I meant."

It was hard to see her face in the dark, so James took her by the arm and stopped her. He moved her so the moonlight could bathe her features. "Since when?" he repeated.

"It doesn't matter."

"I think it does."

Her voice was low and evasive as she took a step away from him. "I think it doesn't."

She could give him all the dirty looks she wanted. He wasn't going to let it rest until he had an answer. "When was the last time you took a moonlit walk on the beach?"

"James, don't." She looked around and lifted her hands in the air, expressing her pleasure. "It's so beautiful out here. Don't ruin it."

"When Samantha?" His words were a low growl that rumbled in his chest. She was keeping something from him. Something personal, something that had to do with the both of them, and he didn't like it.

Samantha hesitated briefly before speaking. "It's been a long day. Please, let's end it with a nice relaxing walk and not an argument."

James watched her tensely. Something wasn't right. "You love the beach, the water, the sand, the sun." He added, "You were practically raised on the beach."

"I did love it at one time."

"What do you mean, you *did?* You don't just stop loving all this." He ran his hand through his wind-blown hair. "Damn it, answer me."

"I haven't been to the beach since I left you," she answered blandly.

"That's been over a year. What does that have to do with anything?"

Samantha's eyes turned as dark as the ocean, which thrashed loudly behind her. Pain and anger swam in the blue murky depths. Her teeth raked over her bottom lip until it almost bled. Hair whipped around her face and she did nothing to try to contain it.

Her expression landed like a blow to James's abdomen. He wanted to grab her and pull her to him but he didn't dare touch her. "Is it because the last time we—"

She raised her hand suddenly, almost frantically.

"—we made love, it was on the beach?" He finished his sentence.

James stared at her as he remembered the night. The water had been cool against their warm skin. The sand had conformed to their bodies as they pressed deep into it. The rough surface had only added to the magnificent sensations they were feeling. She had tasted of salt and passion. Their intense lovemaking had lasted for hours under the soft glow of the moon. Tired, they had lain in the surf, speaking of their love for one another.

"Do you really hate me that much?" he said suddenly.

"Hate is a strong word," she said quickly. "If I hated you I wouldn't be here."

His head cocked to one side, trying to figure her out. "Then why are you here?"

"To take care of your mom."

"No, I mean here." He pointed toward the ground.

She shook her head. "Don't read anything into this, James. I'm living in your house as a nurse. I'm here," she pointed to the sand, "because it's beautiful and I didn't realize how much I missed it until now."

"Now, with me?"

"No. Now, meaning when I moved in your home and it became my back yard. I'm not the one who ruined what we had, James."

"I didn't ruin anything. You were the one who walked out on us."

"You're insane, do you know that?" She pointed her finger at him. "There is no way in hell that you can turn this around and put the blame on me."

"You left. You left me." He squeezed his eyes shut. "Christ, Samantha, we had just made mind-boggling love. It was so intense I feared I'd never recover from it. And you walked away." He shook his head. "Don't you remember what we had? Don't you remember what we shared that night?"

Samantha didn't move.

He couldn't have stopped himself if he wanted to. Moving to her, he pushed the hair away from her face and with both hands cupped her cheeks. He eased her gently to him. "You remember our last night here don't you?"

Her cold eyes never once blinked. Not even when the wind whipped her hair around them.

James grimaced, but wouldn't allow her frosty demeanor to persuade him into believing that she had forgotten. He would chisel away at it until he broke through and found what she was really feeling. His thumbs traced over the arch of her cheeks to the corners of her eyes. "Tell me what you remember."

She refused to make eye contact. "Why are you doing this to me?"

"Look at me, Samantha. Look me in the eyes and tell me you remember." He gently turned her head so her eyes met his. "Tell—"

Her blue eyes caught his gaze and held it. "I remember."

"What? What do you remember?"

Somehow, she mustered up enough strength to shove his hands away. She fought the tears that stung her eyes. "I remember." She was shouting now as she took several giant steps away from him. "I see us in the water making love. I feel our bodies pressing in the sand. I feel you on me, touching me, in me, loving me. But I also see you holding another woman in your arms only hours after we made love. That's what I remember. That's what I think about when I come to the beach." She blinked back the tears that the wind threatened to expose. "Is that what you wanted to hear?"

"Angel—"

She glared challengingly at him. "Are you happy now, or do you want to hear more?"

James hung his head and shook it. "No, I don't want to hear any more."

"Because if you don't remember I can tell you what color dress she was wearing." The tears spilled from her eyes and were spread across her cheeks by the wind. "It was red."

"Stop," he demanded.

"Do you remember the color of her eyes?" she continued. "I do."

"I said stop."

"Green, like jade. I can also tell you the color of her hair and the scent of her perfume." She pushed him hard on the chest with both hands as she gritted the words out. "You were holding her the way you hold me." Her hands turned into fists as she pounded against him again. "Apparently mind-boggling sex isn't enough for you."

"Stop."

"Apparently, giving you my heart wasn't enough either."

"Samantha."

She didn't say anything more. She couldn't. She turned and sprinted down the beach.

"Shit," he shouted into the wind. God, what had he done to her?

CHAPTER TWELVE

Two weeks later, James sat in his office high above town. His arms were crossed over his chest as he leaned back in his chair. He glanced at his watch—twenty more minutes to kill before his next meeting. As he took a deep breath, he rotated the chair in a half circle, stopped the motion with his feet, and stared out the huge window. He didn't feel up to arguing over the minor details his client was complaining about. In his business, details like this inevitably cropped up and would be hashed out, until an agreeable resolution was reached. But at the moment, all of it seemed too petty. Trivial. Unimportant.

Normally, he enjoyed negotiating immensely. It was his specialty. However, his mom's illness had put things in perspective in an abrupt, cruel way. The satisfaction brought on by long hours of hard work, the respect, and the money, didn't seem so important anymore. He would give it all up if it meant his mom would be cancer free. He found it brutally ironic how one could work one's entire life for something and in a single moment it suddenly becomes insignificant.

He drummed his fingers against his chin as he thought about his mom. He had made it a must to stop in and see her at least twice a day. If he knew he was going to be home late, he would run home for a quick lunch. To her surprise, he always managed to find a different bouquet of roses on the way, too. It was one of the small pleasures she looked forward to.

Marie didn't come out of her room much, especially a day or

so after a treatment. The chemo left her too queasy to navigate the stairs and drained what little strength she had left. Despite all of it, amazingly her spirits were still up. Physically she was frail, but mentally she was strong. He smiled gently. She never stopped surprising him. She was as fearless as a warrior and as virtuous as an angel. She was his hero.

James rubbed his eyes briskly with the back of his hands as his thoughts shifted to Samantha. Where did he start with what was happening between them? She, too, was fighting a battle, but it wasn't against some merciless disease; it was with her feelings for him. She was refusing to accept that she still cared for him. Refusing? That was putting it mildly—she was downright in denial. The fact that she wouldn't acknowledge her feelings surprised him, because the chemistry between them was unrelenting. For him, it was undeniable no matter what the circumstances were.

He stood and began to pace. He couldn't even sit still when he thought about her. She got under his skin and inside of him. She unintentionally overpowered all his senses, leaving him to muddle through what was happening between them in complete uncertainty. He was mystified, baffled. He had no idea how to think about what was happening when it came to their relationship.

To say that things were tense was an understatement. She hadn't spoken to him once since the night on the beach; in fact, that was the last time she had even looked at him. He knew she was very busy tending to his mother; however, there were times when she could have spoken to him, if for nothing more than to touch base on how his mother's treatment was coming along. She had left that completely up to his mom.

Moving to the bar, he poured hot coffee into a white cup that had the company logo in gold wrapped around it. As he stirred in a teaspoon of sugar, a slow smile formed. Sure, he was a little confused about what was happening between them; however, there was no confusion about what he *wanted* to happen.

His smile grew even bigger. What Samantha needed wasn't space or time—he had given her plenty of that—but a reminder of what they had shared. He brought the cup to his lips and sipped the warm liquid. She wasn't going to like it, and it sure wasn't going to be easy, but they weren't going to be avoiding each other anymore.

He felt a remorseful twinge deep within him, but didn't allow any guilt to take hold; he had given her more than enough time to settle down, he reminded himself. Somehow, he would find a way to get back into her good graces. And once he did, she better watch out. He wanted her back and he would get her. Starting right now he would stop at nothing until he got what he wanted.

For the moment he was very satisfied. He had a plan and was now in control of the situation; it was a position from which he dominated, so his confidence soared. His sheer conviction was what made him able to return to his desk and prepare for the client who would be walking through the door any minute.

"Mr. Taylor, Mr. Malone is here to see you."

James stared at the speakerphone, lost in his thoughts.

"Mr.—"

His hand shot out and pressed the bar at the base of the phone. "Yes, send him in." He stood and buttoned his suit, straightened his tie, and moved to the front of his desk. "Will, it's a pleasure." He held out his hand when a tall, lean man walked through the door. "I hope your flight was uneventful."

"Smooth the entire way. Very nice jet, thank you."

"Not a problem." He gestured to a large wingback chair in front of his desk. "Care for something to drink?"

"No, thank you."

"I can have Shelly order us some lunch."

"I ate on the jet."

James moved to the other side of his desk, unbuttoned his suit jacket, and sat. Flipping open a file he said, "Then let's get down to business."

It took an exhausting hour of reassurance and several heavy doses of James's hard-to-resist persuasion, but he'd finally managed to satisfy Will Malone. Their contract was still open and in the negotiations process, but basically his company had it. He'd even talked Mr. Malone into having a quick drink before he walked him to the elevator.

Just as the elevator doors closed and James turn toward his office, his pager went off. Slipping it off his hip, he glanced at the number. He waited until he was in his office and the door shut before he reached for his cell phone in his pocket.

"Do you have any information for me?" he asked, hoping that Al would be able to give him some good news. Or as good as news could get when there was a snitch lurking about the company.

"Nothing substantial that's going to lead us to who's leaking information."

"There's nothing on the tapes I had sent over?"

"Nothing."

James punched the air with his fist as he began to pace about the room impatiently. "Shit."

"I hear ya. I was surprised when all the video checked out clean. I watched every single one of them and I noticed nothing out of the ordinary or I wouldn't have believed it myself. You run a tight ship and that reflects on when your people are coming and going. I went a step further and took the liberty of following a few of your managers over the last several days, and they're clean, too. If they're getting information, I don't think it's because one of your employees is selling out."

James pressed his hand against his forehead and pinched his

eyes shut for a moment.

"I think you're right. Someone has hired an investigator to do the dirty work."

"Now what?"

"I have to find out how they're getting the information. I want to look at your computer systems. I think that would be the next best step." Al paused. "Can that be arranged?"

"Of course."

"I'll need all access codes and passwords."

"I'd like to be there when you access the information."

"I understand," Al answered. "Contact me when everything is ready and you want to meet. I think the sooner the better."

"It's going to take me at least a day to get everything. And when we meet it'll have to be after hours."

"Of course."

"I'll call and let you know when."

James clenched the cell phone tightly before he tossed it on the desk, seething with rage. Whoever was responsible for this would pay dearly, he would make sure of it. He pictured McDonald. He would take the man down if all this led back to him.

Marie sat in the deep settee, each elbow resting on the arms, crocheting a pale green blanket. "You know, I'm feeling much better today."

"I told you, you would," Samantha said from the kitchen, where she was filling a large plastic watering container.

"It wasn't that I doubted you, dear." The older woman looped the yarn twice over her needle. "I was so ill I couldn't imagine ever feeling good again."

"I know." Bless her heart, Samantha thought as she lifted the container out of the sink and carried it into the adjoining room. Marie had been such a trooper through it, too. Never once had she complained about anything. And there had been more than one occasion that she could have cried like a baby. God knows, she herself would have broken down if she had to go through half of what Marie has gone through so far.

"It's a good thing I'm feeling better." She shook her head. "Staying in my room was starting to depress me."

"I know. Something as simple as coming downstairs is a nice change, isn't it?"

Marie nodded in agreement. "You'll never know how nice. I've been so thankful for the break in between treatments. I'm dreading this next round. I'll undoubtedly be quarantined to my room again."

"If you'd take—"

"I'm not taking a handful of pills, so don't even suggest it," Marie interrupted sternly. "I know you want me to, but I hate the thought of it. I already take enough with what's mandatory."

"I want you to have the least amount of side effects. The medication will help take the edge off, that's why I'm so adamant about you taking them." Samantha moved around the room watering the houseplants. "But ultimately it's up to you whether you take them or not."

"Thank you for respecting my wishes, but I'll pass."

Samantha turned toward Marie and smiled lightly. "Do these miniature roses get water?"

"Just a little, dear. We don't want them to get root rot."

Samantha went back to the sink and refilled the pitcher. She added several drops of plant fertilizer to the water. "The side effects that you have now are more than likely all you will get."

"I'm not sure if that's a relief or not." Marie tugged on the green fiber to unravel a portion of it from the ball that rested on the floor at her feet. "James has been working late these last few weeks."

Samantha made no comment.

"I think he's been leaving very early, too."

"Really, I hadn't noticed." It was the truth. She hadn't noticed the hours James was keeping because, frankly, she didn't care. She rolled her eyes the second she'd finished the thought. Okay, there might have been a few nights she wouldn't allow herself to fall asleep until she heard his car pull into the drive. But that was it. She cringed. That wasn't true, either. She had also heard him almost every morning out in the hall, checking on his mom. She had even caught him cracking her door and checking on her, too. Of course she had pretended to be asleep.

Marie's hands and crochet hook stopped moving as she watched Samantha. "Are you okay?"

"What? Yes, I'm fine." Samantha pulled herself together long enough to pinch off a dead leaf and stare at it.

"I hate it when he works so hard."

"He works hard all the time."

"Yes, but not this hard. He needs to take a break." She shook her head. "My husband used to say that hard work kept a man young, but I don't think he meant this."

"He knows his limits." She held her voice steady.

Marie sighed loudly. "I'm not too certain that he does. That's what bothers me."

"He'll take care of himself."

"Yes, I suppose you're right." She sighed heavily again. "He might burn himself out though."

"Not likely. He loves his work." She shook her head in disagreement. "James was meant for the corporate world. It races through his blood like an addictive drug."

"That he does. But, I know all this is hard on him." She shifted restlessly in the chair. "It's hard for him to see me sick."

Samantha's smile weakened. "Yes, it is. But he's coping with it. We all are." She turned to Marie and looked at her thoughtfully. "You know what really amazes me? It's the ability we have to muster up strength when we didn't believe there was any." She touched Marie's shoulder. "He's fine."

Marie nodded, but spoke quickly. "But he's alone. He doesn't have anyone." She fidgeted with the yarn. "I have him, but who does he have? Whom will he turn to when it's too much for him?" Her eyes found Samantha's and settled.

Samantha moved away from her and swallowed the gagging knot lodged in the back of her throat. "He has friends."

"Friends can only do so much," Marie insisted. "Besides, his friends are mostly employees and coworkers; they're not true friends. There's a difference."

"Marie, I promise you, he'll be fine."

"I just worry about him."

"I know you do." She smiled as she shifted the subject. "Now, what sounds good for dinner?"

"Nothing."

"You can say that every evening, but that doesn't mean I'm not going to fix anything." Samantha went back into the kitchen and stored the watering can and fertilizer under the sink. She made sure she put everything back exactly where she had found it. Ginger would have her head on a platter if she didn't.

Marie raised her shoulders. "You might as well not. It goes to waste anyway. Every bite tasted metallic, like I'm sucking on a coin. Why bother eating if it doesn't taste good?"

"You need to eat for your strength." She looked across the room. "You'll get your appetite back and when you do it will be twofold."

"I hope you're right. If I lose any more weight I'll look like a skeleton." She tugged on the yarn. "What about take-out?"

"Do you have something in mind?" Samantha asked hopefully. She hadn't thought to suggest ordering out when she had been trying to find something that Marie could keep down. She had been trying to keep it simple. Perhaps what she needed wasn't something plain and bland but something packed full of flavor.

Marie wrinkled her nose. "Not really. But you've cooked every night for the last few weeks. I think you need a break."

"Nonsense. What else do I have to do?" Samantha said as she searched through the cupboards. She was hoping that some unforgotten recipe would pop into her mind when she saw the vital ingredient. There had to be something around here that Marie would eat.

"Well, if you put that much energy into it, the least I could do is eat it."

Finding nothing, Samantha turned and said, "If you could have anything your little heart desired, what would it be?"

Marie thought for a moment. "Chinese sounds good. I love the one down on the boardwalk." She gestured with her hand. "I think James has a menu in the drawer by the kitchen phone."

When the front door opened, then closed, Marie stuffed the blanket along with the remaining yarn into a tote. "How was your day?" she asked when James walked into the room.

"Long, but very productive." His meeting had ended earlier than expected. This had been the first evening in weeks that he had been able to get home this early. "It's good to see you out here."

"It feels good to be out here." She gestured at her tote. "I've even got a little crocheting done, too."

"Wonderful." Seeing her like this made him almost forget that she had cancer. Despite the fact that her hair was thinning and she had lost weight, she looked like her old self. Recently, her life had been nothing more than a struggle to get from one day to the next. It was nice to see this normality, for her sake.

James looked around for Samantha and spotted her in the adjoining kitchen, where she was digging through the junk drawer. Her hair was down, shielding her face from him as she intently searched for something. He would love to thread his fingers through the golden strands, pulling them back at the nape, so he could place a kiss just beneath her ear. Her pulse would beat wildly against his lips in response to his touch. The image caused his body to tighten.

"We're having Chinese take-out. Do you want any?" Marie asked.

James blinked and brought himself back to attention. "Chinese sounds good to me," he answered, reluctantly taking his eyes off Samantha. He sifted through the mail, dropping a few piece onto the table and tossing the rest into the trash.

Marie rose to join Samantha, who was still in the kitchen trying to stuff the bulky contents of the drawer back in so she could close it. "Did you find it?" she asked as she moved beside her.

Samantha looked up for the first time and waved the bright, yellow paper menu in the air. "Yes." She caught James's glance. "Hi."

"It's good to see you."

Samantha held his eyes momentarily before she looked back down at the menu. Positioning it in front of Marie, she said, "What sounds good?"

Marie scanned over the options.

"How about some soup?" Samantha suggested, pointing to the egg drop soup. "This is very light and would be easy on your stomach."

Marie shook her head.

Samantha pointed out a few other items, and when Marie turned them all down, she asked, "Do you see anything you like?"

"Not really."

"We can order something else if Chinese doesn't sound appealing," James said from across the room. His mother's appetite had decreased as her treatments progressed. Finding something appealing was becoming a challenge. He would ship it in from China if that were what she wanted. He clicked opened the gold latches on his briefcase after he set it on the coffee table.

"No, that won't be necessary." Marie searched the menu for several seconds before she looked up. "I have a wonderful idea. Why don't you both go pick something up?"

James shrugged his shoulders, discarding her suggestion. "Whatever you want we can have them deliver. There's no need to go out if we don't have to," he said as he pulled folders from a narrow compartment then arranged them on the table.

Marie disappeared into the foyer and then returned to the living room holding Samantha's sweater, which she'd taken off the hall tree. "Here, sweetie." She held it out until Samantha walked over. "Put this on. It's a little on the cool side this evening."

"Mom, I have work to finish." James motioned to the open briefcase on the table.

"Nonsense. You just walked through the door. Put that briefcase away and start thinking about something else other than work," she snapped.

James looked up suddenly.

"Neither one of you"—Marie looked at each of them—"has been out in weeks." She did nothing to soften her tone; if anything she made it a little more intense.

"I go out every day," James countered. She was looking at him like he was twelve. And why was she reprimanding him in that harsh motherly tone of hers? He had done nothing to warrant it.

Marie tossed her hand in Samantha's direction. "What about Samantha? Do you realize she has only left the house to take

139

me to the hospital and to get food?"

"I've gone to yoga class."

Marie moved over to her son and looked down at him with stern, narrow eyes. "Do you hear that? There is more to life than chemotherapy treatments and yoga."

James sat in stunned silence as he gaped at his mom. It wasn't until she rose a displeased brow that he realized it was his turn to plead his case. "Mom." Oh God, he even sounded like he was twelve. He cleared his throat. "Samantha knows that she can leave—"

Marie brought her hand to her head. "I'm very tired."

"What?" James dropped the pen and papers he was holding and stared at her.

"I'm so tired. And I haven't had the house to myself in awhile. I could use a little time alone." She waved her hands in front of her. "It's always busy here. Something is always going on. I've lived five years alone without your dad and to be quite honest with you, I like my solitude. I've grown used to it."

"I didn't know you wanted to be alone," James said, rising from the couch. He assumed he had thought of his mom's every need. He didn't like the idea that he had overlooked something, especially something as simple as peace and quiet.

"I like having you both here, but I could use some quiet time." She allowed her shoulders to droop.

"If there's something you need, please tell me," James said.

"I just did. A little quiet time will do me good." She put her arm around her son's waist and ushered him and Samantha to the door. "Go out and get some fresh air. And have a nice dinner." She took the car keys from the table in the foyer and pushed them into James's hand.

"What about you?" James asked as he took the keys.

"To tell you the truth I'm not really hungry."

It was James's turn to inflict the narrow eyes on her. "You

were up for take-out just a minute ago."

She smiled weakly when she sensed James's perceptiveness. "I think I'll just grab a little something in the fridge." She eyed them both. "I promise."

"If you're sure," Samantha said, not knowing what else to say. Marie was making it hard to put up an argument. What was her rebuttal going to be? "No, Marie, you don't need any private time of your own"?

"Of course I'm sure. Now, please go so I can soak in a long, hot bath." She winked. "I might even walk through the house naked."

James shook his head, then kissed her cheek. "Lock the door when we leave and call my cell phone if you need anything."

"All right. Have a wonderful evening." Marie leaned against the closed door with a smile.

Chapter Thirteen

"Do you really want Chinese?" James asked as he opened the car door for Samantha. He couldn't believe that he had just been thrown out of his own house, by him mom no less, and he had a nagging suspicion that it wasn't entirely because she wanted to be alone. That woman was relentless.

She shook her head as she slid into the soft leather seat. "No, not really."

"Me neither. If we're going to be coerced to go out together so my mom can"—using his finger, he made air quotes—" 'have some alone time,' we might as well go somewhere we'll enjoy."

She reached for the seatbelt and looked up at him as he held the door open. "Do you really think we've been smothering her?"

"I see her twice a day. I can hardly call that smothering."

"Perhaps I've been too attentive." Samantha said after James climbed into the car and started it.

"No."

She turned to him. "Are you sure? I thought if I kept her busy it would take her mind off things. Maybe I need to pull back a little."

"You don't need to pull back. She enjoys every minute with you." He turned onto the street. "Don't tell me you're buying in to all this alone stuff."

"She sounded convincing."

He sighed theatrically as he muttered her name repeatedly

under his breath.

Samantha smiled. "Stop. There's nothing wrong with being concerned."

"No, there isn't. But trust me, I know my mom. So, where to?"

"I don't care, you pick."

"Okay. I have the perfect place in mind."

James requested a table located outside. Once seated, Samantha took in her surroundings. The open seashore was only several yards away. It was too dark to see the water, but the roar that came from the unlit darkness made the ocean's presence known. The intense tang of salt wrapped itself around them like a warm, familiar blanket.

The small candle placed in the center of the table didn't give off much light, but instead added a cozy feeling. The tablecloth was stark white, floor length, and danced against her legs in the soft breeze.

"I've never been here before," she said as she watched the flame of the candle flicker.

"Neither have I. I just read a review on it. It's supposed to be excellent."

"If the food is anything like the ambiance, it will be wonderful," she said as she glanced at the huge potted palm trees that surrounded them. The long pointy leaves sounded like a dozen baby ducks shaking as they danced in the breeze.

"I agree."

A waiter appeared out of the dimly lit area by the door and moved to James's side. After a warm greeting, he asked, "What may I get for you and the lady?"

James ordered a bottle of white wine and some appetizers. He gave a concise nod as the waiter gave a short bow and slipped away into the darkness between the two palms framing the door.

Samantha leaned back in her chair to look up at the sky. "It's beautiful tonight." The moon was a hazy half crescent. The industrial clutter of civilization that stretched for miles on either side of them went unnoticed. It was as if the world started at the beach and extended outward into infinity.

"Yes, it is."

The breeze pushed her hair forward, wrapping it against her face. "This is lovely." She turned her head, allowing her hair to blow in the opposite direction. She laughed when the wind shifted and it covered her face again. She gathered the strands at the base of her neck and held them firmly as she reached for her purse.

"Don't." James's voice was like a velvet whisper in the night.

Samantha's hand stopped rooting around in her purse and she looked up. "What?"

He shook his head. "Please, don't pull it back."

Samantha let go of the barrette in her hand and set her purse to the side. She didn't move when he reached across the table and took hold of the hand that held her hair firmly in place. The small gesture was temptation in itself.

"It's beautiful when it's down." James gently removed her hand. The breeze caught the silky strands immediately, sending them flying in all directions. He took a handful and held it.

"Your wine and appetizers." The waiter appeared from the darkness, carrying a tray.

James sat back and made room for the food. He ordered for them both and when the waiter had gone he looked back to Samantha. "Why are you smiling?"

"You remembered my favorite entrée."

He watched her for a moment. "I remember everything you like."

Samantha ran her hands over her arms and looked out into the roaring darkness.

"Are you cold?" He stood and began to take off his coat.

Samantha shook her head and motioned for him to sit. "No. I'm enjoying it. Besides, my sweater is in the car if I need it." She lifted her hands into the air. "It's refreshing and stimulating." She enjoyed the breeze blowing over her for a moment and then finally said, "I love it."

"Yes, it is refreshing." There was something in her eyes that captivated him. They came alive as she spoke in a vibrant, content voice. She swayed her arms gracefully through the cool air in a simple gesture that made him want to hold her close beside him.

"It's invigorating, yet relaxing at the same time." She linked her fingers together as she stretched them over her head and smiled. "I think that's why I love the ocean." Her laugh was full and deep in her throat. "I know that's a little contradicting, but when I hear the rhythm of the waves and the familiar scent of the air, all my uncertainties vanish. There's no stress when this surrounds me." She tucked her arms against her body as she rested them on the table. "It's comforting. But at the same time it almost seems to recharge me."

He poured wine into their glasses and nodded. He knew what she meant. He always knew what she meant. She made him feel what she was experiencing and sometimes no words were even necessary. She drew him in, she always had. He envied how carefree she was. How she could let everything go and simply enjoy. That was what was missing from his life. He hadn't simply enjoyed anything in a long time.

"It's like a child's favorite blanket." She took the glass he offered and sipped. "It's a security that calms me almost instantly. It's not as easy to snuggle up to but it's always there, consistent and never-ending." She shook her head delicately. "Listen to

145

me. I'm sorry for carrying on."

"Don't apologize." He loved to hear her speak of things that meant something to her. It was one of her qualities that he found endearing. She was passionate about things that touched her and she never seemed to mind voicing them. She used to be passionate about him, too. When he heard her speak to others about him it left him speechless. He would savor every word she used because each was so descriptive and heartfelt. It never ceased to amaze him how much respect, admiration, and love she held for him. Was it lost forever?

He reached for his glass. "A toast, to my mom. May she beat her cancer."

Samantha raised her glass and tapped his lightly. "To Marie." She took a sip and said, "And she will beat it."

"I know."

She took another sip and set her glass back down. "She had blood work done today. Her counts are lower but still in the normal range."

"That's good to hear."

"She goes in for her next round in two days, providing her cell count remains good."

"It'll be a shame to see all the vigor, she so obviously had today, gone." He offered a plate with square flaky pastries on it.

She nodded in agreement. "It'll be back." She took a taste of the golden pastry. She savored it for several seconds before she spoke. "This is heaven. You have to try this." Without thinking she reached across the table and gave him a bite of hers. "It tastes like spinach and—"

His lips brushed her fingers as he finished her sentence. "Feta cheese."

"That's it." She popped the rest of the appetizer in her mouth—licking every last flake from her fingers. "I think this is going to become my new favorite restaurant."

James reached across the table and with his thumb brushed away the crumbs on her lips. "Mine, too." He allowed his thumb to linger a little longer than it should have. It felt good to be with her like this. He felt like they were the only two people in the world. Nothing existed but them and the elegant restaurant. Bad memories and deadly diseases were worlds away. Right now that's what he needed. That's what they both needed.

When the waiter arrived to serve the main course, Samantha's eyes grew double in size as she looked at the plate he set in front of her. "I'll never be able to eat all of this." She laughed at the huge portion.

James eyed his plate. "I don't think I'll have a problem with mine. After eating soup and salad for weeks on end, I'm ready for this."

"I'm not going to feel too sorry for you." She disregarded his pout. "Ginger said she made several casseroles a week. And countless loaves of bread."

The aroma had James's mouth watering before he'd even taken a bite. He reached for his knife. "True. Mom and I would swarm around it like vultures." He chewed the first bite slowly, enjoying the flavor.

She laughed again as she drove her fork into the huge pile of pasta covered in a spicy red sauce. "I might be going to yoga class twice this week."

Paul's face popped into James's mind. The man was a nuisance. He pushed the image aside. "I know it's not part of your job, but I can't tell you what a relief it's been having you fix the meals." He took another bite, chewed, and then swallowed. "I know Mom hasn't been eating much over the last few months but I was struggling just to remember to go shopping once a week, much less trying to remember that she eat."

"You know I don't mind. I enjoy cooking."

James took a long sip of wine. "I appreciate it."

Samantha smiled up at him. Her eyes darted to his breast pocket when she heard the low ring of the cell phone. "Is it Marie?"

James just shook his head in irritation as he glanced at the number. "Taylor." He listened for a few seconds. "Couldn't this have waited until morning?" There was another pause. "I'm listening . . ."

Samantha leaned in and whispered. "It's fine. Take the call."

The authority and control in his voice as he spoke was that of a powerful man. Impatience with the caller caused the wrinkle across his brow to slowly etch its way into his expression. When James felt her fingers softly glide over the crease, everything inside of him loosened up. As she lowered her hand he looked up to see her mouth the word "better" and wink.

All irritation vanished. She held a power that could make him feel good regardless of the situation. He took her hand in his, not wanting to lose the contact, and stared at her fingers linked in his as he spoke. For this brief moment his world was complete again. It didn't matter that work was on the line. Samantha was there when he got off the phone. It wasn't the dark solitude of his home or the endless amounts of work that would be his only place to turn. Samantha, once again would provide that much-needed balance for him. "As long as we disclosed it in the contract, we'll be fine." He paused. "Have a copy faxed to me by morning and I'll go over it." There was another moment of silence. "Relax, this isn't going to be a problem."

"Everything okay?"

James returned the phone to his pocket. "Yes."

"Are you sure?"

He watched her for a moment. "Of course." And if it wasn't he would make it. That's what he did. He made sure things ran smoothly. "Now, where were we?"

She tore off a chunk of bread and dipped it in a pool of

sauce. "You were thanking me profusely for my culinary skills."

"Was I, now?" He smiled. "You're much better at creating a meal than you are a flowerpot constructed of shells."

She bit the bread and looked up. "It's a lovely pot."

"Yes, I must look at it daily now that it adorns my mantel." He watched her closely. "Did you put it there on purpose to torture me?"

"I merely suggested to Marie that I thought it would look nice there. She agreed." She dabbed her napkin against her lips. "That was wonderful."

"Dessert?"

She shook her head. "I don't think I could eat another bite. I could use a warm cup of coffee, though."

As James spoke with the waiter, Samantha rose and moved to the railing. They were completely alone now. The other couple that had arrived halfway through their meal left moments before. She closed her eyes and let the breeze blow her hair back and caress her face like a thousand gentle fingers. She felt James come up from behind her and drape his coat over her shoulders. She didn't refuse it this time. It was big, it was warm, and it was him. It smelled like him, a deep, warm, exotic scent. The touch was him, ardent and protective. It felt good and familiar. It was like he was holding her, but without having the contact that she feared would drive her crazy. Feeling him watching her, she opened her eyes and looked at him. "Why are you looking at me like that?"

"I just like watching you." He had always enjoyed watching her. He had liked the way she walked into a crowded room—every head would turn, but she never noticed because her eyes were always on him. Like they were now.

"What are you thinking about?" she asked.

He nuzzled his face in her hair and took a deep breath. "I'm thinking how nice this evening turned out."

She looked back into the darkness. "Yes, it has."

He put an arm around her. "Are you warming up?"

"Yes, thank you." She leaned into his embrace. The light contact caused a stir deep within her.

James brought his other arm around her and glanced at his watch.

Samantha looked down at hers, too. "Do you want to go?"

James shook his head and laughed. "Not at all. The last thing I want is for this evening to end." He let his arm fall possessively against her. "I was just noticing we've been gone for an hour and forty-five minutes. My mom is probably doing a victory dance right now."

"Or running through the house naked." Samantha rested her head against his chest. "She's not subtle, is she?"

"She never has been. But the sad thing is, she probably thinks she has outsmarted us."

"There's only four more weeks to go. It will all be over soon."

He turned her around so she faced him. "You're beautiful." The words came out a soft whisper and were almost carried off by the breeze before they reached her ears. Cupping her face he pulled her close, raising her lips to within inches of his. He held the position for an instant. In her eyes he found the unspoken promise that she wanted this as much as he.

The kiss, although gentle, held a year's worth of longing, a year's worth of waiting. While her lips trembled with excitement and anxiety against his, her hands remained steady when they sunk into his hair at the base of his neck. She shifted her weight slightly to get closer. She wanted to feel him. She wanted to feel all of him against her. She hadn't been held or kissed in so long. Carnal instinct took over as she deepened the kiss. He tasted of wine. It was mild and sweet. An old familiarity filled her perfectly.

James pulled her hair to the side and glided the tip of his

tongue along the small of her neck, causing bumps to form in its wake. He nibbled softly as he moved slowly to the base and continued across the top of her shoulder. In the shallow hollow of her shoulder was where he found her need for him bubbling desperately trying to get out. He allowed her pulse to thud against his tongue before moving on. Covering her breast with his hand, he lifted its weight in his palm and began kneading it until a cry passed over her lips.

His other hand was soothing as it roamed over her entire body, trying to feel all of it. God, he wanted to make love to her right here. He was seriously contemplating the thought when he heard his name being spoken, and it wasn't Samantha's heavy voice that found its way to his ears.

"James?"

James turned around, blocking Samantha from the intruders, giving her time to smooth out her hair and straighten her clothes.

James recognized Ed and his wife in the pale light. James shook his hand. "Ed." And then he reached for the woman's hand. "Good evening, Barbara."

"Mr. Taylor, how have you been?"

James nodded briskly and tried to keep the irritation out of his voice when he spoke. "I'm well, thank you."

"Samantha, is that you? By God, it is." Ed slapped his thigh with the palm of his hand. "Well, I'll be damned. You're the last person I expected—"

Ed's wife cut in. "Why don't you introduce us, Ed?" The woman looked apologetically at Samantha.

Ed shut his mouth immediately and then began introductions. "This is my wife Barbara. Barbara this is Samantha, James's—uh—James's—"

James cleared his throat as he watched Ed stutter. "This is a good friend of mine, Samantha."

"It's nice to meet you, Samantha."

Samantha lifted her eyes just long enough to say, "Likewise."

Much to everyone's relief, the waiter immediately ushered Ed and Barbara to a table in the far corner.

Samantha moved toward their table. With a perfectly composed expression, she said, "I think I'm ready to go home."

"The waiter just brought the coffee." James gestured to the cups on the table. He could feel the anger in him starting to rise and he did nothing to try and stifle it.

She didn't even look at the coffee. "I don't feel like coffee anymore."

James would have thoroughly enjoyed placing his hands around Ed's neck and slowly squeezing. He decided that sending him somewhere out of the country for several weeks would suffice. Ed not only hated long business trips, he also couldn't stand to fly. James glared at the table across the room a final time, before turning his attention back to Samantha. He felt her anxiety as he watch her gather up her purse. "Sam—"

"Please, James. I don't know what just happened. It shouldn't have happened. I didn't want it to happen." She pressed the palm of her hand against her forehead. "I can't even think." She looked up. "What I'm trying to say is, this is a mistake."

"What do you mean?" Realizing his voice was a little loud he instinctively lowered it. He was a private man who kept his personal life just that, personal. "What do you mean you don't know what just happened? I'll tell you what almost happened. We just about made love in a restaurant." When she didn't speak, he looked at her accusingly. "Are you going to deny it?" He leaned in closer. "We want each other like—"

"Please, stop." She kept her eyes averted. "I want to go home."

"Running from this isn't going to make it go away."

"I'm not running from anything because there's nothing to run from." She took off his coat and handed it to him.

James shoved it back at her. "Put the damn coat back on."

"I don't need it any more."

"Samantha."

She shrugged the coat back on. "There. Are you satisfied now?"

"What is going to satisfy me is to hear you admit what just happened."

"A mistake just happened."

"Damn it, Samantha."

Samantha glanced over her shoulder at Ed and Barbara, who were trying their best to discreetly eavesdrop. "This isn't the time or the place for this."

He raised his hands in the air, giving up. "Okay, fine."

"Thank you."

Slowly, James rubbed the back of his hand against her cheek. "You will come to me, Samantha. And when you do you won't deny how much you want me." He placed his hand in the small of her back and guided her through the dining area to the car.

CHAPTER FOURTEEN

James walked into his mom's room. The early morning light revealed she was resting on her side, her back toward him. He could see her body rise and fall in the rhythm of sleep. This round of chemo hit her hard, the worst part happening around two this morning.

The commotion had woken him from a dead sleep. By the time he had gotten to his mom's room Samantha was already there. She had moved about the room with efficient speed, taking care of everything, while he stood against the wall like a helpless fool. He couldn't even figure out what was going on, so many things were happening at once. It wasn't until Samantha had run into him twice that she finally shooed him out.

A large green bowl still rested a few feet from Marie's head, a sign of just how weak she was. He swallowed hard. He wanted to talk to her. He needed to touch her. But he knew she needed her rest more than his words and support right now. Besides, didn't he really just want to reassure himself that she was okay? That was part of it, but he also felt like he had to let her know that she was going to be fine.

He cringed inside. How was he going to let her know that she was going to be all right? He was completely helpless to her. Hell, Samantha was more assistance to her right now than he was. He turned his head away and forced himself to leave the room.

He moved down the hall, and stood at Samantha's door for

several moments before he opened it. She, too, was sleeping with her back to him. He moved into the room, quietly closing the space between them.

He took his time as he watched her. The peak of her golden shoulder was exposed, revealing a swatch of the white cotton tank top she wore. Her hair tumbled around her, covering skin and pillow in a haphazard fashion. He wanted to bury himself in the chaotic mess and never find his way out again.

He took a seat next to her. His weight on the mattress caused her to roll onto her back. Even as she slept, he could see lines of exhaustion across her face. Eyelashes, thick and dark, rested against her cheeks like delicate, miniature fans. Her lips were parted ever so slightly. He divided his attention between her face and the curvy gray outline of her body.

He had been so lonely without her. From the outside, it appeared as if he had everything, but inside he couldn't have been emptier. Over the last year his approach to life had become so callous. His steely nature was once reserved purely for work, but it had somehow crept into his personal life, too. He didn't like the man he was becoming. He needed her to balance him, to love him, to tie his two worlds together. He wasn't complete unless he had her by his side.

Samantha's heavy lashes lifted to expose weariness in her eyes. "James?"

His hand moved to her head where he fingered her hair. "Yes." He whispered the word as he leaned down toward her.

"Is Marie all right?" She licked her lips. "Does she need me?"

I need you. "She's sleeping," he said in a calming voice. "She's fine. I just checked on her."

Grogginess drenched her voice when she spoke in a hushed tone. "I didn't think I'd ever get her settled."

He kept stroking her hair. "I know. It was a long night."

Her eyes dropped, then slowly lifted. "She was so sick. I knew the pain must have been unbearable."

He nodded, but wasn't sure she could see him in the dim light. He left her hair and touched her face affectionately.

"I finally had to give her a sleeping pill." She pressed her face against the palm of his hand and snuggled into the pillow. "You're warm." Her eyes drifted closed. "She didn't want to take it. I forced her."

"She needed it," he countered. To his touch, her skin was incredibly soft and tender. His thumb began deliberate lazy strokes. The motion was feathery light and the meager contact was amazingly intimate. He fought the urge to lie down next to her and pull her close to him.

"I think I yelled at her . . . did you hear?"

A smile touched his lips. "No, you didn't yell." Samantha very rarely raised her voice. She was a little more resourceful than that. Last night she had cut to the chase. She had threatened his mother into taking the pill.

"What did I say?" She yawned. "I don't even remember."

"You told her that you'd never have dinner with me again if she didn't swallow the damn pill." He added, "And of course, I'm quoting you."

She eyed him through mere slits. "Well, it worked."

"I'm not saying anything," he said defensively. He was all for whatever got the job done. He had used threats more than once in his line of work, too.

"You'll say something, you always do." She pulled her legs up close. "She was so fatigued—"

Using his finger, he hushed her. "You did the right thing. Rest is vital right now. We both know that. She knows that. Mom just has a phobia about taking pills of any kind." He pulled his hand from the warmth of her cheek and kissed her on the forehead. Her skin was warm against his lips. "You need to rest too."

"It's hard for me to see her like this." She paused, then added, "Even though I'm a nurse, it hurts."

Her eyes remained closed. He wanted to place a kiss on each of them and then work his way down to her lips. It would feel so good if he could just kiss her. "I know it does."

She nestled deeper into the bed. "I love her." She sighed. "I've missed seeing her."

James pulled the blanket up around her, efficiently tucking her in. She looked safe and warm. "She's missed you too."

"I'm so tired." She burrowed down, taking advantage of his efforts. "You should be sleeping. It's too early to be up."

He shook his head. "I can't sleep. If I thought sleeping was hard before you came, it's impossible now."

"Why?"

"Because you're two goddamn feet down the hall from me."

"It feels that close doesn't it?"

"Closer," he grumbled.

"Will you stay? Just sit here until I go back to sleep."

Her simple request packed a punch. He couldn't have left her side even if he had wanted to. She had been endlessly giving herself to the both of them. It was her turn to need someone and he would remain with her for as long as she wanted. It was the least he could do after all she had done for them. "Of course, I'll stay."

He watched her as she drifted away into the cloudy realm of sleep.

"I liked going to dinner with you," she said absently. "And your kisses . . . your lips . . . I liked your lips against mine." She took one long breath and was fast asleep.

He sat and watched her until the clear early morning light broke through the gray dawn. As those first rays of sunshine filled the room he took her fingers in his. He did nothing more but stare at them for the longest time.

As James sat at his desk in his home office, he spoke softly into the phone, because Samantha and his mom were still sleeping. "Shelly, I'm going to be working from home today." He shook his head. "No, don't cancel the meeting. I'll just have it here." He took a sip of the steaming cup of coffee. "That's with Jerry Hancock, right?" Jerry was a specialist in the field of corporate social responsibility. He'd hired the consulting firm two months ago to help the company become more active in the community.

James not only wanted his company to be financially success-ful but also well liked. The relationship between a company and the community in which it operated was very important. Companies like his were expected to get involved with the com-munity, to make a contribution, and not just through providing employment and paying taxes.

"Yes, it's with Jerry Hancock," Shelly confirmed. "I'll call over to his office after we get off the phone."

"What else is on the agenda today?" James listened quietly as Shelly gave him a rundown of the schedule. She also read off all phone messages and any new mail he had received. "Fax that over to me, I'd like to look over it."

"Will do, Mr. Taylor. How is your mom doing?"

"It was a difficult night, but she's hanging in there." He took another sip. "If anything comes up, just call."

Over the next three hours James worked steadily. He held a meeting over the phone that lasted a grueling forty minutes. He reviewed the minutes, which Shelly had faxed over, from the Seattle meeting that he didn't attend. He also went over two proposals that were supposed to go out tomorrow. He spent twenty minutes adding two more items for inclusion for one of them.

Samantha was sleepy-eyed, but showered and dressed, when she stood in the doorway. "I didn't think you'd be home."

"Good morning." He looked at his watch and grinned. "Or should I say, good afternoon."

"That was a rough night."

"Yes, it was."

He pushed away from his desk and moved to her. As he approached her, he caught the scent of fresh morning rain, clean and sweet. The heat of the shower caused her skin to glow a soft rosy pink. Just the ends of her hair were damp. She had allowed it to dry naturally, just how he liked it. A little tousled, not styled to perfection. She wore the comfortable, faded, frayed jeans that drove him to distraction. And there were those perfect red toes, peeking from underneath. This time they didn't twitch. "How are you feeling?"

Her expression was humorless. "Like I haven't slept."

James's lips thinned into a grim line; he knew the feeling. He extended his arms out. And when she walked to him without a moment's consideration, he drew her in close. When she sank against him, he could feel her exhaustion and depletion, all of which should be expected after being up the entire night taking care of an extremely sick person. However, he knew that it wasn't just his mom's condition that was wearing her out; it was also what was happening between them. Emotionally, it was sucking her dry.

Samantha rested her head against his chest. "I feel like I'm burnt out."

"You've been going nonstop for the last few weeks," he whispered as his hand ran the length of her back.

"I'm used to going nonstop." She had done it for the last year.

"You're not used to working around the clock for someone you love dearly. It puts a completely different spin on it when

159

it's someone you care about." He would find something relaxing for them to do to restore her energy, he told himself. She needed a break. He rested his chin on the top of her head. "You're not used to having me around, either." He hadn't been making her job any easier for her. He'd only been adding more weight to her already heavy load.

She pinched his ribs. "Yes, you are a thorn in my side."

He kissed her hair, squeezing her gently to him. "I'll try not to be from now on."

They stayed this way for a moment before Samantha spoke. "What are you doing home?"

He released her but kept an arm around her shoulders. "I decided to work from home today."

"You don't need to stay."

"I want to."

"I can handle anything that comes up."

"I know you can." Her capabilities were clearly not in question. Her skills, without a doubt, were impeccable. Not that there was any, but if there had been hesitation, last night would have resolved all uncertainty. She was amazing and he was simply in awe of how she had handled everything.

"Last night was hard on you," she said softly.

"I think it was hard on all of us. I just needed to be here." He couldn't explain why, so he didn't even try.

"I understand."

Raising his arm, he glanced at the time. "I'll be holding a meeting here in a little while."

Samantha nodded. "I won't keep you." She gave him the first smile of the morning. "I'm going to get some coffee. I hope it's as thick as mud."

With her mug close by, Samantha gathered the ingredients for homemade soup. She prepared it in the slow cooker, so it would be ready for Marie whenever she wanted it. After last night she knew that keeping something down was going to be a challenge. Hopefully, something light would do the trick for her nervous stomach. She went easy on the spices, keeping it bland.

As she wiped down the counters and stored the cutting board, the doorbell rang. She cleaned her hands on a dishtowel and raked her fingers through her hair as she walked through the house.

When she opened the door, a gentleman wearing a black suit, carrying a briefcase to match, greeted her. His expression was serious, and then slowly transformed into one of surprised pleasure when his eyes fell on her.

"Good afternoon, Mrs. Taylor."

Samantha moved to the side to allow him in. "I'm not Mrs. Taylor."

He tensed only for a moment before ducking his head bashfully as he stepped in and closed the door. "I apologize." He tilted his head thoughtfully as a sheepish grin moved his lips. "What's that saying about never assume?" He gave a guilty shrug. "I guess this is a perfect example isn't it?"

Samantha's eyes warmed as she smiled. "An apology isn't necessary." She offered her hand. "I'm Samantha."

"I'm a fool." He took her hand in his as she laughed openly at him. "Does that mean the awkward moment is over?"

"Yes."

"Good. Then might I suggest we start again?"

Samantha played along and swiftly hid her amusement under a straight face. "By all means."

Lowering his voice, he changed his expression to that of a first-time meeting. "Hello, I'm Jerry Hancock."

"Jerry, it's nice to meet you. I'm Samantha, James's mom's nurse."

He turned sincere. "Yes, I heard she was sick. I hope she's

doing well."

Samantha smiled gently and nodded.

"Thank you."

"What for?"

"I have to be honest with you. My nerves were at their limit when I arrived. I've never met Mr. Taylor before and when I was told he wanted me to come to his home, well, let's just say I was very anxious. You have completely broken the tension."

"Glad to be of help. You know, he's not that bad."

"That's not how his reputation precedes him."

"No, I suppose not." She gestured over her shoulder. "He's in his office. Would you like me to show you?"

"Please."

"Here you are." She opened the door for him and gave him a reassuring smile.

James looked up from his desk when the door opened. He paused momentarily before he spoke, for the way his guest was looking at Samantha caught him off guard. He stood. "Mr. Hancock, come in."

Hancock acknowledged James with a nod of his head and then moved quickly across the room to shake his hand. "It's nice to meet you, Mr. Taylor. Please call me Jerry."

Leaning over the desk, James took Jerry's hand even though he had the urge to reject it.

"I've made another pot of coffee," Samantha said as she looked from Jerry to James. "Would either of you like some?"

"I'd love a cup," Jerry said.

"You don't need to bring us coffee." James glared at Jerry. She wasn't his goddamn gopher. "We can get it ourselves if we want some." The last thing he wanted was to have Samantha come back into his office. If she did, that would mean he was going to have to witness the pathetic way Jerry was looking at her again. If that were to happen he would surely hit the man.

"I don't mind, really." She turned. "Jerry, cream and sugar?"

"Please." His features turned soft when he looked at her. "Thank you."

James wanted Jerry Hancock out of his house, preferably as fast as possible. If it weren't for Jerry's extensive experience in evaluating, researching, and developing, James would fire him right on the spot. Jerry was an asset to the company, so James tried to keep his anger in check. He took a seat and gestured for Jerry to do the same. "Thank you for coming, considering the short notice in the change of location."

Jerry was still looking out the door at the backside of Samantha as she walked away. "Of course."

James watched him with irritation. The man's tongue was all but lying on the floor. He would move this along quickly. "I'm very busy today, so I'd like to jump right in. Do you have a list of the different types of charities that my company can get involved in?"

Jerry pulled out several folders. "Yes, I have both volunteer and donation services."

"I'd prefer it to be volunteer."

"I would agree." He passed two folders. "A hands-on company always receives more recognition. Do you want local, in the US, or around the world?"

"Let's start with local," James said, glancing up to take the documents. "I'd also like a list of charities that need corporate backing in order to get themselves known."

"Great idea. There are a lot of hidden benefits when choosing a lesser-known charity." He paused. "Personally, I think it reflects a business that's not afraid to take chances and isn't there purely for the publicity."

"I'm glad you approve," James said dryly as he wrote a few notes and flipped through the papers. "I understand that your firm makes all the necessary arrangements, but I'd like to know how my staff will be notified when it's their turn to volunteer."

"We'll send a monthly schedule, which your employees will have previously signed up for." Jerry passed another sheet to James. "Here's an example."

"That will allow people to contribute when they want to."

"Yes, we've noticed that employees are more apt to commit when they get to decide what and when they are to do something."

Samantha walked in carrying a tray, and Jerry's attention immediately shifted to her.

"Here you are," she said, handing him a cup. "Sugar and cream are on the tray."

James thought Jerry's thank-you was much too effusive and his stare was much too probing. He had the urge to shove him back into the chair when he stood as she came in. He looked up quickly and smiled at Samantha when he caught her eye. "Thank you," he said softly.

She nodded and then left, closing the door quietly behind her.

"Where were we?" James asked.

"Mr. Taylor, I'm not really sure," Jerry said, shaking his head. "How do you do it?"

"What's that?" James looked back down at the folder in his hand, reading over the notes he had taken.

Jerry looked back over his shoulder, almost in disbelief, and then looked back to James. "How do you wake up every morning and leave the house?"

For this he looked up. His nostrils flared when he spoke. "Pardon?"

"She's amazing."

James's hand hit the desk. "Out."

Jerry's eyebrows merged together, openly surprised. "What?"

His expression of shock only irritated James further. "Get out of my house."

"I don't understand. I'm sorry—"

"Jerry, you're a smart man who, at this moment, still happens to have a job. If you want to keep it that way"—James's expression didn't waver—"get out now." James shoved the file to the side of his desk as he made a mental note that he wouldn't have any more home meetings again.

CHAPTER FIFTEEN

James glanced around idly at the crowded lobby, not recognizing any of the faces that passed by them. "What do you have for me?"

"ISAC hired a spy—who happens to be an email-tracking pro," Al said just loud enough for James to hear.

James leaned in. "Are you sure it's ISAC?"

"Yep." Al smiled slyly. "I'm not sure what you're working on but it must be good."

"The sons-of-bitches," James bit out. "What do you mean an email-tracking pro?"

"He can pretty much hack into any type of system. Including your company's. And that's how he managed to steal the data."

"Our computer security is state-of-the-art."

"So are his hacking capabilities." Al's voice turned to irritation. "I'll tell you what, he's a little worm who covers his tracks well. It took me seventeen hours to pinpoint the little bastard."

James raised a brow. "How did you find him?"

"Don't inquire about how I get my information."

"Public records?"

"Sure, if it makes you feel better," Al said flatly. "It will take me a few days to actually pin his location down. I would recommend stopping all email communication and only using verbal communication until we catch this guy."

James nodded curtly.

"After this we're going to have to move quickly. Once the

emails stop he'll know we're on to him. Your company has a conference and expo coming up, right?"

"Yes. I'm going to speak."

"That's good. It's very likely that our little worm will be there. Can you get me a pass for the event?"

"Yes, I'll have it sent to your office by the end of the day." James offered his hand. "Thank you for getting this done so quickly. I appreciate it."

Al nodded. "Unless something comes up I'll meet you at the conference."

James placed the chilled bottle of wine and three glasses on the table. His mouth watered as he eyed the plume of savory smoke that poured from the closed lid of the grill. He could only imagine what was inside. Samantha had forbidden him to look, and wasn't giving a hint as to what she had been marinating in the refrigerator all day.

Samantha had been planning the meal from the moment his mom had woken and said she was starved. It had been almost a week since Marie had been so violently ill that both he and Samantha thought she would never recover from it. Marie's suggestion that she might enjoy a hearty home-cooked meal had caused Samantha to run down the stairs in delight, announcing that she was going to the store. She had snatched up her purse and darted out the door. When she got back, she muscled in three bags of groceries, refusing any help. She didn't want anyone else to know what was for dinner.

Samantha spent the entire day cooking. James had tried to sneak a few peeks throughout the day, resulting in banishment from the kitchen entirely. If he wanted a drink of water he was told it would have to come from the garden hose outside. He had laughed at her announcement, and quickly hid the grin when he caught her heavy glare.

Being prohibited from the kitchen and the enticing aromas was too much for James and Marie. They sat on the couch, because the bar was too close to the kitchen, conjuring up all sorts of different ideas of what was being created for dinner. James had even placed a bet with Marie on what the menu was. What else were they to do?

Now, James moved to the grill, ready to sneak a peek, but stopped instantly when Samantha's words hit him.

"Don't even think about it, James Taylor," Samantha said as she slid open the screen door and walked through. She used her backside to slide the screen shut again. "You've made it the entire day." She looked at her watch. "Just a few more minutes won't make a bit of difference."

"Think about what?" he countered innocently. She was clad in a short summer dress that exposed slender thighs. Her hair was pulled back in a haphazard fashion held by a brown clip. Stray hairs, tugged loose by the wind, danced over her golden shoulders. The thin purple straps of her dress enhanced her delicate frame. Her neckline went on for miles. He eyed the small indentation by her collarbone. The hollow would provide the perfect place for a kiss. He thought about that kiss as he shifted his gaze to the silky opaque slip under the gauzy purple material, which prevented him from viewing the rest of what lay under it.

"No sneaking a peek." She regarded the grill with a nod of her head. "I know what you're thinking, don't deny it," she teased with a smile. "You're practically drooling."

His eyes followed her as she set a green salad along with some dressing on the prepared table. "It's not what's for dinner that's making me drool."

The salad bowl landed with a thump, the wooden spoon chimed against an empty glass as it fell to the table.

James sauntered over to her and held up a glass of wine, offering it to her. "Purple looks good on you."

She took the wine. "It's lavender," she sputtered under her breath.

He considered for a moment, then leaned into her ear casually. "Call it what you want. I'm sure it would look even better on the floor next to my bed." The look she sent him made him grin. "I find the slip underneath a nuisance."

He brushed her hair away and rested his hand on the curve of her neck. His thumb found the slight indentation at its base. He stroked the area before he captured the thin lavender material between his fingers. He played with the strap as he watched her. She didn't back away, he noted, but the wine in her glass vibrated. The small, almost unseen, detail excited him. Her insides were just as fluid and quivering as the beverage she was holding and that's just how he wanted her.

James dipped his head by her ear. "Feel a spark, did ya?"

"Nothing here."

"Nothing?" A single brow arched over daring eyes. "Strange, I thought I felt something."

She took a very long drink of the wine. "Perhaps you were wrong."

He made no attempt to hide his smile. "I'm not often." Using his body to shield her from his mom or anyone on the beach, he moved in front of her. He waited until she looked at him before he spoke. "You know, I like a good challenge."

"I'm not challenging you."

James skimmed his fingers over her shoulder and gently slid them under the narrow spaghetti-thin strap. He moved it in his fingers from side to side considering what should be done with the dainty material. He smiled and slid the strap over her shoulder revealing the full round crest of the top of her breast. He knew exactly what he wanted to do with the whole damn outfit. However, the location posed a problem. He looked up.

"How about now? Feeling anything now, Angel?"

Her skin broke out in goose bumps, her nipples clearly straining against the thin cloth barrier. "I'm glad you're amused by all this."

"I don't think it's amusement that I'm feeling."

"Maybe you're feeling like an overbearing, womanizing cad," she offered in a voice that was weighed down with contempt.

He laughed at the insult and shook his head. "No, that's not it, either."

Her eyes narrowed. "Are you sure?"

"Positive."

Exasperation found its way into her words. "I'll add appalling to the list."

"You don't believe that." There was a short pause. "Your opposition only drives me more."

"It's time to eat." She said the words over her shoulder, and loud enough for Marie to hear, as she headed for the barbeque.

When she turned, James made eye contact with her. "My thoughts exactly." This time amusement was what he was feeling and he allowed it to show in his eyes. He gave her a wink because he knew it would send her into a tailspin. "I'll get the water."

When he was gone, Samantha waited for the bout of faintness to pass. She prayed that it would. Her knees, she needed to put all her focus on her knees. She would die if they buckled. Would God be so cruel? Breathe Samantha, she told herself. She caught herself clenching the wineglass tightly and forced her fingers to relax.

A spark? An explosion would be more like what she was feeling. And challenging him was the last thing she would want to do. She knew what James Taylor did with challenges. He made them his. No matter how unobtainable they might be, he always managed to dominate. It was a fascinating game that he liked to play.

Samantha lifted the barbeque lid, glad that her attention could be focused on something other than James and the traitorous hunger that grew in her body.

"What's that, sweetheart? Did you say something?" Marie said as she stepped out onto the deck.

"Dinner will be ready in a minute."

"It smells heavenly."

Samantha took one last fleeting glance at James as he set the glasses of water on the table and then helped his mom with her chair. He looked so powerful, so confident, it made her head spin. He was arrogant, she thought. Women aren't supposed to find men like him attractive. What was wrong with her?

Conversation flowed freely throughout the meal. Topics included everything from the latest headlines to what the actual diet of a seagull was. As food was passed back and forth, easiness settled over the table, creating chitchat that was of old friends. Good friends.

James couldn't tear his eyes away from Samantha during the entire meal. He had allowed his gaze to drift to his mom during conversation, but it favorably drifted back to Samantha the moment it could. She was too exquisite not to watch, he told himself. With her face beautifully flushed from the wine, and her eyes glittering from all the laughing, it took every ounce of his willpower not to reach across the table and show her how much it pleased him to see her like this.

He leaned back as he finished his meal. This was how it used to be, effortless and comfortable. *Content* was the only word he could use to define what he was feeling as he watched his mom and Samantha. It was this that he wanted. It was this . . . this feeling, this moment, that he must have back. He looked from one woman to the other . . . this was his life, and suddenly it became vitally important. Nothing would stand in his way until he got it.

"James, would you like some more?" Samantha asked the question when she looked over and saw the intense look in his eyes. Whatever he was thinking, it had produced the small line that found its way to his brow.

"No, thank you. Dinner was superb." James rubbed his stomach, satisfied. "You outdid yourself, Samantha." He looked to his mom. "Mom, I'm so glad you got your appetite back."

"Me, too. I think I made up for all the lost meals with this one." She looked at her empty plate and then at Samantha. "Everything was wonderful."

Samantha reached for her hand. "I'm glad you enjoyed it."

James cleared his throat. "Mom, I know you're stalling. Go find your purse and pay up."

Marie's napkin stopped in midair. "Pay up? I won the bet."

James all but gaped at her statement. "How do you figure that?"

"I got everything right, down to the garlic mashed potatoes."

"I said potatoes, too," he insisted.

"Not garlic potatoes."

"It doesn't make a difference what kind they are." James looked to Samantha. "Tell her potatoes are potatoes."

Samantha raised her hands. "I'm not getting in the middle of this."

Marie sat up a little higher and challenged her son. "And you also said bread, not garlic bread."

"Garlic bread is a given." James shot back as he looked toward Samantha expectantly.

"Don't try and drag me into this. I'm not saying a thing." Samantha stood up and began stacking plates.

He watched her rise. "Chicken?"

"I prefer to call it smart."

Marie touched Samantha's hand when she took her plate. "I didn't raise him to be like this." She shook her head as if she couldn't figure where she'd gone wrong.

"Don't blame yourself, Marie, I'm sure there was nothing you could do."

She nodded. "Perhaps you're right, dear. But this type of behavior is improper and quiet honestly, embarrassing."

Samantha shrugged. "Sometimes you just get a bad seed and there's nothing that can be done about it."

Marie nodded methodically at Samantha.

"You did all you could do. Perfect manners can mask only so much; it's bound to come out sooner or later," Samantha said seriously.

James waved his hands in front of the two women, trying to gain their attention. "Hello, do either of you see me sitting here?"

Samantha grabbed the paper napkins and stuffed them between two plates before they blew away. "Did you just say something?"

James just glared at her.

"I hope you left room for dessert," Samantha said as she gathered the silverware and piled it on the plates. "I'll go get it while the both of you duke it out."

James held a hand up. "Wait, don't get it yet." He looked to his mom. "I'll be willing to call the dinner a tie if you agree to having the dessert be the tiebreaker."

"You know I won, fair and square."

James got ready to counter her statement, but stopped when she eyed him.

"However, since we didn't decide how specific we were getting, I accept." She puckered her lips as she raised her glass. "Shall we put it in writing?"

"No." He glanced at Samantha. "We have a witness."

They both followed Samantha into the kitchen. Samantha turned, rolling her eyes at the absurdity of the situation. "Tell me when I can reveal the dessert."

James sniffed the air as Samantha got out dishes and began to brew a pot of coffee. He eyed his mom and knew she too had guessed the rich sweet scent that filled the room.

"Cheesecake," Marie said happily. There was no mistaking it.

"Yes, but what kind?" He leaned on the counter. "This time we are getting specific."

James watched his mom as she sniffed the air a few more times and carefully considered her options. He knew she didn't have a clue what kind of cheesecake it was. However, he did. He knew without a doubt. Every time Samantha and he had celebrated anything together, whether it was she passing her state board exams or he closing a deal, she always made raspberry cheesecake. It was his favorite.

James drummed his fingers across the countertop. "So, what do you think?"

Marie shrugged her shoulders as she contemplated the aroma. "How am I supposed to know what kind of cheesecake it is?"

"How was I supposed to know garlic potatoes?" His retort was a little mocking.

She scowled at him and then looked at Samantha. "There he goes again with that bad—"

"Oh, will the two of you stop it," James said quickly. "I'm tried of you both ganging up on me."

Marie lifted her chin. "Well, it's purely a guess, a safe one I think. I'm going to say cherry cheesecake."

He nodded his head. "A good choice. And yes, it's a safe one."

"I'm glad you agree."

"However, it's not the right one."

Marie glared at James. "Don't count your chickens before they hatch, Son. I raised—"

"It's raspberry," he interrupted.

Marie scowled when Samantha set the raspberry cheesecake on the counter.

James put an arm around his mom's shoulders. "I believe there is a twenty in your purse with my name all over it." He looked at his watch. "I expect payment in full within ten minutes."

Samantha took a long knife from the drawer and began to slice the cake. "You know what I think?"

"I'm sure you're going to tell me regardless of how I answer that."

She turned her attention to him for a minute, making sure he got the full effect of her scornful look. "I think you're not a very graceful winner."

James watched her slip the cake onto three plates before he moved around the counter to her side. "You know what I think?" He said the words as he took her hand in his and studied the long, slender finger that was coated with cheesecake. When he brought her finger slowly into his mouth, he pulled her closer. He meticulously washed the thick sweetness from it. Taking his time, he carefully sucked on the tip before pulling it from his mouth and speaking. "That you make an amazing cheesecake." His tongue traced over the top of her perfectly manicured fingernail. "Mmm, it's still warm."

James had to work not to smile, because inconceivable was the only way to describe Samantha's face at that moment. In fact, she was so astounded she couldn't even utter a single word, although it looked like she was trying desperately to do so. He noticed she became even more flustered when Marie walked into the kitchen.

Marie set the money on the counter and slid the bill to James. "Don't spend it all in one place. And by the way," she added, "I'm never betting with you again."

"That's what you said last time."

"I mean it this time." She turned her attention to Samantha. "Don't ever let me bet with this man." She gestured toward the plates. "Shall I carry something outside?"

When Samantha didn't answer, James spoke. "Nope. I think we've got it." He took the twenty and stuffed it in his front pocket. "We'll be out in a moment."

As James placed forks on each plate he watched Samantha arrange mugs, sugar, and cream on a tray. It wasn't easy to leave Samantha speechless, but clearly he had. He moved behind her. "Don't look so shocked, I've licked cheesecake off more intimate places than your finger," he said in a seductive tone.

When the contents of the tray clattered, James moved quickly around her and took the tray just in time to save everything from toppling over. "Here let me take that." He paused. "What are you muttering about?"

"I'm not muttering," Samantha snapped.

"Sounded like muttering to me." He managed to get the words out without laughing, but the grin wasn't as easily contained.

"Stop looking so satisfied." She pulled her gaze from his mouth to his eyes. "I should wipe that smirk off your face."

His smile was cool, taunting. "You haven't seen me satisfied yet."

"Nor will I." She was completely flustered.

"You will, trust me." His voice was so gentle it went straight to her heart. "Don't pout. Your lips are too tempting when you do."

She lifted her long lashes, and found James staring at her intently. Her chin rose defiantly as she squared her shoulders.

"You wouldn't dare."

His lips found hers in record time. He nipped and teased her plump lower lip, before placing kisses along her jaw line, and then moving near her ear. He made sure he drove her over the edge before he pulled away. "Don't ever dare me, Angel. You should know that by now." If his hands hadn't been full, he would have done justice to the small kiss. It would have to wait.

"Why do you feel you can do whatever you please to me?"

He set the tray on the black granite countertop. He took his time as he looked at her. Why was she so desperately trying to disregard any and all of his advances? Why wouldn't she just put herself out of her misery and give in? Denial was to be expected, but this type of self-control was unheard of. "Angel, you wouldn't be standing in my kitchen right now if I were to do to you whatever pleased me."

"You're forgetting it takes two," she pointed out curtly.

"I haven't forgotten." He leaned in and she pulled back. "Whenever I decide to do what pleases me, trust me, you'll be just as pleased as I'll be." He picked up the tray. "You can get the door for me."

Samantha stood in the kitchen while James went on. What was happening? How had things gotten so out of her control? She had made up her mind that she wasn't going to allow him to affect her like this. What had happened to all that determination she had? Her fingers brushed her lips. She knew it was silly; the kiss had been nothing more than faint contact, yet she felt him on her lips like he had been there for hours. No matter how minor it was, just knowing that his mouth touched her was enough to set fire inside of her. Hell, she had been on fire long before he kissed her. She pressed her hand against her stomach, because her insides shook

She didn't like any of it in the least, but she couldn't help how her body responded to him. It's just been a while, she told herself. She looked up to see James waiting patiently by the screen door. Damn, he looked so sexy. Or was it smug? She decided it was a little of both.

CHAPTER SIXTEEN

As Marie took the last bite of the delicious dessert she wiped her lips with her napkin and moaned a long satisfying moan. "That was delicious. Cheesecake was the perfect way to top off this beautiful evening." She looked to Samantha. "I can't tell you how much I've enjoyed myself."

Samantha smiled. "Would you like some more coffee?"

Marie shook her head. "I'm a little tired. I think I'll turn in now." She stood up and kissed James's cheek. "Good night, baby." She then kissed Samantha. "Good night, dear. As always, everything was just lovely."

Samantha smiled. "Do you need any help?"

"No, I'll be fine." She turned toward the door. "You two just stay out here and enjoy this lovely evening."

James looked at Samantha from across the table when Marie slid the door quietly closed. "She does look tired."

"It was a long day, that's all," Samantha said as she sipped her coffee and stared over his shoulder at the ocean.

"I was beginning to think she would never recover from that last round of chemo." James shook his head, trying to shake off the unwanted images.

Samantha sighed, remembering how draining it was, not only on Marie but on everyone. "Yes, it hit her hard." She turned her attention from the rolling waves to a group of people on the beach standing around a bonfire. "It's almost over. She has one more round next month."

"And that's it?" In one aspect it felt like the treatments were taking forever, but in reality it had all been very timely.

"Yes. Her doctor is very happy with the results. The last MRI showed the cancer has shrunk to almost nothing."

"Does that mean they may not operate?" he asked hopefully.

"They may decide not to. We'll have to wait and see how everything goes next month."

Several people walked by and waved as they made their way to the bonfire that had been started at dusk. There were over twenty people eating, swimming, singing, and dancing on the shore's edge. The large fire snapped and crackled; small sparks shot up in the air, then floated around until they burned out.

"Looks refreshing," James commented, as the shrieks of a couple diving through the white foamy surf drifted up to them. "You want to go for a dip?"

She shook her head. "I have a kitchen full of dishes to clean."

James got up and moved to the chair next to her. When he sat, he said, "You cooked, I'll clean." He reached around her neck and unclipped the barrette. Her hair cascaded in long sheets covering her shoulders. When he ran his fingers through it, a soft fragrance filled the air. "I've wanted to do that all evening."

Samantha tilted her head to the side, pulling her hair from James's grip.

Ignoring her gesture, James threaded his fingers back through her hair.

"Please," she said.

He stared at her for a moment.

"Please, stop."

"I don't want to."

"Why are you doing this?"

"I love the feel of it. I love the way it smells. And I can't get enough of it."

"You know I'm not referring to my hair."

James brought the hair entwined in his hand to his nose. "I believe this is what heaven smells like."

Samantha yanked her hair from his hand and stood up. "This is what I'm talking about. Why are you doing this?" She snatched the clip out of his hand and pulled her hair back. "I will not let what happened the other night repeat itself. It was a mistake. We both know that." She started gathering dishes off the table.

James moved beside her. "Call it what you want. However, I would thoroughly enjoy it if it were to repeat itself." The act of tracing his finger down her cheek and across her lips stopped her instantly. "They taste as soft as they feel," he murmured.

"Stop."

James indulged her but didn't see any reason to move away. She was reluctant because she was afraid. Knowing that, he withdrew his hand and spoke. "You care, Samantha. You can try to convince yourself otherwise, but it'll be futile."

She shook her head. "And how have you come to this conclusion? What makes you so sure that I still care?"

"Dessert tonight tells me all I need to know."

"How so?"

He wanted to pull a strand of her hair loose and twirl it around his finger. However, he fought the impulse. "Raspberries aren't in season."

"And?"

He moved in again and his mouth twitched when he spoke, "Tell me, Samantha, how many stores did you go to before you found fresh raspberries?"

"It's not every day that I can get Marie to eat a full meal, much less request one. I wanted it to be special. Don't read more into this than there really is."

"How many?"

"It's irrelevant," Samantha insisted.

"Then you won't have a problem telling me."

Samantha's voice was low. "Three."

"Such effort and you don't care?" He dipped his head and studied her lips. With a great sense of satisfaction he watched them tremble.

Samantha tried to step back, but the table prevented any escape. "Your little observation proves nothing. Perhaps I did it out of habit."

James was going to toss her on the table if she didn't quit licking her lips like that. "Could be, but I doubt it."

"You're too sure of yourself."

"No one can ever be too sure of themselves," he countered. His possessive look was deliberate, and he knew that it would dissolve her already crumbling will.

"You can," she insisted.

He couldn't wait, if he had wanted to. He needed to kiss her. Taking her face in between his hands, he tilted her head. He licked his own lips and then placed them upon Samantha's. It only took a gentle nudge with his tongue for her mouth to open. A groan traveled across his lips to hers when he tasted her sweetness. He purposely let the kiss linger, enjoying every last detail, before deepening it to savor the flavor.

The kiss built in heat until each of them felt its intensity race through and between them. With his fingers, James moved Samantha's chin, changing the angle of the kiss, igniting even more pleasure.

As their lips parted, James immediately began kissing her cheek, moving near her ear. He didn't want his lips to be off her, not even for a minute. Lifting her onto the edge of the table, he pushed the soft material of her dress up to expose her creamy, soft thighs. Her moan filtered into his ear like a deep growl when he slid his hand between her thighs and stroked the tender skin.

"I've wanted to touch you for so long," he whispered.

At the base of her neck, James could see her pulse pound through her skin. He pressed his lips against it, his heart slamming against his chest as he did so. The tip of his tongue touched the heated vein and flames swept through his body.

"James." His name spilled from her lips, barely audible.

He didn't move his mouth. "Yes."

Samantha knew that if her dress hadn't been so tight she would have parted her legs and allowed him full access. She was in too deep to even care if what she was doing was reckless. Instead of contemplating her actions, she permitted herself to drift into the surprisingly powerful sensations he was creating in her as his thumb lightly stroked the supple skin. If she could verbally beg for more, she would, but words had long been replaced with sensation. A small noise, which came from somewhere deep in her throat, escaped her lips, to convey her satisfaction.

She heard him whisper in her ear, but couldn't make out what he said—the blood rushing through her body and her heartbeat were thunderous in her ears. She had wanted to feel like this for so long. She had longed for her body to come alive again. It was all so overwhelming. "James," she repeated achingly.

"Tell me."

"I've missed you touching me."

"What else have you missed?"

"How you so easily make me want you."

"And."

"I've missed how my body feels when you love me." Her fingers played with his shirt until they found their way underneath it, hot skin and soft hair met her needy hands. "You make me lose control."

"It's okay to lose control." His hand slid up her thigh, parting her legs further as his fingertips touched the soft satin of her underwear.

Whistles, hollers, and clapping swept up the beach toward them. Loud cheers filled the warm air around them. James pulled Samantha to him, shielding her, as he looked over his shoulder in the direction of the bonfire. In the diffuse dusk light, there wasn't much they could make out, but they obviously got the gist of it.

Samantha pulled her hands from his torso like she was being scalded. "We can't do this."

"Don't."

Samantha pushed against the wall of his chest and slid off the table. Once she gained her bearings she stepped away from him, her breath catching as she did.

"Let's go in," he said, gesturing toward the door.

"No."

"Samantha," he said hesitantly.

Samantha shook her head and then rubbed her hands over her face briskly. The night air was cool against her heated skin. She shivered and moved to the table, where she found her hair clip. After securing her hair, she picked up a stack of dishes she had stacked earlier.

"What are you doing?"

She set the dishes back down again as she struggled with her emotions. "I'm sorry."

"Don't apologize to me," James said in a disgusted tone.

Samantha's hand went to her head and she rubbed her brow and looked back at him. "I don't know what's happening to me." She continued to press her hand against her head. "There's probably a word for it in some thick fancy textbook." Her eyes dropped. "There's something definitely wrong with me."

"There's nothing wrong with you." He took the hand that

was at her brow and brought it to his lips. "Relax."

"I can't," she whispered in honest desperation.

"Sure you can." He linked his fingers with hers. "The word's called *lust,* Angel."

She pulled her hand away. "Don't. I can't think when you do that." She closed her eyes while she organized her thoughts.

"There's nothing fancy or complicated about it."

"This is a dangerous game and one I don't want to play."

"This isn't a game, Samantha."

When she opened her eyes they locked intently on James. "You're wasting your time; you know that, don't you?"

James felt like someone had doused him with a cup of cold water "Let me be the one to decide that." He took her hand again; he wouldn't lose the ground he had just gained. He wasn't blind, he'd seen, could still see, the desire she was trying to hide behind a cold veneer.

She looked down at her hand. "Find someone else, because I'm not interested."

"I don't want someone else." Light flickered in his eyes. "I want you."

"You want me because you can't have me." She chewed on her bottom lip. "There are hundreds of women who have nice-smelling hair who would love to be wined, dined, and seduced by you."

"They're not you." With no change in his expression he spoke again. "Besides, your 'you only want what you can't have' analogy doesn't apply to me." His head tilted to the side. "I always get what I want."

Ignoring the underlying warning, she said, "Not this time."

"Always—"

Pure frustration consumed her eyes. "Talking to you is like talking to a wall; it's pointless. Why aren't you listening to me? Don't you get it? I don't want this."

"I am listening to you. I heard you loud and clear at the restaurant the other night, and I sure as hell don't think I was misinterpreting you just a minute ago." He gestured behind him at the bonfire. "I think they heard you loud and clear, too."

"All of it was a mistake."

"It seems like you're making a lot of mistakes lately, Samantha." He waited for a minute. "If the same mistake is repeated many times, is it still considered a mistake?"

"Business slow at work, James?" she snapped.

He was all too aware of where she was going. His eyes turned dark. "Don't go there, Samantha."

"Why not?" She flung her hands in the air. "You've already made it clear that you're looking for a challenge." Her eyes narrowed as she dared him.

James's back went stiff as he felt the anger rise in him. He fought to keep control, for the ground she was choosing to venture into wasn't safe. And she damn well knew it.

"I guess that's what I've become . . . a challenge." She spoke the next words in a mocking tone. "One of James Taylor's little challenges." Her eyebrows lifted slightly in inquiry as her blue eyes flashed. "Is the Europe deal already closed? Or perhaps it's not challenging enough for you. I know how quickly you get bored."

Her sing-song voice shot to his core. Moving his hand to the back of his neck, James massaged the shooting pain that was spreading rapidly. Even with all his determination not to get angry, he felt something deep inside him coil tightly. "Samantha, I would stop if I were you."

"I'm not one of your little workers you can order around."

James's jaw was tightly fixed as he bit back the anger she was dangerously tapping into.

"I'm not a pawn in one of your million-dollar deals. And I'm sure the hell not some company or contract you can manipulate and make yours."

"That's enough." Sure, he had treated other women like they were at his disposal, but never Samantha. Samantha was never a passing fancy. He might have loved her obsessively, possessively, and a little recklessly, but it was because he had been overwhelmed by what he had felt for her.

She took a step back. Her eyes were ice cold. "All you big businessmen are alike. You don't care about the people around you."

"Don't put our relationship in that category. Don't you dare compare what we shared to what others share." It stung to have her strip their relationship down to nothing more than average.

"Why? Are we so different? We've ended up like most of them anyway." She shrugged. "Besides, it belongs there. I was no different than any of the other guy's girlfriends—"

"You were entirely different."

She shook her head. "If I had been, then maybe you wouldn't have felt the need to do what you did. Maybe you wouldn't have wanted to turn to someone else."

James wanted to take her by the shoulders and shake some sense into her. "You don't know what you're talking about."

"I know I was naïve and stupid to think you weren't like them." She used the back of her hand to push the wisps of hair from her eyes. "Name one man who you work with who hasn't cheated."

He remained silent.

"You can't, can you? Endless meetings, extremely long working hours, business trips, conventions, parties, women—"

"Are you suggesting that in my type of business, work and cheating go hand in hand?" He moved closer. "I want to hear you admit it."

She slapped the back of one hand against the palm of the other, in a display of absolute agitation. Her voice rose as she spoke. "You're the one who wants me to admit to everything. Goddamn it, how about you admit that what we had didn't mean a damn thing to you. I want to hear you admit that all of it was a farce."

He stood there watching her vigilantly. His entire body seemed to vibrate.

Samantha's eyes darted over his shoulder to the bonfire and then back to him. Her words were as cold as ice when she finally spoke. "Imagine what you could obtain if you could seduce a company and make it yours. You'd make the *Fortune 500* list for at least a decade."

He inched toward her, infuriated with her accusations. He didn't want to hear any more. "Do I even have to seduce you, Samantha? From your display moments before, not much seduction is needed."

The question hit her full force. "How dare you."

"Afraid to answer the question?" His voice taunted as he watched a turbulent storm flash in her eyes. "Or are we not wasting words over the obvious?"

"You're a heartless monster," she said, her eyes brimming with anger.

He opened his mouth and then shut it again. Moving forward he purposely took the clip out of her hair and let it tumble around his arm. With two fingers he touched the sensitive area behind her ear and ran them down her neck, across her chest, into the soft area between her breasts. "Apparently I am." The kiss he placed on her shaking lips wasn't meant to please.

CHAPTER SEVENTEEN

James craned his neck in an awkward fashion to try to alleviate some of the pain he was experiencing. Goddamn he was sore. He had left Samantha standing on the deck last night and had come to his office, because she had not only infuriated him, she had completely knocked him off balance. He looked up, momentarily pretending he was listening to the person giving a presentation at the end of the long conference table. He was good at appearing interested.

His thoughts drifted again. The last time he had slept on that damn couch in his office had been when Samantha had left him. He had stayed at his office for over two weeks because he couldn't stand being at home or in bed without her. He had left last night for just the opposite reason. She was there. The pain in his neck tensed. He thought about the small tin in the top of his desk drawer that contained aspirin and fought the urge to make a mad dash for it.

The person giving the presentation paused and handed out a packet to everyone. When James got the green folder he absentmindedly creased the first page open with the edge of this thumb. He only heard the speaker's first few words before he was lost in the mayhem of the previous night. He had been outraged when Samantha insinuated that he was some ruthless, heartless man. He felt his grip tighten on the pen; he looked down and saw his knuckles turn white and released it. He wasn't the cold-hearted son-of-a-bitch that she was making him out to be.

He mulled that over for a minute. Okay, that wasn't entirely true. He was a little merciless when it came to business. In his line of work ruthlessness was a prerequisite. But he had never been merciless with Samantha. The hard-nosed trait that allowed him to excel in his profession was never brought home. She had been what balanced it and kept it in check.

He felt himself getting angry all over again. She had been way off base to suggest otherwise. Did she truly believe that he thought she and their relationship was no better than a business deal? No better than some of his colleagues' relationships? What they had was more intense and more real than anything he'd ever experienced. How dare she belittle that.

He took a sip of the coffee that Shelly had handed him over forty minutes ago, when the meeting had first started. She had told him he looked like he needed it as she shoved it into one hand and a thick file into the other. The cold, bitter drink did nothing but ignite the burning that had been smoldering in his stomach. Between the excruciating pain in the top portion of his body and the burning in the lower, all he wanted to do was toss everything off the table, lie across it, and groan until the pain subsided.

When the presentation ended he pushed all his soreness to the back of his mind and focused on the room. It was his turn to take the floor. Looking up, he gave a nod of approval to the speaker. "Very good, Rick." He then looked over to a young man just out of prep school. "Doug, I want you to put together a team to go over to Europe and work on the new merger." He examined his calendar. "Have a preliminary list for me to review by next week. I want to get them over there as soon as possible."

"Yes, sir. However, they want to put together their own team."

Doug started to pass James some papers. "Here is their list—"

James looked up after jotting some notes. "I want our own people there. At least for the first six months."

"I agree. That was going to be my recommendation," Doug said lightly.

"Good." James did little more than glance up. "Then we're on the same page."

"However—"

"I don't like howevers, Doug."

"They are being very persistent—"

"I don't give a damn what they want or how persistent they are being." He took a deep breath to steady himself. "There was nothing in the contract stating this."

Doug nodded. "True. But we never divulged that we wanted our people in there either. They're worried about job security."

"The acquisitions team explained to them there would be some downsizing. Unfortunately, some employees are going to become nonessential because of the merger. This isn't something new to them." James reached for the coffee but didn't take a drink; he didn't think his stomach could take a drop more.

"We have a commitment—"

"To our company, Doug," James said unsympathetically. "I'm making you personally responsible for putting their minds at ease. Reassure them that we've hand-picked the right professionals to head this."

Doug only nodded.

"No mistakes. If this merger collapses it will be costly." James looked down and sifted through some papers, then glanced back at the rest of the group. "I think that's it." He looked to Raymond. "Is there anything you'd like to add?"

"No, I think that about covers it."

James lifted his briefcase from the floor onto the table. "See everyone Monday morning."

In his office he glared at the couch, which was two feet shorter than he was. The expensive piece of furniture was the cause of all the pain that was rapidly creeping across his shoulders and down his back. He couldn't sleep on it again. He wouldn't be able to walk in the morning if he did.

"Mr. Taylor." Shelly poked her head into his office. "I'm getting ready to leave. Do you want me to order you some dinner?"

James shook his head. "That won't be necessary."

"I can get you a blanket and a pillow if you are staying the night again." She motioned over her shoulder. "I think there are some things in the closet in the lounge."

He shook his head. "Thank you, but I'll be going home tonight." He might not be welcomed but he was going nonetheless. His mom would know something was the matter if he didn't come home, and he didn't want her to worry. That was the last thing she needed.

"Is everything okay, Mr. Taylor? I hope you don't mind my saying, but you haven't seemed like yourself lately. Is your mom doing all right?"

"She's doing as well as can be expected." He was going through the list of messages Shelly had set on his desk. He held the dozen or so memos in the air. "Are any of these urgent?"

"Nothing that can't wait until Monday."

He tossed the blue pieces of paper on his desk and looked up. He smiled for the first time that day. "I'm fine, too. Go home to your husband and have a great weekend."

"You try and do the same."

"I will." When he heard the door click shut he stretched his arms over his head. The muscles in his back felt like a mesh of tight cords. They protested against his movement so he dropped them back to his sides. He needed his recliner, an ice-cold beer, and the sports channel.

Samantha saw the headlights through the bedroom window as James pulled into the drive. Her stomach fluttered as she bent to tie her sneakers. She had been hoping to have been gone by now. She looked at her watch; it was her turn to drive to yoga class and she was running fifteen minutes late. Paul would undoubtedly be worried about her if she didn't get a move on it. Taking the bag off the bed she left the room and went down the hall. She looked in on Marie. "I'm going."

Marie smiled over the book she was reading. "Have a nice class, dear."

"I will." She set the gym bag at the door and moved into the room. "James just pulled in, so you won't be alone."

"Did you keep a plate warming?"

Samantha closed the blinds beside the bed. "Yes, just as you requested." She went into the bathroom and turned out the light. "The corn bread is wrapped in foil in the oven and the chili is in the Crock-Pot on low." Before she set a little bottle of pills on the nightstand, she emptied one into a clear cup. "If the pain gets too bad, take one."

Marie regarded the pills. "I'll be fine."

"Don't be stubborn."

"If I take one of those I forget who I am for a day."

"That's why you take them at night." She moved back to the bed and hugged Marie. "Now, you're going to be okay?"

"We already discussed this, this morning. I'm fine."

"Sleep tight."

Marie wasn't reading for more than ten minutes before James walked in. "Hi." He winced as he bent down to kiss her.

Marie leaned forward to meet his kiss. "You must have left

early this morning." She patted his cheek. "I didn't hear you get up."

James didn't look at his mom. Instead he leaned against the wall because standing on his own was too much effort. He crossed his legs at the ankles, and shifted his weight to find a more comfortable position. His attempts were wasted. Nothing was going to put him out of his misery.

"You look tired. Have you had a busy day?"

"Very busy. We're trying to set everything up in Europe."

"Will you have to go over there?"

"Possibly." He reassured her with a smile. "But not for a while yet. Deals like this take time." He would have to go when the merger was closed, but until then he would send someone else, because he wasn't going to leave her. "How do you feel?"

"Good. I think I'm regaining some of my strength," she said brightly.

"That's good to hear."

"Yeah, but the next treatment is going to knock me back down."

His tone lightened. "But it's your last treatment. You're almost done."

"I know." She looked toward the door. "Did you see Samantha?"

He shook his head. "Why?"

"She just left for yoga class."

"I guess I just missed her." It was probably more like she had purposely avoided him. "I went into the office to check my messages before I came up. Why, is something the matter? Do you need something?" He looked at the array of different prescriptions beside her bed. He wouldn't have a clue about what to give her if she did need something.

"No, she just hasn't seemed like herself lately." She tried to keep her look casual and not too prying. "You wouldn't know what's the matter with her, would you?"

"Mother."

"Well, I just—"

"Mother," he repeated. His deep voice commanded that she stop.

"Oh, all right, I'll keep my nose out of it." She waved her hand in the air.

"Thank you."

"Have you eaten?" She smiled when he shook his head. "Samantha made a delicious dinner. She's kept everything warming for you. Wasn't that thoughtful of her?"

"Yeah, thoughtful. Do you need anything before I go?"

"No. I'm going to read for about twenty more minutes, then *Wheel of Fortune* is coming on." She shooed him away with her hand and picked up the book that was folded open beside her. "You go and get some dinner; I need to finish this chapter."

James polished off the last of his chili and sipped his beer as he watched the ball game. He regarded the half-full amber bottle in his hand. He would need about five more to ease the pain he was feeling.

Motion to his left caused him to look up. Samantha stood with her gym bag in one hand and the car keys in the other. Her hair was pulled tightly back into a ponytail. She looked as bad as he did. Their eyes met. "We need to talk."

He took a long sip and then said, "Don't you think we did enough of that last night?" Just seeing her rekindled what little pain he had been able to supress over the last few hours. He fought his building tension. "I don't want to do this again." He closed his eyes, then opened them. "I can't. I know where you stand and how you feel. Nothing more needs to be said."

"No, you don't." Her voice sounded small in the large room. "You don't know how I feel."

Disbelief took over James's expression. His gut twisted into a tight knot. "You can't be serious. You may think I misinterpret things often but I got your point last night."

"I need to explain—"

"There's nothing to explain." James muted the game and stared at her. All the hurt he was feeling surfaced. Damn, he thought he had managed to get control of it. Hadn't he spent the last twenty-four hours stuffing it inside of him? "I don't want to talk."

"But I need you to talk to me. Please, James."

"Do you really think that I'm that type of man?" He shrugged his aching shoulders. "Did I ever treat you like some possession that I wanted to acquire?" He watched her for a moment. "Answer me. Did I ever treat you that way?"

She shook her head as her lashes slowly covered her eyes. "No, of course not."

He slapped his hand on the arm of his chair. "How can you compare what we had to other meaningless and loveless relationships?" For a brief moment he forgot about the pain, he forgot about everything, he remembered only what they had shared. "We never just existed, Samantha. We lived. We loved. Don't twist what we had into something that it's not. What we shared was beautiful and magical, regardless of how it ended."

"You're right."

He didn't speak for a few minutes. "Do you mean it?"

She moved toward him. "Yes. What we had was amazing."

"Then what in the hell happened last night?"

She sighed as she thought about it. There was no plausible excuse for the way she behaved. "I said those things last night because I was mad."

"Excuse me?"

"I was mad at myself for wanting you." She linked her hands together. "I thought if I made you out to be the bad guy then—"

"Then you wouldn't want me," he added for her.

"Something like that." She moved to the couch, too weary to stand. "The things I said last night were not only uncalled for, but untrue." She shifted when he didn't answer. "I'm sorry."

"Why are you fighting this, Samantha?"

"You know why." She shook her head quickly. "I don't want to fight anymore and I don't want to say hurtful things. So, we're not going to talk about it." Her fingers played with the hem of her baggy sweatshirt. "I'm trying to deal with this the best way I know how."

"By not dealing with it at all? You can't ignore what we have, it's too strong." He turned his entire body in the chair, because if he just turned his neck he feared he would die from the pain. "If you would just let me explain—"

"Stop." She held up her hand. "Please don't say another word." It took a moment for her to put together what she wanted to say. "We're friends. I am here because I love Marie and I want to help her. I want to help you, too. That's all." She got ready to continue but then saw the way he was sitting—the odd way he was looking at her. "Are you okay? You don't have to look like it's the end of the world just because I said we're only friends."

"My neck is killing me."

"Your neck?" she said in disbelief.

"Yes. And my shoulders, and my back, and my head. Right now everything pretty much hurts."

"Why didn't you say something?" She moved behind his chair and put her hands on his neck. She felt the tight muscles and began to work them. "You're one giant knot."

"If I turn my head too fast I feel like I'm going to pass out." He winced as she felt around, assessing the damage. "I took some aspirin but it hasn't touched it."

"You know, yoga could take care of this." Her fingers found

their way to his temples, where she applied gentle pressure, using a circular motion that was amazingly effective.

"I'm not getting down on the floor and contorting myself into some crazy position that my body shouldn't be in in the first place."

"Well, that crazy position would relieve this tension."

James rested his head against the back of the chair and let out a long breath. "You seem to be relieving it just fine."

She allowed herself to smile. "You're lucky that I'm not as demanding as my yoga instructor."

"Yes, I'm sure Paul worked his magic on you tonight." His voice was a calm mask of disgust.

Samantha used her thumb and dug into the muscles that covered his shoulder blade. She held the pressure for a very long moment. "As a matter of fact he did."

Yeah, James was sure the jerk had his hands all over her when he was doing it, too. "Is that why class ran late tonight?"

"Are you timing me?"

"Not exactly," he said seriously.

"I had to run by my place."

"I don't like him."

"I do."

"Why? He's not your type," His voice was scornful.

"How do you know what my type is?"

"I just know." He couldn't take the pressure any more. "Okay, ease up."

She reduced the pressure. "At least I'm able to walk upright. A chiropractic adjustment would—"

"Don't even go there, Samantha."

"Fine." She brought her hands to his neck. "That hot tub of yours, which hasn't seen the light of day, might help, too."

"It might," he agreed. "Are you going to get in with me?"

"Not likely."

James sunk a little farther down in the seat and closed his eyes. "I'll pass then. Besides, I've got a full belly, a beer, a ball game, and one hell of a masseuse." He raised the remote and pressed the mute button filling the room with the voices of two overexuberant commentators. "What more could a man ask for?"

Samantha watched the game for a few moments, allowing herself time to relax and regroup. The drive home from class had been pure torture because she hadn't been sure what was going to happen when she got home. She was almost positive her antics had put her job in jeopardy and she was just as certain they would surely destroy the feeble relationship she and James had. When she had walked through the door and had not seen her bags, she'd felt a glimmer of hope.

"We're all right?" she asked, now.

Samantha was surprised when James raised his hands and placed them over hers. Suddenly, he reached over and pulled her over the chair and into his lap. She landed with a thump, her face inches from his.

"I want a confession first," he said as he cradled her to him.

She brushed the hair from her face and studied the warm darkness of his eyes. They reflected power and control. "What do you want me to confess to?"

"I want you to admit you can't ignore what's here." He moved his hand in the small space between them.

It would be a miracle if she could tune out what was between them, she thought. If she could find a way to eliminate and dispose of all the emotions, which seemed to fall in the category of passion, living with him would be tolerable. His request wasn't unreasonable, and after the way she behaved the question seemed meager, so she answered him. "If I could ignore it, do you think we would be going through any of this?"

"You know it's there." His reply wasn't a question, but a confirmation.

The look in his eyes prevented words, so she nodded.

He touched the tip of her nose with two fingers, then her lips, even though he really wanted to kiss her. He studied her beautiful face briefly, and then suddenly tossed her back over his shoulder in one silent fluid movement. Taking each of her hands, he rested them on his shoulders, precisely where they had been only moments before. "There's ten minutes left in the fourth. Whatever you do, don't stop."

CHAPTER EIGHTEEN

James found Samantha stuffing dirty clothes into the washer in the laundry room. He waited until she was finished measuring the detergent before he spoke. "Hi."

"How's your neck feeling?" she said as she bent down and pulled clothes out of the dryer.

"Much better. Thank you. The Rose Festival is today and I was wondering if you think Mom is feeling well enough to go." He didn't give her a chance to answer. "I haven't suggested it to her yet because I didn't know if you thought it was a good idea. She hasn't been out in awhile and I think she would really enjoy going."

"I don't see why she can't. Just try and keep the day short so she doesn't get too worn out." She carried an arm full of warm clothes into the living room and dropped them onto the couch.

James followed, picking up the garments that fell. "Ginger does the laundry."

"Not mine."

He handed her the clothes. "Here."

"Thanks."

"Do you think it's too soon after her treatment for her to go? I know her cell count drops, and all that stuff." He grabbed a shirt and folded it. "We've been so careful, washing our hands and making sure she doesn't come in contact with anyone sick. So far, our efforts haven't been wasted. I didn't want to blow it with one outing."

Samantha smiled. "All that stuff is fine."

"Good." He turned, paused, and then turned back around. "Do you want to come with us?" When she didn't answer right away, he added. "It'll be fun." He needed to be with her.

"Come with us where?" Marie said as she walked into the room. She carried her tote bag with all her crocheting. "Are we going somewhere?"

James turned to his mom. "How does the Rose Festival sound?"

"Just lovely. I had forgotten that it was this weekend." Marie looked over at Samantha. "Oh, you must come. The roses are some of the finest you'll ever see."

"It does sound nice." She looked from one to the other. "Are you sure?"

"Absolutely." Marie said when James nodded.

"Okay, I'd love to go." Samantha finished folding the clothes. She took several stacks of the freshly laundered clothes and then looked at Marie. "Meet me upstairs and I'll help you get ready."

Marie tried another hat on, this time a black one with a large brim. "None of these hats look good on me."

"I liked the sun hat," Samantha said as she sat on the edge of the bed, looking over Marie's shoulder through the mirror.

"I've never looked good in a hat. My forehead is too low, so the band rests on my eyebrows, cutting off half of my head." She set the hat aside. "I don't know why I even bought them."

"Then don't wear one if you don't like them." Samantha looked at Marie, who was trying to brush her thinning hair into somewhat of a style. It had saddened her to see Marie's head of beautiful white hair slowly grow sparse over the last several months. "Come over here and let me give it a try."

Marie sat next to her. "What's it going to hurt?"

"Exactly." Samantha raised a finger. "Just a minute." She darted out of the room and was back in seconds. She held up a large can of hair spray. "We'll have to pull out the big guns for this."

"Extra hold?"

Samantha laughed and looked at the can. She read the small print across the bottom of it aloud. "Super hold." She picked up a comb and began fluffing her hair. She moved around Marie's head, teasing and spraying here and there. She worked the front, then moved around to the side, and after a few minutes she gave the once-limp hair a final spray. "What do you think?"

Marie looked at herself in the mirror and smiled. "How did you do that?" She brought both hands to her hair and patted lightly. It was holding its shape, not collapsing into some lifeless, sparse heap. "That's amazing."

Samantha set the hair spray down, as Marie looked at herself in complete disbelief. Although her hair was thin, it looked very nice, Samantha had to admit. Maybe she missed her calling. Hair could have been her area of expertise. "When I was in high school big hair was in. I learned every trick there was to getting the biggest hair."

"You would have loved the bouffant."

Samantha laughed. She had seen her mom wear the popular sixties style many times. "Yes, I'm sure I would have. If I'm lucky it might just come back in style."

James knocked on the open door as he walked in. "You ladies ready?" He paused as he looked at his mom. "You look wonderful." He hadn't seen her wear her favorite yellow sundress in months and her hair looked amazing.

"Thank you. Samantha did my hair." She took Samantha's hand into hers and stood up from the dressing table. "Isn't it perfect?"

"Yes, it is."

"I'm going to go get my purse. I'll meet you downstairs."

James watched Samantha stand before the mirror and arrange her hair. She then rearranged it several more times, contemplating the style. She wore a long floral skirt that hugged her legs. The ribbed green shirt was cut low. A beautiful gold charm hung near her breasts. Her makeup was kept to a minimum, just enough to accentuate her beautiful features. "Wear it down."

Samantha released the hair she held at the top of her head, ready to secure it with a clip. Looking through the mirror, her eyes found and then settled on James. He was standing over her right shoulder watching, waiting. "What would you do if I cut it off?" She used her hand and gestured at chin level. "Right about here."

James cringed. Her hair was so beautiful. It was shiny, lustrous, and agonizingly soft to the touch. It would be a crime if she cut it. "You wouldn't. It suits you long."

"No, it suits *you* long. What's your infatuation with my hair anyway?" She looked back into the mirror, visualizing the cut. "I think it might be fun."

James moved close. She smelled sweet, the hint of fragrance agreed with him. "You'll never cut it." It was more of an order than a statement. Heaven forbid if she did.

Her amusement vanished, as an intent expression flickered across her face. "Don't tempt me."

The touch was meant to throw her. It was meant to startle and remind. It did all that and more. James's fingers found her lips, her chin, and the corners of her eyes. His mouth barely opened as he spoke. "Don't tempt me." The warning was spoken against her cheek. "Ready?"

The day was a perfect seventy-eight, and the festival drew

crowds. City blocks had been shut down and merchants had set up in the middle of the road, some with white canvas tents and others with nothing more than a few tables. Part of the festival's charm and attraction was the live outdoor music, from local bands. Mix that with good food and beautiful flowers, and it made for a picturesque sight.

Flowers came in every form. Hanging baskets dripped with green foliage dotted with bits of color. Cut flowers were held in white containers, in symmetrical rows, according to type and hue. Marie purchased bouquet after bouquet, because she couldn't resist the arrangements with so much color—every one unique.

Samantha's senses were inundated when they passed a booth that offered every herb imaginable. She stopped and bought some basil and rosemary because the freshness was mouth-watering. She would make spaghetti tonight.

They passed more booths, which were filled with paintings, sculptures, photographs, and other beautiful pieces that revolved around the festival's theme. Local artists had set up mini studios, and James, Samantha, and Marie paused every so often to watch them work.

When they found the American Rose Club's booth, they spent over an hour there. Marie had been a member of the ARC for over fifteen years. She took the time to get caught up on all the latest happenings since she had been away.

The next stop was to gawk over a new miniature rose that she had never seen. Marie clasped her hands together in sheer enchantment. "I must have one. The head size is perfect, the color is superb, and the variegated leaves make it irresistible." She turned to Samantha. "Look how delicate it is."

"It's beautiful." Samantha held the elegant flower head in her hand.

James handed the man some money and took the potted

plant. He watched his mom smile in delight and it warmed his heart. Fresh air and old friends were just what she needed. He had been worried that the outing might exhaust her. But it was doing just the opposite. It was replenishing her spirit and strength. As his mom spoke with a friend, James shifted the bags he was carrying.

"Please, let me carry some of those," Samantha said as she adjusted her purse over her shoulder, preparing to help lighten his load.

James set two of the bags down. "What is she going to do with all these flowers?" He looked down at the dozens of loose flowers nestled amongst baby's breath and green foliage. "I don't think I own enough vases for all of them." His raised the newest purchase. "And now this. I'm going to have to add on another room."

She almost giggled out loud. "Maybe a greenhouse out back."

James shot her a look.

Samantha brought a lavender-colored flower to her nose. "You must admit, they *are* beautiful. Each time I see one I think it's the most beautiful flower I've ever seen. But then I see another and it appears to be more exquisite than the last. I see why Marie enjoys them. And the fragrance is out of this world." She stopped. "What, why are you smiling?"

"I'm just listening." James pulled a single blood-red rose from a bouquet that was neatly tucked in the bag he was still holding. He tore the stem off and placed it behind Samantha's ear. He stood back and looked at her. "Perfection."

She was completely absorbed in his gesture. Looking intently into his eyes, the crowd around them faded away into a molten blur of color and sound. It was just the two of them. Why was he looking at her that way? She touched the rose at her ear and impulsively her hand moved to his face. His skin was soft and warm. Her fingers slid along his cheek and traced over his jawbone. When she brushed his lips, they parted and he kissed her fingertips. How was it that he could mesmerize her so effortlessly?

She stumbled forward when someone bumped her from behind. She looked over her shoulder when she heard sorry muttered from the culprit.

James gripped her shoulder and steadied her. "You okay?" he asked.

She nodded and shook her blond hair out of her eyes. "I guess I should have been paying more attention." She looked at the continual stream of people going by. "Where's Marie?"

"There she is." He retrieved the bags on the ground beside him. He offered Samantha one of them. With his free hand he took hers. Linking their fingers, he pulled her in the direction of his mom.

"No, you don't." James's voice was earnest.

"What?" Marie turned. "It's beautiful." She gestured to the painting before her. "It would go perfectly—"

"Mom, you don't need another rose painting."

"You can never have too many rose paintings." She lifted her shoulders. "It's not just roses anyway." She turned back to the large painting that was mounted on a tall, brass easel. "Look, there's a charming cottage in the foreground." She stepped closer to see the exceptional detail.

"Yeah, and it's surrounded by roses," James pointed out, before he looked at Samantha. She too was admiring the painting. What was it about women and flowers?

Marie looked over at Samantha and noticed the flower in her hair. "Do you know that the rose is the flower for lovers?"

James shook his head. "What?"

Marie caught his look. "Just a little trivia."

"Thanks for the bit of information." He leaned into Samantha's ear. "Are you hungry?"

"A little. Why?" she whispered back to him. "Let's find a place to eat. If we eat that means she can't buy anything else."

Samantha gestured toward Marie. "But look how happy she is."

"I can't hold much more." He pleaded with her. "My house can't hold much more."

Samantha shrugged. "It's a big house."

James squeezed Samantha's hand tightly to illustrate his seriousness. "Will you please work with me here? I'm losing feeling in my right arm. And I lost feeling in my fingers over an hour ago, thanks to the plastic bag that's slowly cutting into my palm."

Her voice wasn't as low when she spoke this time. "If you keep squeezing my hand like that I'm going to lose feeling, too."

"If I have to suffer, so do you."

Marie came up behind James. "I heard that, James Anthony Taylor."

He turned to his mom with a sheepish grin. "I'm starving and in pain."

Samantha didn't know why, but she thought she would bail him out. "I'm getting a little hungry, too. Perhaps, we should call it a day and grab a bite to eat."

CHAPTER NINETEEN

"That was a wonderful day." Marie said as she placed the last vase of roses on the coffee table. She had spent the entire evening making arrangements, thoroughly enjoying herself as she did. The day had been perfect; so had the dinner they all shared in a quaint restaurant downtown. "I think I'm going to call it a night."

"Do you need any help?" Samantha said from the kitchen as she swept leftover foliage into the trash.

"No, thank you."

James got up from the couch and kissed his mom's cheek. "Good night." He surveyed his house. There were roses and flowers in every size, shape, and color. "By the way, thanks for turning my house into a florist shop."

Marie took a deep breath. "The smell is intoxicating isn't it? Good night, all." She waved her hand over her head as she climbed the stairs.

The rose in Samantha's hands fell to the floor. It was a long moment before she picked it up and began walking through the living room, toward the front door.

"Where are you going?" James called after her.

"I think I'll run home and check on things there since I'm not needed here. I haven't been there in a few days. I need to water the plants and get the mail." Where had she put her purse? "My message machine is probably full. I like to leave a light on . . ." Her words trailed off as James stepped in front of her, blocking her path to the door.

"You are needed." His voice was pure seduction.

Samantha eyed the door behind James and then looked back at him. "Marie has turned in for the night."

"It's not my mom who needs you." He stripped away any pretenses she might have with the simple statement.

His words melted into her body, dissolving into warmth that swirled through every fiber of her being. Had he touched her? God, it felt like he had. She focused. "James, your mom's going to be fine—"

He took a step closer. "That's not what I need you for." He eased his fingers into the waist band of her jeans just below her navel. Gripping the denim, he gave a gentle tug toward him. The motion brought her body inches from his. "You know what I need."

Samantha's head was drenched with sensations. The pressure at her waist made her dizzy and did nothing to alleviate the demands that were rapidly forming inside. She shifted her weight to accommodate the hand that slid around her waist. She grasped his wrist, her nails digging into his skin. He was warm, he was solid, and he was real. This wasn't one of the cruel dreams that plagued her too often while she was alone in her bed.

For the first time in her life Samantha was truly indecisive. She was compelled to run to the door and escape any potential harm, but her feet wouldn't budge. She could feel apprehension slowly diminish as his penetrating eyes locked on her.

"Tell me you need me, too." His gaze shifted from her mouth to her eyes, waiting for a reply.

"We can't do this." Even when she spoke the words she knew she didn't mean them. Well, maybe she meant them, but they held no conviction. She didn't want to resist this time. She had no energy left to fight him. Whether she believed it or not, she knew she yearned for this feeling of pure, unrestrained abandon. She wanted him. She needed him. She felt a little lightheaded at the discovery.

"We can do anything we want." The kiss he placed on her lips was unhurried and infused with longing.

She responded to the kiss just as she had so long ago, but this kiss was accentuated with an intense hunger that only separation could create. His tongue probed the unforgettable depths, the taste drawing out old memories.

"You make all the pain disappear when you kiss me." Samantha's voice was broken as she spoke against his lips. "You make me forget."

James held her face firmly in his hands. "It's time to forget, Samantha."

She shook her head as he held it. "I can't. I can't let myself." She pressed her head against his and tried to sort out everything she was experiencing. Her body hadn't been this alive since the last time he had touched her, and it felt so good. Her head swirled with confusion and beautiful sensations. She realized that, in spite of everything, something inside her needed to be with him. It couldn't be denied.

"There's nothing wrong with forgetting." His voice was so gentle it cleared away the chaos from her mind.

When she closed her eyes and tried to focus, she felt him place a gentle kiss on each of her eyelids. Her hands were resting on his shoulders; they clenched in uncertainty. She truly didn't know what to do. She felt like her heart would stop in her chest if she didn't make a decision quickly.

"Open your eyes," he insisted. "Don't think, Angel." He tilted her head and kissed her neck. "Just feel." His words were like soft feathers against her skin. "Like you used to." He worked his way to her lips. "You remember how it used to feel, don't you?"

Samantha had played this scene over and over in her head a

thousand times and it had never been this good. She had thought the memory of how wonderful it was to be with him was enhanced, because she by no means believed she would be with him ever again. Now, that she was standing with him, holding him, feeling him, and tasting him, it was twice as intense as she had ever imagined. She nipped at his lips in a desperate attempt to reassure herself that he was real. "How could I forget? How could I ever forget this?"

James broke the kiss. "Breathe, Sweetie." She looked as if she was going to crumble to the floor. "I don't want you to collapse." He leaned in and placed another kiss on her lips. "At least not until we're near my bed." He took her by the hand and led her up the stairs and to his room.

She was a vision standing at the foot of his bed. It seemed fit that she was washed in moonlight, natural beauty enhancing natural beauty. "You're beautiful."

She reached for him. She needed to touch him. "You used to say stunning."

"There isn't a word suitable to describe you," he whispered as he lifted her shirt over her head.

Impatiently, she helped him tug her pants over her hips. Once she was naked, he laid her on the bed. Half of her body was still illuminated by the moonlight. He ran his hand across the goose bumps that had formed when the cool breeze, which blew in from the window, met with her hot skin. Another dozen prickles were produced when he brought his lips to her heated flesh.

"What about you?" She gestured to his clothes.

He arched a brow when he glanced up. "Not yet." His head dipped down again and found her breast ready and waiting for him.

She arched up to meet him. Her words were a sob of pleasure and pain as she reached for his shirt. "James, don't do this to me." She shuddered as he drew in the pale pink center of her breast. "This isn't fair." Her entire body sizzled with electricity and she didn't know how to deal with it.

"Who said life is fair?"

She felt like she was going to explode if she didn't decompress in some way. His fingers were soft velvet and they whispered over her skin, teasing, taunting, exploring. "James . . ." she moaned his name again before she was able to speak. "Please, it's been so long. I need . . . let me just touch you."

He raised his head and studied her. "There's been no one else? This entire time there's been no one?"

She could only shake her head. She should probably be embarrassed, but the ecstasy that was furiously taking over her body prevented it. Besides, she had never been embarrassed about anything when it came to James, and she wasn't about to start now.

Before he rolled off her, he kissed her senseless. "I'm yours for the taking. Have your way with me."

Her lips turned into a lazy smile and she almost purred. She was going to enjoy this, every painstaking step of it. "Then stand." She wanted to devour him. "I want you standing."

He accommodated her.

Samantha started with James's shirt, easing it over his torso and arms. She tossed it to the side, eager to free her hands so she could touch him. Little by little, she added another article of clothing to the pile. As each piece floated to the floor, her need for him grew more fervent. She experienced an uncontrollable force that she had never felt before. Not even the first time they had made love. Was it the year's worth of pent-up sexual frustration that was driving her to the brink?

As she circled him, she was enthralled by his physique. His body was the essence of maleness. It was defined, broad, and solid. She couldn't resist, she allowed her hand to glide down his back; when it found his tight buttock, it stopped. The touch was burning hot. When she moved in front of him, her eyes met his.

James touched her trembling lips. "What?" Her eyes held a dark yearning he had never seen before. "You can tell me." His voice was a rugged whisper.

Could she? How did she even begin to put into words the crazy energy she was feeling? Primal hunger, a woman's desire, an internal battle with raging hormones, or was she just sex starved? All she knew was that she didn't want it to end. This sexual tension had been sealed deep in her, and now that it was out she was completely baffled and overwhelmed by it. "I don't know where to begin. I don't want it to end." She ran her hand through her hair and tried to still her raging emotions long enough to speak. "God, I feel like I'm going to explode. I want you so badly."

Amusement danced in his eyes. "Let me help."

Their bodies were warm and soft when he pulled her to him in a gentle embrace. He could hear her heart beating wildly. Her state was borderline reckless. His finger moved to her chin, tilting it up so he could see her face. "We have all night. We can take our time."

She kissed him fanatically. She held nothing back. She could hold nothing back. "I can't wait that long."

"Sure you can."

"If you could feel what I'm feeling you'd know that's not true."

"Trust me, I know what you're feeling."

He pulled away, and took his time looking at her. The smile that touched the corner of his lips was pure seduction.

Dear God, would she be able to stand much more? She had to give in to her body's demands, but that wasn't going to happen any time soon with James taking his sweet time. She felt the hunger for him claw at her insides. "I want—"

"You'll get exactly what you want."

She ached for some type of release. "Not if you keep taking your time."

He chuckled. "You're so impatient." With steady hands James guided her to the bed. Her eyes were dazed with dark passion when he stretched out beside her. God she was beautiful, and now, once again, she was his.

CHAPTER TWENTY

James pressed his lips against her neck for a second time. "Wake up, Angel." He smiled when she didn't budge. Threading the silk tie through his collar, he instinctively tied it flawlessly. Once finished, he reached toward the nightstand and took his watch. Putting it on, he looked back at Samantha. She was lying on her back in the center of his bed looking completely content. They had made love most of the night. It had been so powerful it was almost frightening.

There had been a hint of desperation mixed in with the passion that hadn't gone unnoticed. It was like they were making love for the first and last time. He looked down at her as she stirred. This wouldn't be the last time they made love, he promised. He wasn't going to lose her again. Their lovemaking had always been powerful; why should it be any different now? Stop worrying, he told himself.

Remembering his pager on the dresser, he moved across the room and hooked it to his waist. His car keys went into one pocket while he put some change into the other. He made his way back to the bed.

Briefly, he considered and after a moment he knew the perfect way to get her attention. He slid his hand under the covers and felt his way to Samantha's leg. Gliding his hand over the warm, velvety skin he moved to her inner thigh. He sat on the edge of the bed and bent to kiss her as the tips of his fingers sank into soft curls. "Angel." His words were quiet as he stroked her.

Her fingers wrapped around the object that skillfully caused heat to build and spread through her.

"You awake?" James asked, his voice husky.

Samantha shook her head and squeezed his hand between her thighs. "I don't want to wake up." She moved against his hand. "You were in my dreams all night."

James dipped his head and kissed her again. "I was in more than just your dreams last night." He loved the way she looked in the dim light. She summoned images of calm, dewy mornings spent snuggling under covers. "Angel, don't close your eyes again." He pulled his hand away, knowing that it was the only way to get her attention.

Samantha's eyes opened suddenly, but remained dreamy. "Don't stop."

James laughed. "I need to go."

"What time is it?"

"Around five."

Samantha reached for his hand and pulled it back to her. "I haven't woken to a man in over a year. Don't leave yet."

"I have to go."

"Finish what you started," she moaned breathlessly.

He placed kisses on every exposed surface, whispered endearments in her ear, and drove her to the edge, all while he finished what he had started. She arched against his hand and her head rolled to the side, scattering hair across the pillow. He dropped his free hand into her soft mane and felt the deep-seated heat that had consumed him all night return. He pulled away and smiled down at her when she quivered under his hand. "Better?"

Samantha rolled onto her side, dragging the covers with her. "It would've been better if you were in here with me."

"Make sure you're home tonight. No yoga."

Samantha mumbled acknowledgement as she pulled the covers up around her neck and closed her eyes. "I thought you said you had to go," she muttered.

He nuzzled into her neck. "Sure, now that you have what you want from me you're sending me away." Her breath was still slightly labored. "What comes around goes around . . . remember that."

She opened her eyes and grinned. "Yes, I'll remember. Did you get any coffee or breakfast yet?"

He shook his head. "Only you."

"Then what more do you need? You should be completely satisfied."

"Never." He tucked his cell phone in a pocket and made a mental note that his briefcase was wedged between the couch and the end table. "Getting enough of you isn't possible." He bent for one final kiss. "I'll get something at the office. I have to go or I'll be late. Dream about me."

She closed her eyes and mumbled. "I always do."

Sitting at the bar balancing her checkbook, Samantha realized that her day had gone by like a beautiful dream. The night with James had left her invigorated and feeling like a completely new woman. It had been a while since she felt so alive. She had re-awakened at seven, in his bed, and had taken a long hot shower in his bathroom. It felt good, she admitted, but she didn't dwell on it. She took it at face value. She hadn't felt this good in a long time; there was no reason to analyze it.

Marie had received great news when she went in for her last check-up. Her cancer had responded so well to the treatment they weren't going to do surgery. In fact, they couldn't even see a shadow on the last MRI. How could the day possibly get better? She heard the front door open, then close, and her heart trembled in her chest. She wanted to rush to the door and greet him but knew she shouldn't. Instead she allowed her body to quietly respond to him as she remained seated.

James walked in with his arm draped around his mom's shoulder. His smile grew when he saw Samantha. "Mom said her doctor's visit was great."

Samantha glanced up. "Yes, isn't it wonderful news?"

"I think a celebration is in order," he said.

Marie looked over at him when he released her from the tight embrace. "My thoughts exactly. I've already made plans."

An expression of surprise crept across James's face. "Really? What are we doing?"

Marie looked from her son to Samantha. "I'm not sure what the two of you are doing. However, Helen is picking me up in fifteen minutes."

Concern etched its way into his face. "I really—"

Marie cut in. "James, don't tell me how it's not good for me to go out. I went to the festival and I'm fine. Besides, I've stayed home all this time to please you. I've finished my treatments and the doctor says I'm healthy enough to get back to normal activity." She looked over to Samantha. "Right, Samantha?"

"Yes, but he did say do everything in moderation for the first few weeks."

James tossed his coat over the back of the recliner. "Where are you going?" He winked. "I hope it's not bar hopping into the wee hours of the morning."

Marie smiled, happily. "I don't know if you remember but I happen to be somewhat of a card shark." She clapped her hands and rubbed them together. "My poor canasta partner has been on a losing streak since Louise filled in for me." Her eyebrows shot up candidly. "Do you realize what this is doing to our overall points?"

James shrugged, after taking out his cuff links and placing them on the edge of the counter. "I'm afraid I don't." He rolled up his sleeves.

Marie dug around in her purse and found her lipstick. She moved to a massive mirror on the far wall. "Well, let me put it to you this way: If I don't get back in it we aren't going to make the TOC at the end of the year."

Samantha looked puzzled. "TOC?"

"Tournament of champions," Marie replied, before pressing her lips together and returning her lipstick to her purse.

"Of course." Samantha looked over to James, exchanging smirks with him.

"There is a spaghetti feed down at the Rotary Club, so we're leaving early." She looked at James and pointed a finger at him. "Don't lecture me about all the germs I might come across. I will disinfect everything I come in contact with. Thanks to those little wipes you got for me, it will kill ninety-nine percent of them."

James's gaze narrowed at his mom's patronizing tone. His intention had been purely directed on her health, not on inconveniences. "I'm serious about—"

Marie pulled out the little square packet of wipes from her purse. "I know how serious you are, Son. I think I hear her now." She blew them a kiss and left. "Don't wait up for me."

When his mom disappeared, James came from behind. "Almost finished?"

"Yep." Samantha punched several more numbers into the calculator and wrote quickly. She dropped the pen and closed her checkbook. "Done."

"You have enough money in there to take me out tonight?" He nibbled on her ear as his arms encircled her.

The contact was easy, intimate, and it drove her wild. She turned around in the chair and faced him. "Does a night of bar hopping into the wee hours sound inviting?"

He noticed that her hair was down. Reverently he buried his hands in it. Starting at the crown, he combed his fingers aimlessly down its length. "Unless you have a better idea."

"I'm full of ideas," she teased softly. Her fingers slid around his mouth, enticing him.

"I like the sound of that." His voice dropped. "I love being able to touch you whenever I wish." His hand found the nape of her neck.

"I can see that." She smiled. "I also think part of it is that you like to have your way."

He stroked the area that throbbed with her very life. "I'm used to having my way." His lips touched the area where his hands had just been. "Besides, I'm good at it."

"So you say." She was watching him carefully. He looked as if he would eat her alive. She pushed at him. "This is the first time we've had the house alone. How about I make dinner? We can eat in that gorgeous dining room you never use."

He reached out and let his fingers glide between the valley of her breasts. "You know what I would love to do to this area right here? Kiss every inch of it." He glanced up at her. "Slowly."

Samantha pulled his shirt from his slacks. Her hands moved evenly over the soft cream material, undoing one button at a time. Feather-light fingers ran across the dark hair on his abdomen. "You know what I would love to do to this area right here?" She bent down and ran her tongue around the rim of his navel, swirling it gently as she did.

James's head filled with beautiful thoughts as her lips traced over his skin. "Tell me."

Her voice was deep and sexy when she spoke. "Fill it with a hearty dinner."

He smiled as he opened his eyes and looked down at her. He had an appetite but it wasn't entirely for food. "Food wasn't quite what I was thinking."

All seduction vanished as she became serious. "I'm starved. I haven't eaten since lunch and that was some tasteless substance at the hospital cafeteria."

"Since lunch?" He pinched at her waist. "I don't want you to wither away."

She scowled. "I just might."

"Do I have time to take a shower?" He looked at his watch.

Samantha nodded and began to pull items from the cupboards and refrigerator. She stacked them neatly on the counter. "But don't linger."

James swatted her on the butt, playfully, as he left. "If I linger long enough will you come in after me?"

"No, I'll just eat your portion of dinner," she yelled over her shoulder.

Twenty minutes later Samantha had dinner cooking and the table set. She took a few floral arrangements from the living room and placed them between the white tapered candles she had just lit. Dimming the lights, she went back into the kitchen to toss the salad.

The wine glasses she retrieved from the hutch were an exquisite cut of solid crystal. She filled them with merlot. When James walked into the room he caught her off guard. He looked so tall, powerful, and elegant. She took in his essence and then had to remind herself to breathe when she realized she was holding her breath. She exhaled. Why was it when he walked into a room it was if he owned everything in it? No one should have that much confidence.

"Why are you looking at me like that?"

"You can be intimidating at times." She handed him a glass of wine as she took in his extraordinary scent. It was the same scent that had lingered on her skin all day, making it impossible for her thoughts to be on anything other than him.

James took the wine and placed a kiss against her hand. His eyes rested possessively on her. "Do I intimidate you?"

She blinked. "Sometimes."

"Why?"

"You're so intense." Everything about him was intense. When he loved, it was powerful; when he was angry, it was destructive; and when he cared, it was done with endless compassion. He screamed intense.

"You make me that way."

Her mouth curved. "You had it way before you ever met me," she corrected.

He shook his head. "I had nothing until I met you." He traced his fingers over her face. "Dinner smells wonderful."

She had almost forgotten about it. She turned. "Wait until you taste this." She pulled a tray from the oven and used a spatula to slide off a dozen stuffed mushrooms. She put three of them on a small plate and handed it to him. "They're hot." She turned to the sink to rinse a few dishes. "That'll have to hold you over for a little while."

James bit into it, and then rolled it around in his mouth when it started to burn. "I think I've died and gone to heaven."

She turned. "Didn't you say that last night?"

"I actually experienced it last night." He moved to her and pressed his lips to the back of her head. Nuzzling her hair with his nose, he took a deep breath.

Samantha took a step back, pushing him away with a gentle bump of her backside. "Will you let me cook?"

He moved away and raised his arms. "By all means." He snatched another mushroom off the plate.

"Can you get the olive oil for me?" Samantha asked as she lifted the lid on the huge pot of boiling water. Avoiding a burst of stream, she dumped two handfuls of pasta into the water. She moved back to the counter and began to dice the mound of tomatoes; red, yellow, and green peppers; garlic; and fresh basil she had just washed and let drain in a colander.

James retrieved the oil from the pantry and handed it to her;

somehow he refrained from kissing her. It was almost becoming impossible to keep his hands off her. He plucked up his wine and went into the living room to turn on some music. The distance would do him good.

As he popped in the CD and pressed PLAY, the music along with the aroma of the sautéing garlic filled the room. He sipped his wine and watched Samantha move about the kitchen preparing their meal. It was a domestic act that millions of couples did every day, but somehow it seemed exclusive to only them. He had thought he would never see her in his kitchen, their kitchen, again.

Finding his way to the recliner, he put his feet up and watched Samantha as she took a huge green bowl and filled it with pasta. She moved to the stove, stirred a large pot of simmering sauce, and brought the wooden spoon to her lips. "I love to watch you," he said.

Samantha looked up. "Did you say something?"

"I love to watch you."

Samantha licked the sauce off her lips as an unexpected flare of heat erupted inside of her. Just the look in his eyes made her so breathless she couldn't speak.

James savored the moment before he spoke. "I could never get tired of watching you." He smiled. "Don't blush. It's the truth." He crossed his feet at the ankles. "After last night, the last thing you should be doing is blushing when I give you a compliment."

"I'm not blushing. It's hot in here."

"How hot?"

She tossed some fresh herbs into the sauce. "Stop teasing me."

"I only do it because you look so cute when I do." He took a drink and held it in his mouth for a moment, enjoying the flavor. "You're lucky I'm across the room."

The wooden spoon she was using dropped. She retrieved it and looked toward him. "Not another word until I'm finished cooking."

"Let's go for a walk on the beach." James looked down at his empty plate and pushed it to the side. "I can't think of a better way to end this scrumptious meal."

Samantha nodded in agreement. "Sounds wonderful."

James scooted his chair out and offered his hand. He led her out of the house, across the deck, and down to the edge of the water. He curved an arm around her waist as they began walking the beach.

"Look at the moon," James said.

Samantha looked out over the ocean. The moon was masked with an eerie orange haze. "If I hear a werewolf cry, I'm running back to the house," she laughed.

James pulled her closer. "You have no faith that I could protect you?"

"I have faith that my legs could get me back to the house mighty fast."

He picked her up and spun her suddenly. His voice was a low teasing growl when he stopped. "Don't make me show you how manly I can be."

She tucked her head under his chin and laughed again. She knew how male James was. There was no need for any type of demonstration. When next to him she felt like nothing could touch her.

As James set her feet back on the ground he said, "Let's go for a dip."

Samantha viewed her blouse and skirt. "I can't swim in this."

James pulled her close. His fingers slowly undid the buttons on her blouse. "I agree. I wouldn't want you to ruin your clothes." He slid the material off, leaving her in a lavender bra.

"You know that color is really starting to grow on me." He traced a finger over the soft lace. The wind started to pick up. It covered their bodies in a cool, salty breeze that swept across the ocean to them.

Samantha sucked in a deep breath as he teased her nipple. "What if someone sees us?"

It was dark and the beach was deserted. "No one will see." He found the zipper at the small of her back. The skirt fell to the sand, revealing a swatch of matching lace. He hooked a finger through the string bikini underwear. Moving his hand under the fine material and filling his hand with her buttock, he gave a gentle squeeze. "Remember what I said this morning?"

Samantha nuzzled closer to him, enjoying the fact every time he clenched her bottom it pressed her closer against him. "As I recall, you weren't there when I woke up." She pushed her lower lip out in a sexy pout. "All I remember is being rather lonely."

"Lonely?"

She nodded. "However, I do recall a little something. It's vague but I do remember bits and pieces. It was quite early." Her voice was sexy and teasing. "How about you give me a littler reminder?" She puckered her lips and ran her tongue along them slowly, purely for his benefit. "Something to jog my memory."

James didn't need any more of an invite than that. He slid his hand to the front of her panties and buried it in the soft curls. He worked the area gently, caressing until it became almost painfully sensitive. He deliberately took his time. He knew what she wanted and how she liked it. "Are you remembering anything now?"

"It's all coming back to me." Her voice was nothing more than a whimper.

"Glad to see you haven't forgotten."

"Yes, it would be a shame if your efforts were wasted."

He nibbled on her ear. "What goes around comes around."

Samantha pulled herself away and boldly ran her hand down the front of his jeans. Her eyes were heavy with want. "And just what do you think is coming to you?" When James tried to reach for her she darted around him and dove into the surf.

James was naked in seconds and following just feet behind her. When he caught up with her he grabbed her around the waist and pulled her to him. "Going somewhere?"

She laughed as waves crashed over them, sending them tumbling under the water. When she surfaced, James's lips were hot against hers. He unhooked her bra, freeing her breasts. His gaze roamed over the soft mounds and then moved to her eyes. They glistened like the moonlight bouncing off the water. His heart tightened when he realized they weren't sad eyes any more. He closed his eyes momentarily as their bodies bobbed with each swell. She was happy again. Somehow that was all that mattered to him.

Samantha felt James quiver as he threaded his hand through her wet hair possessively. "What?"

He just shook his head and pulled her closer to him.

She smiled sweetly. "You drive me insane." She pressed her body as close as she possibly could.

"That's likewise, Angel."

"Tell me," she whispered in his ear. She wished that the moon was fuller so she could see his expression. "Tell me. I want to know everything you're thinking. Everything you're feeling."

Overcome with emotion he nearly choked the words out. "There are no words. Remember?"

Samantha's appetite was just as insatiable for him as it had been the previous night. Her voice was a dark whisper on the waves. "Make love to me, James."

He couldn't talk. He could only show. He ran his hands over her body, exploring each delicate curve that the water seemed to enhance. The exploration created a helpless sensation deep within him. For an instant everything stopped. His breath, his heart, and time.

Chapter Twenty-One

"We have a problem," Raymond said as everyone rushed to take their seats. He had called the meeting forty minutes ago and was anxious to begin.

James sat at the head of the table looking at his board members, who quickly arranged themselves. His gaze fell onto Raymond as the man spoke in a hurried tone. Of course there was a problem, he thought. It was very rare that a meeting was called on such short notice. "What kind of problem?"

Raymond took a seat and turned the floor over to George. "George will get us all up to speed."

George stood, and there was anxiety on his face and in his voice. "The Opposition Commission wasn't notified of the merger,"

The cup in James's hand stopped in midair. His insides turned as still as the air in the room. "What?" This wasn't just a problem, this was a major crisis. His eyes darted to Raymond. Raymond merely raised his hands in the air, indicating that he was just as baffled as anyone else.

"The Opposition—" George began to repeat.

"I heard what the hell you said." James leaned forward suddenly. "The Commission must be notified of the merger before the actual implementation of the proposed merger." He slammed his hand on the table causing everyone to jump. "That is the first goddamn step of any merger this size." The words seeped from his mouth and spread through the room like venom.

No one spoke. They all knew the gravity of the situation.

"Who the hell was responsible for the notice?" James's voice held authority.

Brian spoke up. "That would be me." He wasted no time explaining himself. "I was under the assumption that the combined assets weren't over four hundred million. If they're not over four hundred million, then no notification is required." He swallowed visibly. "I caught the error this morning."

"When you work for me there are no goddamn assumptions. Got that?"

"Yes."

"Don't ever assume again." He ran his hand over his face as he thought about how he was going to fix the situation. They would have to act fast. "Have you already obtained a merger form?"

Brian nodded and he rose from his chair to hand James the thick document. "It's been completed. It's ready to send."

James shook his head as he snapped the papers out of the other man's hand. "We don't have time to go through the proper channels. This merger is supposed to be closed in a few weeks. It will take the Commission that long to process the goddamn paperwork." This merger would create a powerful bridge between the two companies and there was no way James was going to lose it because of an oversight.

Raymond spoke up. "What do you suggest?"

James took a breath. All eyes were on him. Like anything tossed at him, this, too, could be dealt with. Business boils down not to what you know, but whom you know. Knowing the right people was critical for success. James prayed they knew the right people. "Who do we know that works over at the Commission?"

All the board members dropped their heads as they thought. This was not a good position to be in. Rumors had been flying that this was one of the biggest mergers of the year. A lot was at stake, and if the deal fell through it could be disastrous.

"Rodger Cates is on the board over there." Raymond said abruptly.

"Call him. If he's not available, then we find someone else." He looked at each individual member. "No one is leaving this room until we find someone who can sign this off." He tossed the merger form onto the center of the large table.

James flung open the door to his office and then slammed it shut. His hands found his hips and he began to pace. They had gotten through to Rodger and with any luck they would be free and clear by morning. He had cashed in every favor he had, but it was worth it. Nothing could go wrong with this merger.

He was fuming inside and desperately trying to hang onto the restraint he had shown in the boardroom.

He needed her. Right now more than anything he needed her.

He picked up the phone in his office that connected directly to his secretary. "Shelly, if Rodger Cates calls please ring him through to my cell phone." He glanced at his watch. "I'll be leaving in a few minutes."

"Yes, Mr. Taylor."

"I'll be at lunch for about an hour."

"Lunch?"

She didn't have to sound so shocked. "Yes, it's the meal that comes mid-afternoon. The one after breakfast and before dinner."

"I know when it is." There was a hint of attitude in Shelly's voice. "I just didn't think you did. I haven't seen you take one in a very long time."

He signed his signature to several pages. "I haven't had a reason to take one."

"Care to share it with me?"

It was so unlike Shelly to ask personal questions. He put the pen down and gathered the loose pages into a neat pile. "Maybe later. I just finished those signature pages you requested."

"I'll get them before I leave. Enjoy your lunch, Mr. Taylor." She paused. "Enjoy who you're having it with even more."

"I plan to." James hung up his phone and immediately called home.

When Samantha answered the phone and heard James's voice on the other end she said, "I was just thinking about you."

The only time she hadn't been in his mind was when business pushed her from it. "Meet me for lunch."

"What's the matter?" Samantha held the phone tighter and tucked her hair behind her ear.

"I need to see you."

"Are you all right?"

"I will be when I see you."

"Come home and I'll fix something."

"No, I don't trust myself with you at home."

She pressed her lips together. "That's why I want you to come home." She was shameless. She couldn't get enough of him and she wasn't about to hide it.

James groaned into the phone. "Angel, you don't know what you're doing to me. Meet me at Simian's Bistro in twenty minutes."

James studied her as she moved through the small room toward their table. It was sweet torment watching her. He had chosen a table in the back purely for this purpose. His body tightened as he took her in. Her hair trailed behind her as it caught the breeze her stride created. The deep red shirt stretched perfectly over her breasts and gathered around her slender waist. Her smile was gentle and polite as she passed other patrons. Her eyes found his. The only way to describe her was sinuous.

Everything in him began to calm.

He stood when she reached the table. "Hi." He took her hands in his and pulled her close so he could kiss her.

When they broke away Samantha cupped the side of his face in her hand, her finger touched the crease between his brows. "You look worried."

"Some things came up at work. Nothing that I can't take care of, though."

"You're sure?"

He nodded.

Her smile was tormentingly lascivious. "You feel safe here?" she asked, as James pulled out her chair. She waited for him to move around the table and take his seat. Sliding her foot out of her shoe she found his leg.

He felt the tip of her toe glide over his calf muscle. "Nowhere is safe when it comes to you."

Her laugh was profound and meant only for him. "This is nice." She looked around the room.

"It's good and quick. The guys come down here all the time." He took a sip of the water the waitress had brought when he arrived. "How's Mom?"

"She was resting when I left."

"Was her night out too much for her?"

Samantha shook her head. "She's hasn't stopped talking about it. Apparently, she was successful at canasta last night. She informed me that not only had she and her partner won, they had, and I'm quoting this, 'kicked butt.' "

James just shook his head and laughed.

She smiled her thanks as the waitress handed her a menu and placed a glass of water before her. "We have one last visit today at three."

"What's that for?"

"So, the doctor can release her." She gave him a heartfelt smile. "She's done."

Her sincerity touched him deeply. Yes, she was done. She had made it. All three of them made it. He couldn't think of a better time to give her the gift, so he handed her a wrapped box that was sitting on the floor next to his feet. He had been out getting the present when he had received word that an emergency meeting had been called.

"What's this?" She tucked her hair behind her ears.

"Something I owe you."

"Well, you've definitely sparked my interest." She slid the lace bow off the package. Lifting the lid she folded back the tissue paper. She caught sight of the beautiful lavender lace bra and panties and her eyes shot to James's.

"I figured the least I could do was replace what floated out to sea." James enjoyed the way her eyes turned heavy with hunger, with the heated need that swept through her, which she didn't try to hide. It was satisfying to see her look at him that way. It was also deeply satisfying to know that he was the only one who could produce such a reaction. She was his. No one could take her away ever again. He wouldn't allow it.

She leaned forward. "Thank you." The kissed she placed against his lips conveyed what was to come. She pulled back and stared at him. "Perhaps tonight I'll see if it fits."

"It'll fit." He smiled as the waitress approached the table to take their order. "Trust me, it'll fit."

James held Samantha close to him and smiled with great contentment. He was getting used to waking up next to her, seeing her as his eyes first opened, and reaching for her soft body in the middle of the night. He would get used to it but never take it for granted. He knew what it was like to have it all taken away and he would never risk it again.

He kissed the top of her head and opened his eyes. It was early; the sun hadn't risen yet, but the sky held an amazing glow that seemed to fit his mood. He tightened his arm, pulling her closer. "Are you awake?"

"A little," she mumbled, her lips brushing his skin.

"I heard you murmuring in your sleep." His hand found her hair. "What were you dreaming about?"

Samantha nuzzled against him. "I'll never tell."

"Is that so?" He pressed his lips against her forehead. "I'm sure I can think of way to pry it out of you."

"I'm sure you could."

He was quiet for a long time and then he spoke. "I want you to stay here with me. Now that Mom's treatment is over, I want you here permanently. What do you think?"

Samantha stiffened momentarily and then relaxed when she tilted her head and kissed him deeply.

James pushed the hair from her face and ran his fingers across her lips. "I like that," he whispered. "How about doing that every morning for the rest of my life?"

She kissed him again, this time lingering longer.

James broke the kiss and studied her curiously. "Why aren't you answering me?"

"Make love to me."

When she moved on top of him and dipped her head next to his ear, he stopped her. "Samantha."

"Shh, don't talk."

"Answer me." When her head fell into the pillow next to his, he didn't move. "What is it?"

"I can't."

"You can't what?" She tried to roll away but he caught her. Holding her firmly in place with his legs he said. "What is it that you can't do, Samantha?"

"I can't talk about this," she said as she wiggled. "I can't stay."

"Why?"

She slid off the top of him, when he released her. "Because nothing has changed."

"Everything has changed." He flung back the covers to expose their naked bodies. "You're lying here next to me in my bed. Don't tell me nothing has changed." He was angry. "You just asked me to make love to you." He took her by the chin. "Dammit Samantha, look at me."

"None of this matters. This is purely physical."

His expression turned dark and he didn't speak.

"All of this is wonderful but it is also temporary."

"Temporary?" The word sprang from his mouth. "I can't believe what you're saying. Nothing has ever been temporary with you." When she did something she gave one hundred percent. When she gave her heart she gave it completely. It was all or nothing. They were both that way. "This isn't a fling."

She reached for the sheet but James wasn't giving it up.

"Dammit, don't try and cover up." He shook his head, as he looked at her so beautifully naked on his bed. "Don't do this."

"Don't make it more than it is." Samantha turned her eyes away. "It's time for me to go. Marie is in remission," she explained. "Her doctor said she'd be strong enough to move back home in a week or so. There will be no reason for me to stay."

"There'll be me." When she got out of bed he followed her. He watched her hastily collect her clothes, which were spread around the room. "Will you stop and talk to me?"

She rolled the clothes in her hand into a ball and held them close. "This isn't going to work. It can't work."

"It's working right now. It's worked over the last few weeks. We are rebuilding what we had."

All she could do was shake her head.

"I'm not going to hurt you again. I swear on my life I won't ever hurt you." He took her by the arms. He needed the contact that she was trying so desperately to take from him. "Say you believe me." At that moment it seemed like the most important thing in the world for her to say yes to.

"It's too late."

His stomach tumbled. "You're wrong."

"No, I'm not wrong, James. You can't even begin to imagine what it's like to be hurt the way you hurt me."

"The hell I can't. You hurt me too."

She suddenly pulled her arms free from his grip. "I hurt you?"

This time when she moved from him, he made no attempt to pursue her. "You walked out on me. You left without even telling me where you were going."

"You didn't have a right to know," she flung back.

"Bullshit! I had every right to know that you were safe, that you had found a place to live."

"You lost that right when you decided to be unfaithful."

James stood very still. Controlling his emotions had never been very hard for him; however, he was struggling right now. He bit his words back so they came out slow and restrained. "I had a right to know. I had the right to explain."

"It doesn't matter. Nothing matters," she condemned him unemotionally.

Everything matters, he thought. She matters. What they had shared, were sharing, mattered. Watching her face, he saw the same unmistakable pain he had seen the first night on the beach. It was raw and sensitive.

"I don't trust you." Samantha held his eyes. "What do we have if we don't have trust?" Her voice was harsh when she spoke. "We have sex. That's all."

Her assertion tore painfully through him. James didn't move. He couldn't.

The phone broke the defining silence that had lapsed between them. James moved to the nightstand, not taking his eyes off Samantha once. "Yes." He listened to Raymond speak for several moments. Jesus H. Christ, could things get any worse? He could do nothing as he watched the woman he loved getting dressed at neck-breaking speed, so she could get as far away from him as possible, while he listened to the details of one of his biggest deals slowly come unraveled. "Why the hell wasn't I notified? This shit doesn't fall apart over night."

He paced in short fast steps.

James spoke quickly when Raymond had finished. "I'll be there in thirty minutes. I want the entire team on that goddamn jet with me. And make sure Gregory is there, too. Call Shelly and have her cancel all my appointments. Also contact Al." He ran a hand through his hair as he searched his mind for anything he might be forgetting. "I don't want anyone in Europe to know we're coming. If there's a leak, you're fired. Hell, if there's a leak, we'll all be fired," he added abruptly. He turned the phone off and tossed it across the room.

Completely dressed, Samantha flinched when the phone shattered as it made contact with the wall. The air sizzled with emotion and Samantha felt the weight of it pressing down on them. She moved farther away from him.

"I need to go to Europe." His voice was uneven as he spoke, found his clothes, and then quickly dressed.

Samantha nodded slowly. "I'll stay with your mom."

Why did she have to look at him that way? All he wanted to do was take her in his arms and hold her close, yet from the looks of her, if he were to do that she would fight with everything she had to prevent it. "I'm not sure how long I'll be. It could take about three days or possibly a week."

Samantha watched him walk into the closet, come back out, and then start grabbing items around the room and stuffing them into a small brown leather bag. "Take as long as you need."

"I'll leave numbers," he said as he zipped the carry-on shut. "I'll have Shelly call with all the details in a few hours." He felt like a little piece of him was being cut away. The awful void was ripping back open and there was nothing he could do about it.

"We'll be fine."

Their gazes locked momentarily. Neither one spoke, only stared. Samantha could hear her own heart pounding in her ears. James felt like he was slowly losing everything he had ever wanted—all over again.

"What do you want from him?" Marisa asked as she pushed the coffee aside and took Samantha by the hands. It had been twenty minutes since she had arrived and Samantha had filled her in on what had happened.

Samantha sat at the table and stared blankly through the glass door at the ocean.

"Sam, look at me and answer the question."

After a long moment Samantha looked at her friend. "Nothing." Lifting her shoulders she added, "I don't want anything from him."

"That's a lie. We both know that's not true." Marisa's grip tightened. "If that were true you wouldn't be reacting this way."

"I'm reacting this way because I foolishly got caught up in emotions that were based solely on lust," she said regretfully.

"I disagree. I think you've duped yourself into believing they're based on lust. I think they're based on love."

Samantha shook her head quickly, not even considering it.

"Are you saying you don't love him? Look me in the eyes and tell me you don't love him." After a moment she said, "That's what I thought."

Samantha's pain-filled eyes brimmed with tears. "I can't love a man who's cheated on me."

"What if he didn't?" Marisa whispered as she stroked Samantha's hair softly. "What if he's telling the truth?"

"I know what I saw."

"You know what you think you saw," she offered gently as she wiped at her friend's tears.

"Whose side are you on?"

"Yours. Why else would I be up at this godawful hour?"

The makings of a smile touched Samantha's lips.

"I'm not going to tell you what you want to hear," Marisa warned.

"I know you're not." Samantha sighed and after a moment of thought, she said honestly, "I thought it was lust at first but now I'm not so sure."

Marisa nodded in agreement, encouraging her to continue with the thought.

"I still love him," she whispered to herself.

Marisa pulled Samantha to her and wrapped her in a big hug. She held her tightly, giving her time to let it sink in.

"I love him," she whispered again.

Slowly releasing her, Marisa pulled from the embrace. "When I got here, you asked me for my opinion—here it is. I think you need to hear him out before deciding what you're going to do."

"I don't want to know all the details."

"Of course you don't. But you need to know them. There is a difference." Reaching for her purse she flung it over her shoulder. "Come on."

"Where are we going?"

"To see James. I'm sure he hasn't left for the airport yet." When she saw the reluctant look cross her friend's face she took her firmly by the shoulders. "Sam, what do you have to lose? More importantly, let's look at what you have to gain."

Samantha hugged her friend tightly to her. "Thank you for being the voice of reason."

They spoke little as they drove through town. Thankfully the morning traffic was light, so Marisa was able to make good time. Once they turned off the freeway and headed toward the narrow high-rise buildings located downtown, they were almost there. Dodging a few street sweepers, they pulled up to the curb and Marisa put the car in park.

She turned to Samantha. "Are you ready?"

"As I'll ever be."

"All you have to do is hear him out," she said reassuringly. "You don't have to make any decisions, just listen to him."

"I know."

Right at that moment both Samantha and Marisa looked out the window. James was exiting the building and heading toward a waiting limo a few cars ahead of them. He paused for a moment as if he was waiting for someone. When he was joined, Marisa was the first to speak. "Who the hell is that with him?"

Samantha couldn't take her eyes off the woman, whom James was helping into the limo, with a gentle hand against her back. "It's her."

"Are you sure?"

"Yes, I'm sure. I don't think I'll ever forget what she looks like."

Marisa reached for her door. "The son-of-a-bitch. I'm going to give him a piece of my—"

Samantha stopped her by grabbing her arm. "Don't. He's not worth it." It was funny; she thought she'd have to fight off the tears, but nothing came. "Let's go."

CHAPTER TWENTY-TWO

Samantha shot up off the couch when she heard the loud bang on her front door. It echoed through her apartment like a gunshot. She took a deep, steady breath, knowing immediately who it was. Her hand went to her midsection, trying to soothe the rolling, which had come on instantaneously and was so fierce she thought she might throw up. Her body was motionless, her mind racing.

The knock came again, this time even louder and more persistent than the last. She looked at the closed door and had half a mind to leave it that way. However, she was smart enough to know that James wasn't the type of man who would just go away if she refused to let him in. She would have to give him the chance to say what he wanted to say; it was the only way she would be able to end everything completely.

She coolly collected herself as she moved to the door and eyed the gold-toned safety chain. The inhalations she took were long and even, though they were anything but calming. As she slid the chain to the side and let it drop, the door suddenly swung open. James pushed past her, knocking her off balance, causing her to stumble back.

"It seems you have a tendency toward walking out on me," James said. Anguish and rage etched its way across his face.

As Samantha recovered from the sudden motion, she moved to the other side of the room in an ungraceful wobble. She didn't like the way he looked. There were dark circles under his eyes and several days' worth of stubble on his face. His hair was devilish and his suit looked like it had been slept in. The rolling in her stomach turned into a nauseating tidal wave. "I didn't walk out. It was time for me to go."

The veins in James's face bulged as he reached behind him and slammed the door shut. His strides were lengthy as he moved toward her. "I didn't say it was time."

Samantha noted the anger in his voice and stepped into the kitchen. It was the most distance she could put between them without running down the short hall into her bedroom. She fought the urge to do just that. She had never in her life feared James, but right now she didn't trust his judgment. "James, calm down."

"I don't feel like calming down. I leave for two weeks, come home, and find you gone. No note, no phone call, nothing."

"I don't have to notify you of every move I make."

"Not every." The pitch of his voice dropped, he remained perfectly still. His eyes never shifted from her.

Samantha didn't like his tone—it was leaden and driven by resentment. "I made sure Marie was completely moved back into her place." She raised her shoulders. "What did you want me to do? Stay at your house and wait for you to come home?"

"That would have been nice." He rubbed a hand across the coarse stubble along his jaw.

"I'm not your girlfriend or your roommate."

"No, you were just sleeping with me and living in my home." The words oozed with sarcasm.

Samantha flinched as the crudeness of his words hit her. "I was your employee. You were my boss," she pointed out. "The job was over, so I left." She said the last words quietly.

"The job wasn't over."

"Marie is fine," she countered. "I spoke with her this morning."

James sent her a cautious look. "We aren't over."

"We never started," she flung at him.

"We never goddamn ended." The back of his jaw clenched tensely.

"I already told you—"

"I hope you're not about to remind me that all we were having was sex. That would not be wise right now, Samantha."

"You coming here isn't wise."

James's eyes narrowed momentarily.

"What do you want, James?"

"You."

"You want her, too."

"What the hell are you talking about?"

"I saw you with her before you left. I watched her get into the limo with you."

"What?"

"Like a fool I went after you." Tears of utter humiliation clouded her eyes. "I'm not going to be foolish any more."

An intimate look, a look of disbelief, crept into his dark eyes. "That morning, you—you came—"

"Get out," she said with a cold-hearted stare.

"You came for me?"

"Get out."

"Not a chance." He took a step. "Why did you come after me?"

"I said get out." Her hand shot to the door. "Leave."

"I'm not going anywhere. Tell me. I want to know why."

"Tell me, why is it after we make love you have to go to her?"

Every muscle in his body reacted. His fists balled at his sides as his pulse jolted. "Find your keys." The words came out as a direct order.

"Excuse me?"

"Get your keys, Samantha. You are coming home with me."

His peripheral vision remained on her as he glanced around the room. "Right now."

"I'm not going anywhere with you."

The veins at James's temple started to protrude again. He cleared his voice before he spoke. "If I have to toss you over my goddamn shoulder and carry you to my car, I will." He spotted her purse on the kitchen table, retrieved it, and then pushed it into her hands. "Don't tempt me Samantha, I'll do it."

"You can't just pick me up and cart me off."

He took a step forward. "You want to bet?"

Samantha shook her head.

"Good." He took her hand in his and headed out the door. He deposited her in the passenger seat and moved around the car. He looked at her briefly over the hood. By the end of the night she would know everything that had happened. If she chose not to stay with him after she heard what he had to say then he would let her go. His stomach started to churn at the thought of her leaving him. He tried in vain to disregard the notion as he slid behind the wheel and started the car.

The ride across town was thirty minutes of uncomfortable silence. The tires squealed around every corner and he slid several feet when he stopped in front of his house. He flung open the car door and met Samantha on the other side of the car. Once in the house, James gestured up the stairs. "My room."

Samantha was about to say something, but the look on James's face silenced her. She followed him up the stairs.

James's hand shot out when they entered the room. "On the bed."

"I—"

"Sit on the bed, Samantha." The words were said sharply as he disappeared into the huge walk-in closet.

Samantha sat on the very edge of the mattress. She didn't dare look over her shoulder at the bed. Images of their lovemaking were already dancing through her head. For some strange reason she felt guilty for thinking about it, for her body responding to it. Noise from the closet caused her to look up, relieving her of any more culpable thoughts.

When James quietly reappeared, he leaned against the wall and stared at Samantha. "That night on the beach—"

Samantha shot off the bed. "I don't want to hear this."

"I need to tell you what happened that night." His voice lowered. "And regardless of what you think, you need to hear it."

"No, I don't." She twisted her hands together. She would rather die than hear him admit that he had been with another woman. "It's not going to make a bit of difference. I know what happened. I saw what happened with my own eyes. I saw her get into the limo and I saw her in the lobby kissing you." She looked around the room hysterically. "I want to go home."

"You're being unfair."

Samantha turned suddenly. Her temper sparked. "What would you have done if you walked in and saw me kissing another man the way you were kissing that woman?"

"I'd probably beat the living shit out of him."

"And you think I'm being unfair just because I don't want to hear all about it?"

He moved across the room and stopped several feet from her. "I don't want to lose you again."

"You never got me back." She watched his eyes dart over her shoulder to the bed as he walked toward her. She knew what he was thinking. "James, I can't explain it. My body wants you but my heart won't let me forget." There was no emotion in her voice. She was purely stating the obvious.

"It's not just physical, Samantha. I don't care how much you try to convince yourself of that. You wouldn't have let me make love to you unless you loved me."

"It had been over a year since a man had even touched me. I think that had more to do with it than anything."

"Your reasoning isn't going to work." For a moment he stood perfectly still. "I love you."

Her blood pressure spiked. She could actually hear the blood pounding in her head, pushing through her veins. "How can you stand here and say that?"

"Because it's true."

"You lying son of—"

"This is how I can stand here and say I love you." He pulled a black velvet box from his pants pocket. He held it in the space that separated them.

Samantha's hand went to her mouth as she watched James open the small box and take out a solitaire diamond ring.

"I planned to give this to you the night we made love on the beach." He tried to control his voice. "I was going to ask you to marry me."

She smacked at him wildly. "You son-of-a-bitch." Her voice was pure venom as she smacked the ring out of his hand. "How dare you? How dare you do this to me?" She pushed his chest hard. "Does she know that you were going to propose to me?" She shouted in his face. "Does she know that we made love? Does she know—"

"Stop," he said as he gathered her hands. "This isn't about her, this is about us. I love you. Don't you get it?"

She shook her head and felt her lip tremble as she caught it between her teeth. "I will never forgive you for this."

Reaching into his coat pocket he took out his phone and flipped it open. He dialed a few numbers. "It's Taylor. You need to get over to my house immediately. No, it doesn't have anything to do with that—this is personal." He shook his head briskly. "I don't care about your goddamn policy." Each word seeped through teeth clamped so tightly they began to ache from the continual pressure. "If you don't come here, I'll come there. Take your pick. I don't give a damn about the repercussions." There was a pause. "No, that's out of the question. Fifteen minutes or I'm coming over."

When the conversation was over and the phone was tucked back into his pocket he looked at Samantha. "We can wait downstairs."

"I'm going home."

He reached for her arm. "You're going downstairs."

Exactly fifteen minutes later the doorbell rang. James shot Samantha a stay-put look and went to answer the door.

The woman, who was dressed in sneakers, jeans, and a white T-shirt, was hot on James's trail when they walked into the room. Her dark brown hair was pulled gently back into a long ponytail and a look of hard anger lit her jade-green eyes.

Recognizing her immediately, Samantha stood and headed for the door.

"Goddamn it, sit Samantha," James demanded.

"I'm leaving."

"No, you're not." He grabbed her arm. "Not until you've met Alicia."

Alicia looked directly at James, paying no attention to Samantha. "I don't know what in the hell you think you're doing. How dare you put me in this type of position?"

James blew out a long breath. "Al, tell Samantha what you do."

"Mr. Taylor, I don't care who you are, what company you run, or how much money you pay me—we have a contract."

"I understand. However, this is important. I promise you—"

"I don't want your promises. I want you to abide by the contract you signed." Her face was an uncompromising stare. "You know how I feel about this."

"I can't let it slide again." He had slowly died inside the first time for keeping his mouth shut. It would kill him he if he did it again.

"That's not my problem."

"It is now."

"You signed a confidentiality clause which provides for serious consequences if it is ever breached—"

"Sue me," James snapped. "Just tell her who the hell you are."

"What's going on?" Samantha said, desperately looking between the two.

"I don't care if I lose everything," James continued. "She needs to know the truth."

"We went over this last time," Alicia insisted.

James directed his words to Samantha but continued to look at Alicia when he spoke. "Al is a former U.S. intelligence officer. She retired from the Department of Defense two years ago. She now owns and operates an investigations company, which specializes in corporate espionage."

James turned to Samantha. "I hired Al a year ago when I thought my company was being spied on."

Samantha felt the color drain from her face. She shook her head in denial. She couldn't believe what he was saying. There was too much at stake if she did. All this couldn't just be a simple misunderstanding. "No."

"Yes, Samantha. I hired her again, a few months ago, because we have a new product being released very soon and our competitors were trying to find out what it was."

"They were trying to steal it," Alicia reluctantly corrected under her breath.

Samantha's eyes were filled with torment and regret when she looked at him. "But she was in your arms. I saw the both of you kissing." The words fell out of her mouth in dismay.

James looked at Alicia frantically. "What you say will never leave this room. I swear on my life. You can't expect me to do this again."

"I was undercover," Alicia said after a very long and thoughtful moment. "I do whatever it takes to get the information." She took a deep breath and looked over to James and then back to Samantha. "People don't know who I am. I have to keep it that way. I pretended to be Mr. Taylor's girlfriend." She lifted her shoulders. "I've also been a janitor, a man, and an opera singer. It's all a part of what I do. I take on whatever role that allows me to get the information I need." She cleared her throat. "I was the one who called that evening. I got word that there was a party, which posed the perfect opportunity for Mr. Taylor and I to get near the suspect. Trust me, I got an earful when he told me I interrupted what he said was the most important moment of his life."

Samantha looked to James when he spoke. "She couldn't get into the party without me. I needed to go," he explained. "I called her the morning I left for Europe because whoever was trying to steal information was also trying to collapse the merger."

Alicia nodded in agreement.

Samantha began to shake. "Oh my God, what have I done?"

James tore his gaze from Samantha and looked to Alicia. "I'll show myself out," she said as she turned.

"Al—" James began.

She stopped. "I was never here."

James closed his eyes briefly. "Thank you."

When they were alone, Samantha shed tears that were pure anguish. She had let the man she loved with all her heart go because of a mistake. Because he was doing his job. The onslaught of emotions threw her off balance. Would she ever be able to forgive herself? Would he ever be able to forgive her?

"You couldn't tell me," she said in sudden understanding.

"Not if I wanted to keep my job." He shook his head. "Why didn't you trust me?"

They weren't the actual words that he said that caused Samantha's heart to drop into the pit of her stomach; it was the way he said them. She felt his pain. No words would ever be able to convey how terribly sorry she was.

"In the beginning all I wanted to do was make you understand what really happened." He lifted his shoulders. "But after a while I got to thinking, what kind of relationship did we have if you didn't trust me? I became angry and started resenting you for leaving."

"I don't even know what to say." She touched his arm, though she really wanted to wrap her arms around him and never let him go. "I'm so sorry I doubted you. How could I have not trusted our love? Your love for me."

"When I saw you that first day in my mom's room I knew none of it mattered. I didn't care that you didn't trust me. I wanted you back. I wanted to tell you I was never unfaithful and I never stopped loving you but I knew you wouldn't listen. I knew you wouldn't believe me."

The moment he touched her, she lifted her head and nestled it into the crook of his neck. "So, now what?"

He pulled away and smiled. "Angel, I'm never letting you go."

She wiped the onslaught of tears with the back of her hand.

He took the ring out of the box. "Now, it's time to put this where it should have been for the last year."

She looked down at her shaking hand as he slid the brilliant ring onto her finger. She was humbled. All she had ever wanted—and he was sitting before her offering her everything. "All I've ever wanted was for you to want only me."

"I've never wanted anyone but you."

She smiled through her tears. "Have I told you how much I love you?"

"Not lately." He pressed her back on the bed, his body resting snuggly beside her. "We have the rest of our lives to tell," he kissed her deeply, "and show each other."

ABOUT THE AUTHOR

Aris Whittier is a freelance writer who lives in northern California with her husband and two children. She is the author of *Fatal Embrace,* a *Cosmopolitan* "Red-Hot Read," and the hilariously funny book *The Truth about Being a Bass Fisherman's Wife.* Aris enjoys reading romance just as much as she does writing it.